The door flew open
and there she stood
wearing a pale blue nightgown

"Were you asleep?" Garret asked.

"Of course! It's two o'clock in the morning." Panic replaced the sleepy look in Krystal's eyes. "What's wrong?"

"I need to come in."

"If you came here to check on me, it's not necessary. I'm not sick."

"I know. You're pregnant." That stunned her into silence. He waited for her to say something, but nothing came out of her mouth. "It's true, isn't it?" he said.

She moistened her lips, then said, "Yes. I'm sorry. This is all my fault. If I hadn't practically begged you to take me to bed, we wouldn't be in this—"

Garret cut her off. "Wait a minute! Are you saying I'*m* the father?"

Dear Reader,

As a child I spent many hours with a length of clothesline in my hand. My friend Susie would be on the other end and our friend Joanie would be in the middle, jumping as we twirled the rope and sang one of the many ditties created especially for skipping rope. Our favorite was the one that ended with "First comes love, then comes marriage, then comes Joanie pushing a baby carriage."

It's a refrain that echoed often in my head while I wrote this book because my heroine, Krystal—like a lot of women—believes she's going to fall in love, get married and have a baby—in that order. Then she does a favor for a friend and discovers that her plan has suddenly been thrown out the window. Now she finds herself wondering if it's possible to have a baby first, then get married and then fall in love.

As you read this story you'll find the answer. You'll also meet the women who live at 14 Valentine Place, a wonderful old Victorian house where love has a way of sneaking up on its tenants when they least expect it. I hope you'll enjoy your visit with them.

If you'd like to write to me, I love to hear from readers. Send your letters to Pamela Bauer, c/o MFW, P.O. Box 24107, Minneapolis, MN 55424, or you can visit me via the Internet at www.pamelabauer.com.

Warmly,

Pamela Bauer

Books by Pamela Bauer

HARLEQUIN SUPERROMANCE

A Baby in the House
Pamela Bauer

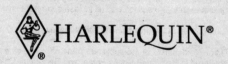

HARLEQUIN®

TORONTO • NEW YORK • LONDON
AMSTERDAM • PARIS • SYDNEY • HAMBURG
STOCKHOLM • ATHENS • TOKYO • MILAN • MADRID
PRAGUE • WARSAW • BUDAPEST • AUCKLAND

ISBN 0-373-71163-8

A BABY IN THE HOUSE

Copyright © 2003 by Pamela Bauer.

Visit us at www.eHarlequin.com

Printed in U.S.A.

For the baby in our house,
Aedan Paul.
What a joy you are!

And a special thank-you to
Michelle Rudolph for sharing her
professional insights with me.

PROLOGUE

KRYSTAL GRAHAM SPOTTED Garret Donovan across the ballroom, briefly locked her eyes with his, then glanced away. She waited only a moment before allowing her gaze to slowly wander back to his, giving him a smile that said, *You know what I'm thinking and it's a bit naughty.*

The flirtatious move hinted at an intimacy that didn't exist and was part of a plan to make Samantha Penrose jealous. It worked. Samantha couldn't keep her eyes—or her hands—off Garret.

As Krystal stared at Garret, she could see why. He was cute. Not exactly her type, but still cute. And sexy. That realization rocked her for a moment. She hadn't thought of him in that way before. He'd always been her landlady's son. A friend. But tonight he looked good enough to send a little jolt of pleasure all the way down to her toes.

She shook her head. There was no point in thinking of Garret in that way, because she was making a new start with Roy.

She glanced at her watch, wishing she were with him now. As if Garret could read her mind, he came toward her and suggested they leave.

She slipped her arm through his as they said goodbye to his colleagues. Seeing Samantha across the room watching their movements, she whispered to

Garret, "If you kiss me now you can make your old girlfriend very jealous."

He looked her in the eye and said, "As tempting as that offer is, when I kiss a woman it's not for someone else's benefit. It's because she wants me. Do you want me to kiss you, Krystal?"

She did, only she wasn't about to admit that to him. It was a startling discovery and one that kept her quiet as they walked through the hotel corridors to the front entrance. When they were waiting for the parking lot attendant to bring his car around, she knew she needed to say something about the sexual tension that seemed to have come out of nowhere between them.

"Garret, the reason I came with you tonight..." she began.

"I know why you're with me, Krystal. My mother asked you to be my date, but contrary to what you—or my mother—may think, I don't need help when it comes to my relationship with Samantha Penrose."

It wasn't the first time she'd heard those words. When his mother had suggested they go to the hospital ball together, Garret had objected to the idea, but it had been a good-natured objection. Now he sounded angry.

"Look, it's still early. Why don't you go back inside and I'll take a cab home," she suggested.

"You aren't taking a cab anywhere. I brought you here and I will take you home."

His tone made her sound like an obligation. "I wasn't planning to go home. I thought I'd go to Roy's place."

"Old unfaithful, huh?" He slowly shook his head.

As her friend, he knew about her on-again, off-again relationship with Roy Stanton. Until tonight, however, he'd kept his opinions of the other man to himself.

"He's changed." She felt the need to defend her decision to give Roy another chance.

"I'm glad to hear that," he stated. She wished she knew if he truly meant those words, but as usual, his face revealed nothing of what he was thinking.

The parking lot attendant had brought the car around, and he held the door open for her. Reluctantly, she climbed inside. Garret didn't speak as he drove except to ask for directions. She should have been used to it by now—his penchant for silence. It had been that way since the first day she met him. She'd never known a man who could get so lost in his own thoughts.

When they reached Roy's apartment complex, he said, "Wait. I'll walk you to the door."

He was the dutiful escort, making sure she arrived safely inside the dimly lit lobby. "Thanks. It's right here." She motioned to the lower level apartment. "Someone's home. I can hear music."

"So can half the neighborhood," he said dryly.

"You can leave. I'm fine."

He surveyed their surroundings with a critical eye, then said, "I'll go back to the car, but I'd appreciate you signaling when you've made it inside."

She nodded and watched him walk away before pounding on Roy's door. She knew it wasn't likely he'd hear her. The music was too loud. She figured he was probably stretched out on the sofa, watching videos on MTV and missing her.

Krystal dug deep into her purse for a key she'd never returned after one of their earlier breakups. She inserted it in the lock and pushed open the door.

"Surprise! Party was over sooner than I expected," she announced as she stepped into the room.

Only the party wasn't over in Roy's apartment. He

was indeed on the sofa with music videos playing on his big-screen TV, but he was definitely not missing her. Next to him was a woman. A naked woman whose limbs were entwined with his.

The blood rushed to Krystal's face and pounded in her temples. For a moment she was too stunned to speak, but then her anger erupted.

"You scumbag! How could you do this to me?" She screamed at him. "You told me being in the military had made you realize how important I was to you, that you were never going to look at another woman again. You…you…" she stammered, struggling to get her breath, so great was her fury. "You are a disgusting pig, Roy Stanton, and I can't believe I was stupid enough to believe you could ever change!"

"Wait, I can explain," he began, but she wasn't going to listen to one more word he had to say.

She threw the key at him, bouncing it off his bare chest. She turned and ran out of his apartment, sickened by what she'd seen. To her surprise, there were no tears flooding her eyes.

As she stepped outside she saw that Garret's car was still at the curb. He saw her coming toward him and got out to open the door for her. She slid inside.

He didn't say a word to her until he was behind the wheel. Then he said, "Change of plans?"

"Yes, change of plans," she managed in a voice that was surprisingly calm.

"Where to now?"

When she looked at him she didn't see her land-lady's son. She saw the man who'd looked at her with desire in his eyes. "Did you mean what you said earlier this evening?"

"You ought to know by now that I don't say things I don't mean," he answered in a voice that sent a shiver of awareness through her.

"Then take me to your place."

CHAPTER ONE

"I'M SORRY YOU HAD TO WAIT, Angie," Krystal said as she escorted her eleven-o'clock appointment to her workstation.

It was an apology she issued often in a typical workday. No matter how hard she tried to stay on time, she usually failed. Not because she was slow, but because she regarded styling hair as an art form and one that shouldn't be hurried. Creating the right look for a client was more important than staying on schedule.

Angie brushed away her apology with a flap of her hand. "No problem. I needed the downtime and your reception area provided a very nice distraction. That construction site across the street is crawling with men in tight, dusty jeans. Have you seen the size of the arms on some of those guys?"

"I try not to look," Krystal told her, shaking out the black plastic cape before draping it over Angie's shoulders. "A guy I used to date works there. A real zero. Cute with a great body but—" she pointed to her head "—nothing up here."

"Yeah, I know what you mean. A good personality can make a guy look attractive, and you can always drag him to the gym and work out together to get his body in shape, but if he's dumb as dirt, what's the point?"

"There isn't one. So what are we doing today? The usual?"

"Uh-uh. I need a change. Chop it off."

"Oh-oh. If you want me to cut it, you must be having guy trouble."

She grinned. "You know me well, don't you?"

Krystal knew most of her regular clients very well. She regarded them as friends and she often found herself privy to information some of them hadn't even shared with their closest family members. She knew that before this woman left, she'd know all about her breakup with her boyfriend.

"Any ideas as to what you want me to do?" she asked, running her fingers through the blond tresses.

"Take it up to about here." She used her hand as a measure, raising it to just below her ear. "I'll let you decide how you want to style it."

Krystal studied the hair from all angles, lifting and rearranging strands as she mentally sculpted a new style. She loved it when a client gave her carte blanche. Creating the right look for someone was a challenge and she took great satisfaction in knowing that if she did her job well, she would make a woman feel better about herself.

While Krystal shampooed and rinsed the woman's hair at the sink, the client filled her in on her troubled love life. Krystal didn't mind. She was a people person and enjoyed hearing what was happening in their lives—the good and the bad. It was one of the aspects she loved most about her job—interacting with others.

"So how are things with you?" the young woman finally asked Krystal when she was once more sitting facing the mirror.

It was a question Krystal expected to hear from all of her regular clients at some point during their visits. And usually her life was an open book, with many of her customers knowing as much about her personal life as her friends did, but not today. A page had been written she wasn't ready for anyone else to read. At least not yet.

"Things could be better," she said, tossing the wet towel into the bin behind her.

"Does that mean you and Roy have split up again? The last time I was in you told me you were giving him one more last chance to make things work."

"I did and that was a mistake."

"It didn't work out?"

She chuckled sardonically as she reached for a comb. "It lasted all of three days. I wanted to believe that serving in the military had changed him. I was wrong."

"You don't sound brokenhearted over it," Angie observed.

"Because I'm not." It was the truth. Looking back now she could see how foolish she'd been when it came to her relationship with Roy, seeing only what she wanted to see. She'd wasted her time trying to recycle an old love—only it hadn't even been love, just a misplaced devotion. She wished it hadn't taken her so long to realize that.

"I suppose you've already found one…or two…or three guys to take his place," she said with a sly grin.

"Uh-uh. My juggling days are in the past. Gone for good," Krystal said on a note of finality.

"You're kidding!" Wide eyes met hers in the mirror. "You are like the queen of the dating scene."

"Not anymore I'm not. I need a break from dating."

"You and me both," she seconded, then went on to lament the lack of decent men in their age group, concluding with the statement that life would be less complicated without men.

Krystal knew that *her* life certainly would be if she hadn't let one particular man into it. When she'd finished styling her client's hair, she handed her a mirror. "What do you think?"

"It looks fabulous." As she climbed out of the chair, she pulled a folded ten-dollar bill from her pocket and gave it to Krystal. "Thank you so much for the great cut."

"Thank *you*. I'm glad you like it."

"Oh, I do. And I appreciate you letting me whine about guys," she said as she straightened her skirt.

"Hey—we all need to do it now and then," Krystal told her.

"Yes, we do, and especially with someone who understands what it's like out there in the dating world. You, Krystal, are one smart lady when it comes to men," she told her, then, with a grateful wave goodbye, headed for the front desk.

A few minutes later one of Krystal's co-workers approached her with her lunch—an order of take-out barbecue ribs. "Want some? I'll share." She held up the package invitingly.

The aroma hit Krystal the way heat blasted her face when she stepped outside from cool air-conditioning, causing her stomach to revolt. She uttered, "No, thanks," then bolted for the bathroom. She barely managed to get there before she was sick.

As she washed up at the sink, she stared at her reflection in the mirror and thought, *Oh yeah, I'm real smart when it comes to men.* She clicked her tongue in disgust, dried her hands and went back to work.

GARRET WAS TIRED. He'd spent most of the night at the hospital with a patient and after only a few hours of sleep on a cot in the doctors' lounge, he'd had to make his morning rounds, fill out a mountain of paperwork and attend a staff meeting. Now he'd promised one of the nurses at the clinic that he'd stop in and check on her mother who was a patient in a nursing home.

Garret knew that if Dolly Anderson still lived in her house on the east side of St. Paul, she'd be outside in her large floppy hat tending her vegetables. But at eighty-nine, a broken hip had marked the end of her days as a home owner and landed her in the nursing home not far from her old neighborhood. Although her bones had healed, she'd never regained the strength and agility to return home. That hadn't stopped her from gardening, however.

When Garret arrived at the nursing home, he found her outdoors tending to the plants on the tiny patio outside her room. One hand rested on a cane helping her stand, the other clutched a plastic watering can.

"Got any pumpkins in that patch?" he called out as he made his way across the lawn toward her.

She looked up at him. "It's a good thing you're a brilliant doctor. You'd stink as a farmer. Pumpkins need room to spread." As he drew closer she added, "You look tired. You'd better go easy on the women for a while and catch up on your sleep." She gave him a crooked grin.

"Oh, Dolly, you ought to know you're the only one for me." He'd never been much for flirting with women, but with her he couldn't resist. "How come you're not wearing your sun hat?"

"Don't want to mess up my hair." She turned back to watering her plants. "Just had it styled. I always get it done on Tuesdays."

He didn't correct her and tell her it was Wednesday.

"What brings you here?" she wanted to know.

"I was in the neighborhood and thought I'd stop and see how you're doing."

She slanted a look at him. "Liar. I know Mavis called you."

He didn't deny the accusation. "She's worried you might have a cold."

She harrumphed. "Can you believe it? My daughter is fifty-nine years old and she still doesn't know the difference between a cold and allergies. If I cough, it's because the pollen count is high. It tickles my throat. It's been that way ever since I was a child."

"That's why I told you to stay inside in air-conditioning this time of the year," he said with a gentle wag of his finger.

"Can't. Have to take care of my garden."

The garden to which she referred was comprised of large pots holding a variety of vegetable plants on her patio. To his amazement, she had cherry tomatoes, radishes, green peppers and even a bean plant, which she'd staked with a yardstick.

"Don't they feed you here?" he asked.

"Of course they do. That isn't why I have my vegetables and you know it," she scolded him.

Yes, he did. On more than one occasion she'd told him that she'd planted her first garden during World War II when Americans were encouraged to grow their own vegetables as a sign of support for the troops. When her husband had been killed in the war, she'd decided to continue the tradition in honor of his memory. She'd been planting her victory garden for over sixty years.

"I brought you something," he told her.

"Not more pills to swallow, I hope."

"No, something sweet."

That had her setting her watering can down and

giving her attention to him. "Ooh. Gingersnaps," she cooed, when he pulled a box of cookies from his bag and handed them to her. "What do I have to do for them? Take off my clothes?"

He saw the twinkle in her eye and smiled. "You know me well, Dolly." Not many of his patients did, but he had a soft spot for this octogenarian with her sharp mind and keen wit.

"You're not going to take my word for it that it's only the pollen, are you, Dr. G.?"

"I'd like to, but I'm afraid if I don't give you a clean bill of health, Mavis won't get any sleep tonight. How about it? Should we put her mind at rest?"

She hesitated momentarily, then said, "All right. To please Mavis." She moved slowly but with a gracefulness few women her age possessed. He slid open the patio door for her and followed her inside.

"You're not going to make me get back into bed, are you? Once I'm up and dressed, I don't like to even look at that thing," she told him with a wave of her hand in the direction of her bed. "Someone around here is always trying to get me to nap. I'm not a nap person. Never was, never will be."

He patted the leather chair. "How about sitting right here."

Sitting had never been easy for someone as active as Dolly and today was no different than any other time he'd visited her. She squirmed and fidgeted, but he managed to complete the exam and was relieved when he found there was no cause for alarm.

"Okay, that'll do it,"' he said, stuffing his stethoscope back into his bag.

"I'm as right as rain, aren't I?"

"You are. How's the hip?"

"The only thing wrong with my hip is that it kept

me from getting my hair done yesterday because I had to go to physical therapy,'' she grumbled.

He looked at her white curls. ''I thought you said you had your hair done today?''

''I did. My gal came back this morning. Made a special trip for me. Isn't she just the sweetest thing?'' She didn't wait for an answer but continued on. ''I think you'd like her. She's pretty. Really pretty.''

''Now don't go getting any ideas, Dolly,'' he warned.

''I know better than to do that,'' she said with a flap of her wrinkled hand. ''Kryssie's got too many boyfriends the way it is. She gets flowers all the time from this one or that one. They usually end up here…the flowers, that is. She doesn't want reminders of a bad date.''

Garret didn't comment and she continued on, ''You wouldn't be interested in her anyway being you're not looking to settle down just yet. You have too many things to accomplish.''

''Yes, I do,'' he agreed.

''Are you still thinking about the Doctors Without Borders program?''

Because Dolly's husband had been in the Red Cross, Garret had told her about his interest in doing relief work. She'd shown him journals her husband had kept during his tour of duty overseas and shared stories of what it had been like to be a doctor's wife during the 1940s. Besides being a very interesting woman, she was easy to talk to and encouraged Garret to use his medical training in whatever way he felt was best.

''I don't think I'll be leaving until after the first of the year,'' he told her.

''I'll miss seeing you, but I'm happy to share you

with the rest of the world," she said with a gracious smile. "You remind me so much of my husband. Dedicated. Passionate about helping people. A true gentleman."

"Thank you. I wish I had known him."

"You would have liked him. He was a good man." A wistful expression came over her face as she talked about him. "We only had a few years together, but they were wonderful years. It's too bad everyone can't have a love like ours. There'd be a lot fewer divorces."

"You were lucky."

"Yes, we were. No amount of time can erase what we had together. True love is like that. It'll go on forever…" She trailed off, her eyes glassy with a distant expression in them. "Even after all these years I still have so many clear memories. And of course I have Mavis. There is no greater reminder of a love shared than a child. Don't you agree?"

"I certainly do. And your daughter should sleep well tonight. Your lungs sound fine, Dolly."

"I told you it was only my allergies causing me to cough."

"Yes, you did," he said, snapping his bag shut. "Do you have any questions before I go?"

"Oh, you're leaving so soon?" she said, suddenly sounding very childlike. "I was hoping you could stay and talk."

"I wish I could, but I have appointments this afternoon. I'm sorry." His apology couldn't have been more sincere. It was one of the aspects of his job he wished he could change—there were never enough hours in a day. He regretted not being able to spend more time with his patients and it frustrated him that he had to spend so much of his workday doing paperwork. He wanted to be helping people, which was why he was interested in doing humanitarian work.

She nodded her head in understanding. "Mavis said you're the hardest-working doctor at the clinic."

"I don't know about that. All doctors work hard, Dolly."

She sighed. "You don't need to tell me. When you do finally settle down, you'd better make sure it's with someone who understands that."

"Of one thing you can be sure, Dolly, and that's when I do finally get around to doing just that, you'll be the first to know." With that statement, he left her with a smile.

THE FIRST TIME KRYSTAL HAD walked into 14 Valentine Place she'd felt at home. If houses had personalities—which Krystal believed they did—this one's was warm and inviting and definitely female, just like its owner, Leonie Donovan.

Contentment resonated in the polished wood floors and mahogany-trimmed walls. Krystal noticed it every time she stepped through the front door. Her landlady said it was because it had been home to a happy family. Three generations of Donovans had lived in the house and there'd been no divorce, no bitter battles over who owned what, no kids coming and going in split-custody arrangements.

It was only after Leonie's husband had died unexpectedly that the big old Victorian structure had been converted into a boardinghouse. Everyone understood why Leonie had decided to rent the rooms to women. She'd raised four sons and had reached a point in her life where she wanted to connect with the feminine side of life.

Krystal had been one of the first women to rent a

room and, like everyone else who would live at 14 Valentine Place, was treated like a member of a family. It was an extended family that included Leonie's sons, her daughters-in-law and her grandson. It was a family rich in history, just like the house, and hearing the Donovan brothers talk about their childhoods reminded her how very different their lives had been from hers.

That's because home to her had been a series of house trailers, none of them double-wide. What little furniture they'd had was either rented or purchased at a garage sale or flea market. There had been no family heirlooms handed down from generation to generation. While Leonie's home often smelled of lemon-scented furniture polish, the mobile homes where Krystal had lived had reeked of stale cigarette smoke.

Not that Krystal had been unhappy with her childhood—she hadn't. It was just very different from the one the Donovan boys had experienced, and not just because they lived in a house with a concrete foundation and plaster walls.

She'd grown up in a house of women. She'd never known her father, she didn't have a brother and she seldom saw her grandfather. If her mother had men friends, she and her sister Carly never saw them.

Krystal knew it was because she was trying to be a good role model for her daughters. To Linda Graham, the most important lesson she could teach her daughters was not to make the same mistakes she had. She'd had not one but two teen pregnancies, and she'd made it clear that she wanted her daughters to have a different life than she'd had. It was why she had imposed such strict rules when it came to dating.

No matter how hard Krystal and Carly had tried to convince her they were teenagers who could be trusted, their mother had refused to allow them to date until they were seniors in high school. Both had thought their mother was unfair, but only Krystal had rebelled against her authority, willing to risk punishment for a chance at romance.

The strict rules may have been a good parenting tactic in Linda Graham's eyes, but to Krystal they had only created distance in their mother-daughter relationship. Her love life became a frequent source of conflict between them that continued into her late teens and early twenties.

It was one of the reasons Krystal had been eager to move out of Fergus Falls. Besides the limited employment opportunities, the town was small enough that it was difficult to keep her personal relationships private. And as long as she lived there, she felt as if her mother was looking over her shoulder into her love life.

Until she moved into 14 Valentine Place, she'd thought most mothers were probably like hers—critical of whomever their children dated. Then she met Leonie. Even though her landlady was a romance coach, she seldom interfered in her sons' love lives.

Leonie rarely gave anyone unsolicited advice, yet she was always there for moral support when it was needed. Not only did she encourage the young women who rented rooms from her to feel free to come to her if they wanted to talk about relationships, she designated the living room in the house as the great room where discussions of men and romance became a regular occurrence. It wasn't long before Krystal came to regard Leonie as a second mother, only with this mother she could talk about everything and anything.

At least she had been able to until a few weeks ago. Now that aspect of their relationship had changed. Krystal had made a mistake. A big mistake. And it was one she was reluctant to admit to anyone, and especially to her mother and Leonie.

Instead she would keep it secret. Not easy for someone who usually blurted out whatever was on her mind. Worried that Leonie would be able to detect that she was keeping something from her, Krystal did her best to avoid seeing her landlady.

Today, however, was Tuesday, which meant Leonie wouldn't be at home. She'd be teaching a class on the dos and don'ts of dating at the community center and that meant the only other person in the boardinghouse would be Dena Bailey, since the third-floor apartment was still vacant.

As she expected, Dena was in the kitchen. When she saw Krystal she said, "Oh good! You're home. I was hoping I'd see you." She motioned for Krystal to come sit beside her. "Come join me for a glass of lemonade."

Krystal shook her head. "I'll pass on the lemonade, thanks." She did go over to the refrigerator, however, to get a bottle of water. When she opened the door, the aroma of the leftover parmesan chicken she'd had the night before nearly caused her to bolt toward the bathroom. She didn't understand how something could taste so good warm yet smell so bad cold that it made her wish she'd never gone near it.

But then so many things made her stomach queasy. Like when she was in an elevator and someone stepped in wearing perfume. Or the pungent smell of gasoline at the service station. Or the tiny bit of oatmeal left in Leonie's bowl each morning.

Krystal shuddered and willed her stomach to settle itself. When she sat down at the table, she saw Dena had a bridal magazine spread open in front of her.

"What's up with that? I thought you and Quinn were going to elope."

"I thought we were, too, but then we sat down to make plans and before I knew it, we'd reserved the church and booked the reception hall. It's amazing what that guy can talk me into."

"Must be the power of love," Krystal remarked, noting the glow on Dena's cheeks. "So when's this big day going to happen?"

"September sixth." Seeing Krystal's jaw drop open, she quickly added, "I know, it doesn't give us much time, but we've hired a wedding coordinator who assures us it's possible. Still, I feel as if I have too much to do."

"I would think so. Is there anything I can do to help?"

"Actually, there is. You could be one of my bridesmaids."

The invitation caught Krystal by surprise. "You want me to be in the wedding?"

Dena nodded and looked at her expectantly, waiting for her response, only Krystal didn't know what to say. "That is so sweet of you to ask me, but..." She paused, searching for the right words to decline without hurting Dena's feelings.

"But I shouldn't have asked because we haven't been friends all that long," Dena finished for her, looking embarrassed. "I'm sorry, Krystal. I didn't mean to put you on the spot."

Krystal reached for her hand. "You didn't. I'm honored that you asked me. The fact that you did says a lot about our friendship."

"But you still don't want to do it."

"I want to, but..." She hated to bring up the subject, but knew she had no choice. "You know I'm pregnant."

Dena gave her a blank look. "Yeah, so what?"

"So all eyes are supposed to be on you, the bride. By September sixth I'm going to be just far enough along that people will be wondering if I'm having a baby or if I'm just getting fat. You don't need that kind of distraction at your wedding."

"Have you been talking to Maddie? She's worried about the same thing and I'm going to tell you what I told her. It doesn't matter if your belly sticks out like a watermelon, which it won't. I want you to be in my wedding."

Maddie Donovan was a dear friend to both of them. Although she'd already married Leonie's son Dylan and moved to France before Dena had moved into 14 Valentine Place, her friendship with Dena went back to their college days when they'd been roommates. Had it not been for Maddie, Dena wouldn't have rented her old room at the boardinghouse and she and Krystal wouldn't have become friends.

"Is Maddie going to be in the wedding?" Krystal asked.

"Yes. I convinced her that I had found the perfect dress to cover what she refers to her as her walrus-shaped body, although I can't imagine Maddie looking anything but gorgeous no matter how much weight she gains."

"Are there dresses that can hide pregnant tummies?"

"Actually, there are." She thumbed through the magazine until she'd found the page she wanted, then shoved it toward Krystal. "Look at this plum one. See how high the waistline is? It's perfect for you and Maddie…and my sister-in-law, Lisa, too. She's going to be my matron of honor, and having had three kids, she also wants to hide her bulges.''

''Don't dresses in these magazines take months to order?''

''Not a problem. Quinn's sister has a friend who works in a bridal shop and she says she can put a rush on them and get them in time, but I do need to get moving on this, which is why I really need an answer from you…like today.'' She gave her an apologetic grin.

Krystal wanted to say yes. Dena had only lived across the hall from her for six months, yet in that time they'd become good friends. She also liked Dena's fiancé Quinn, who was the only man Leonie had allowed to live upstairs. A close friend of the family he had become like a brother to Krystal, as well.

''Would it make it any easier for you to say yes if I said you could bring Roy as your date?'' Dena asked when she continued to deliberate.

''Good grief, no!'' Her response was forceful enough that Dena apologized.

''I guess that means you haven't worked things out.''

''No, and we aren't going to.''

''I'm sorry. I thought…with the baby…'' She trailed off, looking a bit self-conscious.

Krystal reached across and gave her hand a squeeze. ''I'm the one who should be apologizing. I should have told you before now that Roy isn't the father of my baby.''

Dena tried not to look shocked, but Krystal knew she was. Although she'd dated many men, Roy had been the only serious relationship she'd had since living at 14 Valentine Place. It was only natural that people would expect that she was carrying his child. Krys-

tal knew it was what most of her friends would think
when they learned of her pregnancy.

"Have you told the father?" Dena asked in a quiet
voice.

Krystal shook her head. "Not yet. I want to, but it's
complicated." She wished she could tell her just how
complicated it was, but she couldn't. Not with the
wedding only weeks away.

"Well, if there's anything I can do to help, you'll
let me know, right?"

Krystal nodded. "Thanks for caring, but I'm afraid
the only thing you can do is not mention to anyone
that I'm pregnant."

Dena held up her hand. "That goes without saying.
I won't say a word."

"What about Quinn? He was the one who found
my home pregnancy test in the bathroom," she reminded her.

"Yes, but I'm not sure he even realizes it was yours.
At the time I told him it could belong to any one of
a number of your friends who'd stayed with you.
Don't forget. He's lived upstairs so he knows how
popular you are."

"I usually do have people coming and going, don't
I?" she said, hoping Dena was right about Quinn.

"Yes, but if you're worried, I can speak to him
about it."

"Would you mind?"

"No, not at all. Now, back to my request," Dena
said with an endearing smile. "Will you be my bridesmaid?"

As tempting as it was to decline her request, Krystal
could see by the look on Dena's face how important
it was to her. "If you're sure you want me, then yes,
I'd love to be in your wedding."

Dena leaned over to give her a hug. "Thank you. It'll be so much easier for me to do this whole wedding thing knowing you and Maddie will be there."

Easier for Dena maybe, but more difficult for Krystal. "How many people are coming?"

"We wanted to keep it small, but that's not easy to do when your fiancé is a professional hockey player." She flipped open her day planner. "Here's what's been decided so far."

They spent the next two hours discussing everything from what music should be played at the church to what lingerie Dena should take on her honeymoon. It was exactly the kind of girl talk Krystal needed and she appreciated the fact that Dena made no other references to her pregnancy.

"So now you know why I'm so nervous," Dena said as she stacked her day planner on top of the bridal magazine. "By the time this wedding is over, I'm going to be a basket case and you are going to be happy to be rid of me."

"I most certainly will not be. I hate the thought of you leaving," Krystal said sincerely. "I'm glad you decided not to move out until after the wedding. Do you know if Leonie has found someone for the third floor?"

"You haven't heard?" When Krystal gave her a blank look, she continued. "I thought you would know all about it. You see more of Garret than I do."

Krystal frowned. "Know what?"

"Your plan worked."

Krystal was puzzled. "What plan?"

"Going with him to the hospital ball to make his old girlfriend jealous. It must have worked."

Krystal had a bad feeling in her gut and it had nothing to do with morning sickness. "He's seeing Samantha again?"

"He must be. Why else would she be moving in here?"

Krystal gasped. "No! Oh please, tell me it isn't true!" she begged.

"Isn't she the one you said had so many ruffles on her dress at that party that she looked like she could set sail if a gust of wind came up?" Dena asked.

"Yes, and it's too bad it didn't," Krystal retorted.

"Wow! You really don't like her, do you?"

Krystal could see the curiosity in her eyes and knew she needed to give an explanation. She would have liked to have told Dena the real reason she hated to see Samantha Penrose move into the house, but the bride-to-be didn't need to get drawn into the melodrama her life had become.

So instead she said, "Don't pay any attention to me. I'm just in a witchy mood. This early stage of pregnancy is like having PMS 24/7." She brushed the hair from her forehead and sighed.

"It's all right, I understand," Dena assured her.

"Will you please just forget I made a fuss, because I shouldn't have said anything. That night of the hospital ball I hardly spoke to Samantha. For all I know she could be a very nice person."

"I don't think Leonie would have rented the apartment to her if she didn't think she would fit in here. You know how she is about her tenants," Dena pointed out.

Krystal nodded. "I'm just surprised she gave her Quinn's old place. I didn't think Leonie liked her because of what she did to Garret. You do know that she was the one who left him."

Dena nodded. "If Leonie had any hard feelings toward her, they're gone. She spoke very highly of Samantha when she mentioned her to me. Said she was lovely and that she thought we'd get along with her just fine.''

Krystal had to stifle the laughter that nearly spilled out of her. Fortunately Dena's cell phone rang at that moment.

''I'm sorry, Krys, but I have to take this. It's Quinn. You don't mind, do you?''

Krystal shook her head, excused herself and went up to her room. As she climbed the stairs, her legs felt like undercooked pasta. The first thing she did when she got inside her apartment was to collapse on to her bed and stare at the ceiling, stunned by what Dena had told her.

Samantha Penrose would soon be living above her.

If it weren't so tragic it would be funny, Krystal thought. She threw her shoe at the ceiling and groaned in frustration. This couldn't be happening to her. Was fate so cruel or had her life suddenly become a black comedy?

She could only wonder what the lovely Samantha was going to say when she found out her new neighbor was pregnant with her boyfriend's baby.

CHAPTER TWO

"WHAT DO YOU THINK? Wing collar or lay-down?" Quinn Sterling held two pleated shirts up for Garret's inspection.

Before he could answer, Shane Donovan leaned close to them and said, "Whichever one doesn't make you feel like you have a rope around your neck." He made a choking gesture with his hands.

"He *does* have a rope around his neck," Dave Duggan was quick to add with a cocky grin.

Shane's and Dave's kidding brought back memories of their teenage years when the four of them had been the best of friends and someone was always making a wisecrack. Garret pointed to the shirt on his right. "Go with the wing collar and don't pay any attention to these guys. Marriage is going to be a good thing for you and Dena."

"So speaks my brother, the bachelor," Shane drawled sarcastically.

"Hey—his turn will come. Some woman will get her hooks into him sooner or later," Dave warned.

Quinn put one of the hangers back on the rack of starched white shirts. "My money's on later."

"I'd say sooner, judging by the way women eye him once he puts on that white coat," Dave teased.

"Quinn has you on this one, Dave. Come the first of the year, Garret's going to be overseas practicing medicine," Shane said.

"That doesn't mean he can't get married," Dave pointed out.

Garret would have preferred not to have his bachelor status be the topic of discussion, but he knew you couldn't put a group of men in a wedding wear shop and not have the usual banter involving women and marriage. Since the only other single guys in the wedding party were hockey players and everyone apparently expected them to be bachelors, Garret was the prime target for their quips.

"Just for the record, as happy as I know married life can make a man, I think I'll stay single for a while...like five or ten more years," he added with a huge grin.

"I hope you told that to Samantha Penrose," Dave remarked.

That had Quinn asking, "Who's Samantha Penrose and how come I haven't met her?"

"She's just a colleague," Garret answered.

Dave elbowed Shane. "Did you hear that? Just a colleague? Is that any way to talk about your old girlfriend who's hot for you?"

Quinn shot Garret an inquisitive look. "All right, out with it. What did I miss?"

"Nothing important," Garret answered. "Samantha and I dated while we were in medical school. Then she left to do her internship, but recently she moved back to take a position at a hospital here."

"She's not the doctor who's taking over my apartment at 14 Valentine Place, is she?" Quinn asked.

It was the first Garret had heard of it. He turned to his brother. "Has Mom rented the third floor to Samantha?"

"Yes and I can tell by the look on your face she

didn't ask you about it before she did,'' Shane answered.

No, she hadn't, and it annoyed him. He wondered what his mother was up to. First she'd finagled him into going to the hospital ball so that he would see Samantha again, now she was moving her into the boardinghouse. It wasn't like his mother to meddle in his personal life, so just what was going on?

Dave slowly shook his head and whistled through his teeth. ''It's not a good sign, Garret...your old girl-friend moving into a house where there's a match-maker.''

''She's not a matchmaker,'' Garret corrected him. ''She's a romance coach.''

Dave shrugged. ''Same difference. She hooked Quinn up with Dena, didn't she? And Dylan with Maddie. Has she had any tenants move out who weren't getting married? I mean, they move into that place single and the next thing you know...'' He clapped his hands. ''Bang. There's a wedding in the works.''

Shane shoved his hands to his hips. ''I hadn't thought about it before, but you're right. All of her previous tenants are married.''

When Dave began to hum a funeral dirge, Garret stopped him with a raised palm. ''You can cut the music. *If* I ever get married, it will be to someone of my choice, not my mother's. And I say *if* because I'm telling you guys, my plans at this time don't include marriage.''

It was the truth. Right now all he wanted to think about was his career. To finally have the freedom to choose what he wanted to do with his medical training was exhilarating. It made all the struggles he'd been through the past ten years worthwhile.

"Come on, buddy. Are you going to say you don't have any time for women in those plans?" Dave asked him on a note of disbelief.

"Women yes, marriage no," Garret said with a sly grin.

Quinn clapped him on the shoulder. "That's exactly what I said right before I met Dena."

Garret was relieved that a wedding specialist chose that moment to arrive, and for the next half hour, talk was of tuxedos and accessories. While they were measured and fitted for the formal wear, they discussed their roles as ushers and groomsmen at the wedding and reception.

When a question arose regarding which groomsman would be escorting which bridesmaid down the aisle, Quinn said, "I'm not sure. That's Dena's territory."

"I'll take the hot redhead who lived downstairs from you," one of the hockey players offered with a huge grin.

"You mean Krystal."

Upon hearing her name Garret's blood stirred. It had always been that way, even before he'd spent the night with her. Someone would mention her name and he'd be aroused. He blamed it on the fact that the first time he'd seen her she'd been half-naked. He could still remember the look of surprise that had been on her face when he'd pushed open the laundry room door at 14 Valentine Place and found her sorting her dirty clothes clad only in a lacy bra and pants.

Ever since that day he had fantasized about what it would be like to see all of that delectable body unclothed. Never had he expected it to happen, and certainly not on the night of the hospital ball. Only it *had* happened and now he was having trouble forgetting how she had looked lying naked in his bed.

"Is she seeing someone?" the hockey player asked.

"Are girls that hot ever not seeing someone?" Dave wanted to know. "She probably has guys lining up halfway around the block to take her out."

"I bet I could get to the front of the line," boasted the hockey player.

Garret didn't doubt that he could. He looked like the kind of guy Krystal would find attractive. She liked men who looked as if they spent more time at the gym than they did at a job and dressed as if they were on their way to a *GQ* photo shoot.

He wondered what everyone would say if he announced that he had been to the front of the line. That he'd spent the night with her and she was everything a fantasy should be and then some.

He chuckled to himself. They probably wouldn't believe him. Not that he could blame them. He and Krystal were as different as night and day. No one would expect that someone as fun loving and outgoing as Krystal would be attracted to a man who spent most of his free time reading medical journals.

"Knowing Krystal, I bet she already has a date lined up for the wedding," Quinn commented.

Garret suspected he was probably right. There was no shortage of men in her life. He only hoped that the man she did bring wouldn't be Roy Stanton. After the way Roy had betrayed her, Garret didn't want to think she would ever let the creep back into her life. Yet he knew the possibility existed. History had proved that she'd forgive him for almost anything.

"Will you be bringing this Samantha as your date to the wedding?" Quinn interrupted his thoughts.

"Ah...I'm not sure," he said evasively. Until now he hadn't considered taking anyone, but if he needed a date, Samantha would be a sensible choice. She was, after all, more his type than someone like Krystal.

Again his thoughts returned to the beautiful, impulsive hairdresser. He wondered if she ever thought about their night together, or had she simply written it off as a night she wanted to forget. Judging by the way she'd avoided him whenever he'd stopped in at 14 Valentine Place lately, he guessed it was the latter. He knew he should do the same. Forget about her, forget about that night.

Only he couldn't. He'd messed with a fantasy and his life would never be the same.

"I'M SO GLAD YOU WERE OFF today and you could help me move," Samantha told Garret as she filled a shelf with books.

Because she'd hired professional movers, there was little to do except help her unpack boxes. To someone as organized and as efficient as Samantha, it was a task that didn't take long to accomplish.

"I believe that's the last of it and just in time," she told him as she dusted her hands off on her blue jeans. "I'm ready for lunch. Where do you recommend, since this is familiar territory to you?"

"Dixie's is good and it's close."

"Great, I'll just make a couple of phone calls and we'll go." She leaned over to grab her phone from her desk.

"I'll wait for you downstairs. It'll give me a few minutes to talk to my mom," he told her, then headed down to the first floor.

He found his mother in the kitchen seated at the large round oak table. She wasn't alone. Krystal sat across from her, a pair of scissors in her hands. Her expression was one of concentration as she cut clippings from a magazine.

Dressed in a T-shirt and jeans with her hair pulled back from her face and held in place by a barrette, she looked like an innocent and very different from the woman who'd seduced him the night of the hospital ball. She'd been all glitter and glamour and his body tightened as he remembered what had happened after they left the party.

"All finished?" his mother asked when she noticed him.

"Yes." He didn't miss the way Krystal kept her eyes lowered and focused on her task. Usually she greeted him with a grin and started a conversation, but not today. He'd expected that after the way they'd parted the next morning, things would be awkward between them, but not this awkward.

As he moved closer to her he saw what had her attention. Spread out on the table were what looked to be paper dolls, only they were all men wearing swimsuits and none of them had heads.

"What's up with that?" he asked, gesturing to the clippings. "Are you venting your frustration with the opposite sex?"

"We're working on a game for Dena's wedding shower," his mother answered.

"What kind of game has headless male swimsuit models?" he asked.

"A fun one," Krystal answered, cutting around a pair of men's legs.

His mother used her scissors to point to a small stack of paper heads. "The object is to match the celebrity's head with the body. Each match is worth a point. The person with the most points wins. It's as simple as that."

"But Quinn is five points," Krystal corrected.

"Quinn? You have his body in here?"

"Of course. He *is* a celebrity," his mother reminded him. "Although it wasn't easy finding him in a swimsuit. He's usually photographed in his hockey gear."

Garret peered more closely at the headless paper men on the table. "Which one is he?"

"You can't tell?" his mother asked.

He chuckled. "No, Quinn has clothes on when I'm with him." That comment caused Krystal to smile, but she didn't look up at him. "Won't this give Dena an unfair advantage? She's probably the only one who's seen that much of Quinn's skin."

"That's part of the fun...seeing if she can identify her own fiancé without his clothes," Krystal answered.

She glanced up at him then and, from the look in her eyes, he knew she was remembering what he looked like without *his* clothes. If his swimsuit-clad body was in the game, he wondered if she would be able to identify it.

She looked away and he knew that what had happened the night of the hospital party had definitely changed how she felt toward him. The old Krystal would have flirted with him and made a comment regarding the two of them sharing a secret. The new Krystal looked as if she wished he wasn't in the same room with her.

Just then Samantha appeared in the doorway to the kitchen. In her usual take-charge manner, she strode in and greeted his mother.

"I'm glad you're all settled," Leonie said. "Have you met Krystal?"

"Yes, at the hospital ball," Samantha extended a hand, but Garret could see her smile was forced. "It's nice to see you again."

Krystal stiffened and for a moment Garret thought she might bolt right out of her chair, but to his surprise, she smiled brightly, shook Samantha's hand and said, "You're right. You had on the dress with all the ruffles."

The two women made small talk about the food and music at the party. Garret tried to remember Samantha's ruffled dress, but all he could recall was the slinky dress that Krystal had worn. It had been a bright blue and cut to a vee in the front revealing a generous cleavage that had drawn the eyes of every man in the place. Then there had been the slit up the side that had spread whenever she walked, revealing a thigh that was ever so…

"Garret, I asked if that's all right with you?" Samantha sounded a bit impatient and he realized he'd missed what she'd been saying.

"I'm sorry, what did you say?"

"Your mother offered to show me how to use the laundry facilities. You don't mind waiting a few minutes longer, do you?"

She didn't wait for his response but headed out of the kitchen.

Leonie followed her out and suddenly he found himself alone with Krystal for the first time since the party. She didn't look at him but continued cutting out the paper dolls. Before today it would have been unusual for there to be quietness between them. But then it would have been unusual for anyone who was in Krystal's company. She could talk enough for two people and often did.

Only she wasn't talking now. She wasn't even looking at him. And he knew why. They'd had a one-nighter and nothing would ever be the same between them again.

"I'm glad we have a few minutes alone," he finally said, breaking the awkward silence. "I wanted to talk to you about Samantha living here."

"If you're worried I'm going to slip up and let the cat out of the bag that I wasn't a real date that night of the ball, you can relax. I'm not going to say anything," she told him, her concentration on the trimming of a brawny chest. She must have made a mistake because she crinkled the paper and tossed it aside.

"It was a real date, Krystal...or have you forgotten?" He deliberately made his tone seductive, wanting to get a response from her and he did. Her cheeks turned a light pink. "Besides, the cat's already out of the bag," he added.

That brought her head up with a jerk. "You told her the truth?"

"Is there a reason why I shouldn't have?"

"Yes! What happened between us was private," she said, her eyes sparkling with emotion. "I didn't think you'd tell anyone."

"I meant I told her the truth about why you went with me to the ball. She doesn't know what happened after we left and I don't plan to tell her. Or anyone else for that matter."

She looked relieved. "Then she thinks we're just friends."

"We are friends, aren't we?"

"Yeah, sure."

He wasn't so sure she wasn't simply agreeing with him because she didn't want to get into a discussion about what had happened between them. "Is it going to be awkward for you having her living upstairs?" he asked.

She rolled her eyes. "I'm not going to lose any sleep over it, if that's what you're thinking."

"You have no idea what I'm thinking."

She looked directly into his eyes and said, "Then why don't you tell me?"

He couldn't because, if he did and his mother and Samantha were to walk back into the room, they'd hear that he'd made love to her. Because that's what was running through his mind right now—the memory of that night they'd spent together. How incredibly good sex had been with her. How he hadn't been able to forget that it had happened—or that the only reason it had happened had been because she was trying to ease the pain of Roy Stanton's betrayal.

But he couldn't tell her any of those things so he said, "You know Mom likes to think that everyone who lives here is one big happy family."

She set down her scissors and stared at him. "So that's it. You're not worried about things being awkward for me. You want to make sure I'm nice to her."

"That's not what I meant at all," he denied firmly.

"Isn't it?" She jumped up from the table. "I've got to go. I have things to do."

"Krystal, wait," he called out to her as she hurried out of the room.

She kept walking, saying, "You don't need to worry, Garret. I'm not going to be mean to your girlfriend."

"She's not my girlfriend," he said, but she was already gone.

KRYSTAL AWOKE TO the feeling of something not being quite right in her world. It didn't take her long to remember exactly what it was. Before even lifting her head from the pillow, she reached for the soda crackers on her nightstand. After several bites, she gingerly rolled out of bed, relieved that the home remedy for nausea worked for her.

As she did every morning, she showered then examined her naked body in the mirror, looking to see if it had changed enough that other people would notice she was pregnant. So far it hadn't. Except for the slight thickening of her waist, which wasn't any different from the bloating that usually accompanied her PMS, she looked the same as she had ten weeks ago. She wondered how much longer that would be true.

She hoped to keep her pregnancy secret until after Dena and Quinn were married. Weddings were supposed to be happy occasions and with so many Donovans involved in this one, the news that she was expecting Garret's baby could make things uncomfortable for people she cared about, including Dena. She wasn't going to take that risk. A pregnancy lasted forty weeks. Whether she told Garret now or in four weeks wouldn't change that. Postponing the news would, however, make Dena's wedding a more joyful celebration.

Which was why, after dressing in a pink polka-dot chiffon skirt and a white tailored blouse, she went straight to her car instead of stopping for breakfast in the kitchen. She felt confident that she could keep her secret from Leonie, but Samantha was a doctor, trained to diagnose such things as pregnancy. She didn't want to be around her any more than was necessary.

On her way to the mall, she stopped at a convenience store for a bottle of orange juice and a container of blueberry yogurt, which she ate in her car. Next she tackled the shops with her usual zest for shopping.

When she'd purchased everything on her list, she glanced at her watch and saw that it was past noon.

Her stomach growled in hunger, reminding her that, although she was plagued by morning sickness, there was nothing wrong with her appetite during the middle of the day.

She drove home expecting she'd have the kitchen to herself. Only as she pulled into the alley, she saw not only Samantha's car but Garret's, as well.

"Is it going to be awkward for you to have her living upstairs?" Garret's question echoed in her mind.

She couldn't believe he'd even ask such a thing. Of course it was awkward. She'd slept with the woman's boyfriend. The only thing that made her even more uncomfortable was seeing him, which was why she didn't want to go inside when she knew he and Samantha could very well be having lunch together in Leonie's kitchen.

For the first time since she'd moved to 14 Valentine Place, the boardinghouse did not feel like home. And after everything that had happened the past few weeks, if there was one thing she needed, it was the comfort of home.

As she sat staring at the big old Victorian house, she realized this wasn't the only place she called home. Lately she hadn't been back to Fergus Falls, but ever since she'd moved to St. Paul she'd gone back to her hometown when she needed to be with people who loved her unconditionally.

Today she felt that need. Carly already knew about her pregnancy, but she'd been avoiding telling her mother about the baby for fear of what she'd say. Maybe the time had come for her to trust in that unconditional love and ease the burden of her secret a little.

So instead of parking her car next to Garret's and

going inside for lunch, she drove right on through the alley and out on to the city street. Within a few minutes she was on the interstate and heading west. She made one stop on the way—to pick up a chocolate milk shake at the drive-through window of a fast-food restaurant.

When she reached the city limits of Fergus Falls, it was the middle of the afternoon. As always when she returned to her hometown, she felt a rush of nostalgia. Nothing had changed since the last time she'd been back, except lawns that had been green were now brown from the extended hot spell.

The mobile-home park where her mother lived was on the north end of town. It, too, looked the same. A row of long metal boxes parked close together. Her mother was outside her pink-and-gray box home sunning herself on the small patio next to it. A woman Krystal recognized as her neighbor, Edie Fellstrom, was in the reclining lawn chair next to hers. Both wore two-piece swimsuits that were tinier than any Krystal had ever owned. White cotton balls covered their eyes.

They looked oblivious to everything going on around them. Country Western music played loud enough to drown out the sound of her tires crunching on the gravel. It wasn't until Krystal slammed her car door that her mother removed the cotton balls and lifted her head.

"Well, look what the cat dragged in."

Krystal was used to her mother's sense of humor and didn't take offense to the greeting.

"Hi, Mom."

"What's wrong?" she demanded to know.

"You make it sound as if I never come to visit you unless something is wrong."

Her mother swung her legs to one side of the reclining lawn chair and sat up. "Why aren't you at work?" she asked suspiciously.

"When I work Saturdays I get a weekday off. This week it's Tuesday." She watched her mother spritz arms already a deep bronze with cold water. "You should watch how much you sit in the sun, Mom. Too much isn't good for you. It can cause cancer."

"Everything causes cancer. Smoking, drinking, eating, breathing…" She shook her head. "I might as well just crawl into a box and wait to die."

Krystal knew it was useless to argue with her, so she didn't.

Edie said, "You don't have to worry about your momma, Krystal. She takes good care of herself," she assured her. "She uses sunscreen. We both do." She held up a bottle for Krystal's inspection.

Krystal forced a weak smile to her lips.

Her mother said, "Are you hungry? There's chicken salad in the refrigerator."

Only a few hours ago she would have jumped at the chance to eat. Now her appetite had deserted her again, replaced by an indifference to any food. She was learning that when it came to eating, as a pregnant woman she had a short window of opportunity.

"It's too hot to eat," she told her mother.

"It's cool inside."

Still Krystal shook her head.

Her mother rattled off several more food options before finally giving up. "Suit yourself. I hope you have more of an appetite by dinnertime. There's a new Mexican place just up the road I'd like to try. Are you going to stay the night?"

She hadn't thought that far ahead. She shrugged and said, "I suppose I can. I don't have to be at work until noon tomorrow, but I didn't bring any clothes."

Her mother's brow wrinkled. "You didn't call to tell me you were on your way, you didn't bring a change of clothes...what's up with you? There is something wrong, isn't there?"

Edie saw the questions as a sign for her to leave. She reached for a terry-cloth beach wrap draped over the back of her chair. "I gotta get going."

"You don't have to leave because of me," Krystal told her.

"I'm not leaving because of you, sweetie. I'm leaving because I'm getting toasted." She pushed the strap on her bra aside briefly and said, "See?" Then she downed the remainder of her beer, picked up her sunscreen lotion and slipped her feet into a pair of flip-flops. Posed to go, she asked Krystal's mother, "Are you planning to go to the candle party at Jilly's tonight?"

"Not with Krystal here I'm not. Tell her to bring the booklet to work and I'll order something there."

"You don't have to miss it because of me, Mom," Krystal insisted.

Her mother flapped her hand in midair. "It doesn't matter. I didn't really want to go."

"Me, either. I was just going to see Jilly's new place."

Krystal turned to her mother. "I think you should go, Mom. I'll visit Carly while you're gone."

"If you're sure you don't mind...it would be kinda fun..." She trailed off.

"Then it's settled. You're going," Krystal stated firmly.

Edie waved goodbye and called out as she left, "I'll pick you up at seven-fifteen."

As soon as Edie was gone, her mother turned to Krystal and said, "Okay, so what's wrong?"

Despite the fact that Krystal knew it was impossible to lie to her mother and get away with it, she said, "Nothing. Really."

Her mother gave her a look Krystal had seen often. It said, *I'll let you think you're fooling me, but we both know you're not.* She motioned for her to come inside the mobile home. "I want to show you what I've done to the place."

Because her mother had told her she'd made some changes, Krystal expected to find new curtains on both the kitchen and living room windows. To her surprise, however, the entire inside had been paneled in white, replacing the dark walnut walls.

She did a three-sixty and spread her hands in wonder. "You did all this yourself?"

Her mother nodded. "Edie and I went to a couple of those classes they have at the home store in Alex. It's not the most professional-looking job, but it's good enough for this place."

"It looks nice, Mom," she told her, noticing she'd made a new slipcover for the sofa. Instead of the blue-and-green-plaid fabric that she and Carly had soiled on many an occasion, there was a polished cotton floral print. "I like what you did to the sofa. It adds a lot of color to the room."

"And look. I finally got air-conditioning." She pointed to a window unit humming quietly as it blasted cold air into the small home. "I had to. This summer is a killer. If you want it colder, just turn the knob."

"No, it's fine," Krystal said, still looking around in amazement.

"Sit down. I'll put on some clothes and then we'll catch up."

Krystal knew it wasn't going to be easy to tell her

about her pregnancy, not considering their history when it came to talking about sex. She hoped that, because her mother had been a single mom, she'd understand that what she needed most of all was a mom who was there for her.

"Even if you're not hungry you must be thirsty. There's beer and soda in the fridge. Help yourself," her mother said as she moved through the tiny kitchen area.

"I'll just have some water, thanks."

"I don't buy that bottled stuff. What I have comes straight out of the tap," she warned before going into her bedroom and closing the door.

Krystal pulled a tumbler from the cupboard and filled it with water. Before sitting down at the table, she went over to the wall to look at the pictures hanging there. Most of them were of her and Carly when they were kids. She wondered why her mother didn't have pictures of them as adults. She'd gone to all the trouble of replacing the paneling in the mobile home, yet she'd hung the same old pictures on the wall.

She looked to the far end of the living room and, as she expected, there hung the watercolor of the Eiffel Tower—a gift from one of her mother's friends who'd been to France. It had to be close to twenty years old and had survived several moves in which many of her mother's possessions had been carted away to the dump. Linda still hadn't given up on her dream of someday visiting Paris.

When her mother returned, she had on a pair of capri pants and a scoop-neck top that made her look much younger than her forty-five years. "You look good, Mom."

The compliment brought a smile. "Why thank you, dear."

Again Krystal looked around. "I really like what you've done with the house."

"It looks good, doesn't it? I should have spruced up the place years ago, but there were always other things that needed my money."

"Yeah, me and Carly."

She chuckled. "One of you was always needing something." She grabbed a bottle of beer from the refrigerator, twisted off the cap and took a sip. "Are you sure you don't want a beer?"

Krystal shook her head. "No, I'm fine."

Her mother sat down across from her. "So why are you here on a hot summer day when you should be at the beach on one of those beautiful lakes they have down there in the cities?"

Krystal looked at her glass and shrugged. "You know I'm not a beach person."

"No, but you're a city person. You didn't have any trouble making that transition, did you?"

"I like the fact that there are so many people. There's an energy there…always something going on, always something in motion."

"You don't miss your hometown?"

"I miss you and Carly."

She could feel her mother's eyes on her. "Everything going okay at work?"

She nodded. "Yeah, work's going good."

"You must be putting in long hours. You look tired."

She was tired, but not because of extra hours at work. "I've been busy and then it's been so hot. You know the heat always drains me." Even with the new window air conditioner, she felt warm and swiped at her brow with a napkin.

"Maybe you want to take a nap before dinner," her mother suggested.

She nodded. "I would, but first I need to talk to you about something."

Her mother's brow furrowed. "So you didn't just come because you wanted to see me. I should have known."

"Mom, that's not fair. I come up here all the time and very seldom do I ever ask for anything."

Her mother reached for her hands and gave them a squeeze. "I'm sorry. I shouldn't have said that. Oh, before I forget." She jumped up and went over to the tiny bookshelf in the corner. "I have a new book for you."

Krystal read the title aloud. *"How to Marry Your Soul Mate in One Year Or Less."*

"I heard the author talking about it on TV," her mother said, her voice full of excitement. "She knows her stuff, Kryssie. Take it home with you and read it."

She nodded and murmured a thanks, knowing perfectly well that she'd take it home and add it to the pile of self-help books her mother had given her over the years—most of them about how to find a mate for life. She knew it was important to her mother that Krystal find her soul mate. Really important. Which made it all the more difficult for Krystal to tell her she was pregnant, yet it had to be done.

She set the book aside. "Mom, I need to talk to you."

Her mother frowned. "Something's bugging you. What is it? Are you having money problems? Is that it? If you need to borrow some, I have a little put away," she told her.

Krystal pushed a stray red strand of hair back from her face. "I don't need money, Mom."

"But you need something. I can see it in your face."

Krystal took a deep breath and clenched her fingers, aware that the moment she'd been dreading had arrived and there was no turning back. "I do need something, Mom. I need your understanding."

"About what?" she asked slowly.

Krystal tried to get the words out, but they stuck in her throat. She swallowed with difficulty, trying to stop the emotion that threatened to make this even more difficult than it already was. When moisture pooled in her eyes, she knew she'd lost the battle.

Her mother saw her distress and demanded, "What is it? What's wrong?"

A tear slipped down her cheek and she swiped at it with the back of her hand. "I messed up big time, Mom."

"Messed up how? You didn't get fired, did you?"

She shook her head. "It's not about work, Mom. I already told you that."

"Then tell me what it is about. You're sitting there looking as if you've lost your best friend. Is that it? Did you and Shannon have words?"

Krystal reached into her purse for a tissue and blew her nose. She knew there was no easy way to tell her mother and blurted out, "I'm pregnant."

In the blink of an eye her mother's hand slapped her face, stinging her cheek. For a moment, Krystal was too stunned to move. Then she jumped up from her chair, grabbed her purse and headed for the door.

She expected her mother to come after her, to tell her she was sorry, that she'd reacted emotionally and she regretted it.

But she didn't. For all Krystal knew she could still

be sitting at the kitchen table. She certainly wasn't making any effort to stop her daughter from leaving.

With tears streaming down her cheeks, Krystal climbed into her car and started the engine. And for the second time that day she felt as if she were running away from home.

CHAPTER THREE

WHEN KRYSTAL PULLED IN TO Carly's long driveway she saw her sister sitting on the porch swing. Beside her was Emily, her four-year-old daughter. As soon as they saw Krystal's car, they came running across the lawn to welcome her.

"I'm glad you came here," Carly said, wrapping her in a sisterly hug.

It was the only place in Fergus Falls Krystal could go. Since she'd moved to St. Paul she'd lost touch with many of her friends. Most of them had moved away, but of the ones who remained, none could give her the emotional support that Carly provided.

As children they'd been like other close siblings, rivals one minute and best friends the next. Being older by fifteen months, Krystal had often played the role of protector, looking out for the smaller, more innocent Graham girl. It wasn't until the emotional turbulence of adolescence that their roles reversed, with a calm Carly being the one who kept a watchful eye on an impetuous Krystal.

"Did Mom call?" she asked, although she already knew the answer.

Carly nodded. "I'll tell you about it in a minute."

Emily tugged on Krystal's hand saying, "Auntie Krys, guess what? I get to go with Grandma."

Krystal stiffened as she looked to her sister for an explanation.

"Relax. She means Joe's mother," Carly explained.

"I get to eat supper at Grandma's, then go get ice cream at church," Emily boasted.

"It's an old-fashioned ice-cream social." Carly then said to Emily, "Go get your backpack from the house. I think I see Grandma's car coming." As she skipped away she said to Krystal, "You didn't tell me you were planning to tell Mom you're pregnant today."

"I didn't know. I just got in the car and came up here on the spur of the moment." She shook her head. "Boy, was that a mistake."

Carly placed a hand on her arm, her eyes full of compassion. "Are you okay? You're trembling."

"I know. I should probably eat something. I haven't had anything since breakfast except for a milk shake," she told her, not wanting to begin a discussion with Carly's mother-in-law in the driveway.

"I'll make you something as soon as Joe's mom leaves with Emily," she said with a comforting pat on Krystal's arm.

Krystal nodded and tried to act as if nothing was wrong as the three women made small talk. It was a typical August afternoon with the humidity making it feel much warmer than the temperature indicated. By the time Emily and her grandmother finally left, perspiration tickled the back of Krystal's neck and she felt light-headed.

Carly noticed her paleness and looped an arm through Krystal's. "Come. We're going inside where it's cool and I'll get you something to eat."

Carly's house was definitely cooler than her mother's, but then it was nothing at all like the homes in the trailer park. It was two stories of brick with tall ceilings, lots of windows, and a design that was as elegant as any of the model homes she'd seen in the cities. It had everything she and Carly had dreamed about as children, including a swimming pool in the backyard.

"Would you rather sit outside by the pool?" she asked when Krystal glanced through the patio door.

"No, this feels good." As she passed the family room she saw a piano. "Where did that come from?"

"Joe's parents bought it for Emily." She nudged her toward the kitchen. "You sit while I make us some tea and get you something to eat. What sounds good?"

"Nothing," she answered honestly.

Carly grinned. "I know that feeling. How about if I toast you an English muffin? I have some fresh raspberry jam."

Krystal shrugged. "That's fine." She took a seat at the breakfast counter on one of the tall stools and watched her sister move about a kitchen that looked like something out of a magazine.

"So tell me what happened at Mom's," Carly ordered as she set two china cups on the counter.

"What did she tell you?"

"Not very much," she answered, filling the teakettle.

Krystal knew her sister was being diplomatic. "You don't need to worry about my feelings, Carly. I know Mom's upset. I'm sure she sees my being pregnant as just another one of the many things I've done to disappoint her."

"We both know she has high expectations of us," she noted.

"Yes, well her expectations were met when it came to you. You have a beautiful house, a great husband, and an adorable daughter." She sighed, not out of envy but because she knew it was the truth. Carly had fulfilled their mother's dream for her. She, on the other hand, hadn't even come close.

Carly frowned. "She didn't drag my name into it, did she?"

"No, she didn't say anything at all. There was no time. I blurted out, I'm pregnant, she slapped me and gave me this wounded look, then I left."

Carly gasped. "She slapped you? She didn't tell me that!"

"It's probably not something she wants to admit." The memory was enough to make Krystal's eyes misty. "If there was one thing Mom never did to us when we were growing up it was hit us."

"No, which means she must be really upset to strike you now," Carly concluded.

"*She's* upset? What about me? How does she think I feel?" They were rhetorical questions she didn't expect her sister to answer. "The one time in my life when I could really use her understanding, she treats me as if I've shamed her."

"You haven't shamed anybody."

"Tell that to her."

"I already did. I'm on your side, Krys. You ought to know that. I always have been." She reached for Krystal's hand and gave it a squeeze.

"Thanks, but I don't want to put you in the middle between me and Mom."

"Isn't that where I am anyway?"

Krystal nodded soberly. They both knew that their mother had put them in that position by setting "married with children" as a standard by which she judged her daughters. Krystal knew it made Carly just as uncomfortable as it did her, but there was really nothing they could do about it.

"Part of the problem is she takes everything so personally,'' Carly continued. ''As if every mistake we make is her fault.''

''You mean every mistake I make,'' Krystal corrected her. ''Let's face it. I'm the one who was always getting into trouble. And she hasn't liked one single boyfriend I've brought home.'' Her voice broke as she struggled not to cry.

''I can sure tell you're pregnant.'' Carly handed her a tissue.

Krystal blew her nose. ''I thought I was emotional before I got pregnant. Now it's ten times worse.''

''Maybe it's better if we don't talk about Mom. Let's talk about you.''

''Then for sure I'll be mopping up the tears,'' she warned her.

''Aw, come on. It can't be that bad.'' Carly came around to Krystal's side of the counter and put her arm around her. ''Where's that 'the glass is always half full' sister of mine?''

''She discovered her glass is almost empty,'' she said miserably.

''No, it isn't,'' Carly contradicted her. ''You are going to be a mother, Krystal. That in itself is a miracle and a blessing.''

''I know, but right now I'm having trouble seeing the blessing part,'' she confessed.

''Of course you are. It's too early in your pregnancy for you to see this as anything but unexpected and scary. But you have a little person growing inside you. Someone who's going to be so happy to have you for a mom.''

She sniffled. ''Someone's who going to wish I also had a husband.''

''Listen to me.'' Carly grabbed Krystal by the shoulders and forced her to look into her eyes. ''You don't need a husband to be a good mother. And your baby has a father—a man you've told me is a good guy and one you know won't turn his back on his child.''

Krystal nodded. "I know. I'm trying to stay positive about all of this, but it's just such a big mess."

"A mess that can be straightened out," Carly stated reassuringly. "I know you want to wait until after Dena's wedding to tell Garret about the baby, but I wish you'd do it now. You need to know what he plans to do. His reassurance that he's going to be a part of the baby's life would ease some of the stress you're feeling. Plus then you wouldn't have to keep this big secret from everyone."

"You're right. I will feel better once Garret knows, but I have to wait to tell him, Carly," she insisted. "Do you realize what it's going to be like at 14 Valentine Place when everybody hears of this pregnancy? Leonie's the unsuspecting grandmother who lives downstairs, Samantha's the unsuspecting girlfriend who lives upstairs, and Dena's stuck in the middle trying to plan a wedding, one in which most of the Donovan family has a part. In a few weeks she'll be married and it won't matter what's going on in the house, but for now I don't want my problems spoiling what should be a happy time for Dena."

"All right." Carly hopped down off the stool to tend to the teakettle that whistled on the stove. "I won't bug you about it again. Let's talk about something fun. Tell me about the wedding. I want to know all the details. It's not every day my sister's a bridesmaid in a professional hockey player's wedding."

Krystal told her about the wedding shower and just about everything she could think of that Dena had told her about her plans, including the list of celebrities and professional athletes who'd be attending. It was the diversion Krystal needed to forget about the scene with her mother.

When Joe didn't come home for dinner, Carly ordered a pizza for the two of them. By the time they'd finished, they were laughing and they'd forgotten the tears that had been shed earlier in the day. Even though she'd had the scene with her mother, Krystal was glad she'd driven to Fergus Falls for the day. Carly gave her something no one else could—a sister's love and understanding.

When it came time for her to leave, she wasn't surprised when her sister said, ''I think you should go back to Mom's. She cares about you, Krys.''

''Don't you ever get tired of playing peacemaker between me and Mom?''

''Uh-uh. I love you both. And I know she loves you. And if you had heard her on the phone today, you'd know she does, too.''

Krystal sighed. ''I'm not sure she's ever going to speak to me again.''

''Of course she will.''

Krystal looked down at her fingers. ''You didn't see the look in her eyes when I told her I was pregnant.''

''You broke the most important rule she ever set for us. Do as I say, don't do what I've done.''

''That's why I thought maybe she'd understand where I'm at emotionally right now. I don't need another critic. I have enough of them, but I could use a mother.'' She hated that her voice faltered.

Carly placed a comforting hand on her arm. ''Then don't go home angry. Go back over there,'' she urged her. ''Mom will have had some time to think about this and to get over her initial shock.''

''You really think I should?''

Carly nodded. "The two of you need to talk."

"I'm not sure we can. You know what Mom's like. Did she show you the latest book she bought for me?" When Carly shook her head, she said, "It's *How To Marry Your Soul Mate in One Year or Less.*"

Carly grimaced. "She just wants you to be happy."

Krystal groaned in frustration. "She wants me to be married. How are we going to be able to have an honest discussion about my being pregnant?"

"You've got to try, Krys. For your sake and for Mom's," her sister pleaded with her. "You should listen to me on this one. I don't have pregnant hormones messing with my emotions. You do."

As difficult as it was, Krystal took her sister's advice and went back to the trailer park. When she got to her mom's, there was no one home. Krystal figured she'd gone to the candle party with Edie after all.

She found the spare key under the clay pot with the red geraniums and let herself in. Feeling a craving for something sweet, she opened the freezer, grateful to see that her mother hadn't changed. Inside was a half gallon of her favorite ice cream—mint chocolate chip. It was Krystal's favorite, too.

She ate two scoops, then stretched out on the sofa. She turned on the TV, trying not to think about what lay ahead when her mother returned.

Only her mother didn't return. At eleven Krystal looked up Jilly's number in her mother's address book.

"Hi, Jilly, it's Krystal. I heard you were having a candle party tonight. My mom isn't still there, is she?"

"No, Kryssie," the older woman replied. "She never came to the party. Edie said she went with a friend to hear some band play over in Alex."

Friend meaning *man,* Krystal deduced, since if it had been one of her girlfriends Jilly would have said her name. It didn't matter. She wasn't going to wait and find out, because with her mother it was always the same old story.

Krystal got in her car and drove back to St. Paul. The house at 14 Valentine Place was in darkness when she arrived. She was glad. What she didn't need was to find Samantha and Garret in the kitchen at two in the morning. She used the side entrance and quietly climbed the stairs to the second floor, relieved to find her room was once again the haven it had always been. She shed her clothes and crawled into bed.

KRYSTAL AND HER MOTHER HAD argued in the past, but never had they gone for more than a day or two without talking to each other. Now more than a week had passed without any communication between them. Krystal had called and left several messages after returning home, but now with each passing day, it became more difficult for her to pick up the phone, especially when she wasn't sure if her mother would hang up on her.

But it wasn't only the possibility of her mother rejecting her that kept her from calling. Pride stood in the way of her making a peace overture. Normally Krystal wasn't one to hold a grudge, but lately nothing seemed normal when it came to her emotions.

That's why, when she arrived home from work on the day of Dena's bridal shower and found her mother sitting in Leonie's kitchen, she found herself angry. She struggled to keep her feelings in check, unsure what had transpired between her landlady and her mother, who sat with their heads together over coffee.

They looked as comfortable as if they were the best of friends, which shouldn't have surprised Krystal. Leonie had a way of making guests feel at home in her kitchen. Krystal could only hope that Leonie's empathetic nature hadn't evoked any great urge on her mother's part to pour her heart out on the subject of her daughter's pregnancy.

"Mom! I didn't expect to see you here." Krystal could feel Leonie's eyes on her and she hoped she didn't sound as uneasy as she was feeling.

"Isn't it a lovely surprise?" Leonie asked with her usual cheerful grin.

Lovely was not the adjective that came to mind for Krystal. *Scary* was more like it. In less than two hours the house would be filled with people showering good wishes on Dena, and her mother had chosen today to visit. Since she rarely drove to the city, Krystal wondered if she'd come to scold her or to reconcile with her.

"We've been getting to know each other better," Leonie said as she rose to get a refill of coffee.

Krystal eyed her mother suspiciously, wondering what she'd said to her landlady. Had she told her they'd been fighting? Or worse yet, had she revealed the reason for the tension between them? Judging by Leonie's jovial expression, Krystal didn't think she had.

"Leonie told me you're giving Dena a bridal shower tonight," Linda commented.

Krystal nodded. "Yeah, and I have a lot to do before the guests arrive, so I should go upstairs."

"Maybe I can help," her mother offered.

It was her peace offering and Krystal knew she should behave like a grown-up and accept, but she'd discovered that during pregnancy her moments of maturity had a way of escaping when she least expected it. "No, I'm fine. I can manage."

She could see she'd shocked Leonie. Her landlady

leaned over to her mother, patted her forearm and said, "That's very sweet of you to offer to help, Linda. We can always use an extra pair of hands in the kitchen."

Only Krystal knew that her mother's smile was forced. "Just give me an apron and tell me what to do."

To Krystal's dismay, that's exactly what her landlady did. Her mother listened intently as Leonie launched into a description of the melon baskets and vegetable crudités they were going to serve. Krystal felt as if the rug was being pulled out from under her feet. She needed to talk to her mother and she needed to do it soon.

"Mom, maybe before you get started down here you could come with me upstairs. I have the party favors in my room and we still need to decorate the great room, too."

"No, you don't," Leonie told her. "Lisa was over earlier today and took care of the decorating. Wait until you see what she's done. She has white paper streamers everywhere and lots of balloons."

"Oh, that sounds lovely," Linda beat her to a response. "I'd love to take a look."

"Go ahead," Leonie instructed with a wave of her arm. "It's just down the hall and around the corner."

Krystal suppressed her sigh of frustration. "We can take a look when we bring the party favors down from upstairs." She motioned for her mother to follow her out of the kitchen.

She planned not to say another word until they were in her room, but at the top of the landing her mother said, "Your landlady's a nice person. She's very easy to talk to."

Krystal turned to face her. "Just what did you tell her?"

"Nothing about—" she paused, then lowered her voice to a near whisper "—your condition."

Krystal heaved a sigh of relief. "Thank God. My life is enough of a mess without having Leonie upset with me."

"Oh, I see. It's okay for you to have your mother upset with you but not Leonie?" she snapped.

"No, it's not okay, but I'm not the one who hasn't been returning phone calls this past week," she shot back.

"I had my reasons."

"And they would be…" she prodded.

"This hasn't been easy for me, Kryssie."

"And you think it has been for me?" She didn't want to sound defensive, but that's exactly how she felt. "You know, this really isn't the best time to be having this conversation. I'm supposed to be getting ready for the shower. Why did you come down here today of all days?"

"Because I don't want the next week to be like this past one has been. This nontalking has got to stop."

"I'm not the one who hasn't been talking!"

Aware that Dena could come home at any time and find the two of them arguing on the landing, Krystal pulled her mother by the arm into her room. She didn't bother to ask her to sit down, but stood facing her, her hands on her hips.

Her mother stated the obvious. "I know you're angry with me."

Krystal folded her arms across her chest. "How do you expect me to feel? You wouldn't even listen to me when I came to see you." She hated the way her voice quivered when she spoke.

"I know and I'm sorry. It was just such a shock

hearing that you'd done the one thing I'd prayed you'd never do. I thought I'd raised you to have values.''

''I do have values. I'm pregnant, not morally bankrupt, and if the only reason you came here was to tell me I've done a bad thing, I got the message loud and clear last week.'' She wished she could express herself without getting so emotional, but she was dangerously close to tears. ''A stinging palm on my cheek, not coming home, not returning my calls... I believe I know exactly what you think of me, Mom.''

''No, you don't, and I am sorry. For everything, but especially for slapping you. You know how I feel about mothers hitting their children. I've always taken pride in the fact that I raised you and Carly by myself yet I never laid a hand on either of you. I was ashamed of what I did.''

Krystal could hear the regret in her voice, see the sadness in her eyes. ''Then why did you do it?''

Linda shrugged. ''I don't know. Maybe it was because I saw myself in you.''

''Mom, I'm not a teenager who got caught having sex.''

''No, you're a grown woman who should have known better.''

It wasn't anything Krystal hadn't said to herself a hundred times, but she didn't need to hear those words from her mother. ''You know what, Mom? I should have known better but I didn't. I messed up.'' She threw up her hands. ''There. I've admitted it. Are you happy?''

''No, I'm not happy.''

''Well, that makes two of us because I'm not happy, either. I'm scared. Damn scared. And it would be nice if I could talk about that with my mother instead of feeling like I'm the world's biggest loser of a daughter." There was no stopping the tears. They flooded her eyes, shook her shoulders and wrinkled her face. She turned away, but within a few moments she felt a pair of arms around her.

Her mother pulled her close, soothing her with the same words she'd used so often when she was a child. "There, there, now. It's going to be all right."

"I don't think it is, Mom. I don't know what I'm going to do," she sobbed into her shoulder.

"You'll figure it out," Linda said reassuringly. "And I'll be there to help you."

"Do you mean that?" Krystal asked on a hiccup, straightening.

"Of course I do." She handed her a tissue. "That's why I'm here."

Krystal tried to smile but failed. She swiped at the tears with the back of her hand. "We shouldn't be talking about this now. I have to get ready for the shower."

"Then we won't talk about it anymore," her mother said with a maternal authority. "Now stop crying so those splotches go away."

She glanced in the mirror and moaned. "Oh great! My eyes are all puffy."

Her mother scrutinized her swollen lids. "Do you have any cucumbers?"

"I'm sure Leonie has some, but I don't think I have time to sit with them on my eyes. I've too much to do."

"Then we'll have to think of something else." Linda gave her a gentle shove. "You go get in the shower and let me get started on your to-do list. What should I do first?"

"The party favors have to be taken downstairs." She gestured to the tray on her dresser that was covered in tiny champagne cups filled with candies. "Mom, you have to promise me you won't mention my pregnancy to Leonie or anyone else you meet tonight."

Linda made a sound of indignation. "Of course I'm not going to say anything."

"Good. This is Dena's night. I can't seem to even mention the baby without getting weepy and if there's one thing I don't want to do, it's spoil the bridal shower by being a wet rag."

"Doesn't anyone know about the baby?"

"Dena does, but she's the only one. Are you planning to stay the night? You can sleep on my futon if you want," Krystal offered.

"Why don't I wait and see how late it is when the festivities end?"

Krystal nodded. Some of her apprehension must have shown because her mother said, "You can take that worried look off your face. I'm not going to reveal your secret. I've walked in your shoes and I know what you're going through."

"Then help me get through it. Please," she begged, again getting weepy.

"I will, sweetie. I will," her mother said, giving her another hug.

"And please whatever you do, don't say anything to Leonie about the baby," she repeated.

Linda sighed impatiently. "I've already told you I wouldn't."

Yes, she had and Krystal needed to trust her.

During the bridal shower, her mother spent most of her time in the kitchen. When it came time for the food to be served, however, Leonie insisted that she join the party and eat with everyone in the great room.

It was a long night for Krystal, not because she

worried her mother would slip and mention the baby, but because of the look in her mother's eyes as she listened to Dena talk about the wedding. It was what she'd always wanted for her daughters—the white dress, the elegant reception, the romantic honeymoon.

Later, as they cleaned up the kitchen, she knew she hadn't imagined the wistful look in her mother's eyes. "Bridal showers are such happy occasions, aren't they?"

"Mmm-hmm," Krystal agreed, rinsing plates in the sink before putting them in the dishwasher.

"It sounds as if Dena and Quinn are going to have the kind of wedding most folks only dream about."

"I'm sure it'll be nice."

"She showed me a picture of her dress. It's gorgeous."

"I know. I was with her when she picked it out."

"They've hired a live orchestra for the reception. It's at the country club," Linda told her, as if it were news. "It's amazing what they've planned in such a short time, isn't it?" She didn't wait for Krystal to comment but added, "Which just goes to show you that you can have a beautiful wedding on short notice."

"I suppose you can...if you want one," Krystal said on a weary note.

"Every girl wants one."

Krystal didn't say a word, but continued working in silence until her mother said, "You want one, don't you?"

"No, I don't think I do."

"Krystal!"

Without glancing at her mother she knew the look on her face. It was the shock and disappointment that always accompanied that tone of voice. When Krystal did finally look at her she saw that she was right.

"Are you telling me you're giving up your dream of a wedding with all the trimmings?" Again she didn't wait for an answer. "Just because you're—" to Krystal's relief, she stopped herself before saying the word *pregnant* "—doesn't mean you can't have a wedding."

Krystal had heard enough. She wiped her hands on a dish towel and tossed it aside. "I'm going outside for some fresh air."

She should have known her mother would follow.

"You can have as big a wedding as you want, Krystal." Linda stood beside her, pleading her case. "You just need to do it quickly and, if that's what's worrying you, I can help with the plans. Dena is proof that it doesn't take long to set the plans in motion. Look at what she's accomplished in just a few weeks."

Krystal was tired, too tired to be having this discussion, but she had to say, "I don't have any plans to set in motion."

"Not right now, maybe, but you're going to have to make some soon. Time is not on your side. You need to think about this."

Think about getting married was what she meant. Her mother had jumped to the conclusion that because she was going to have a baby she was going to get married.

"Now if it's money that has you worried, I've got a little put aside. You know I helped Carly with her wedding and I want to do the same for you."

"You can keep your money. I don't want to get married, Mother," she stated firmly.

"What do you mean you don't want to get married?"

"Just what I said. I don't want to get married," she repeated, enunciating each word slowly.

"Of course you want to get married. Do you know how many times you and Carly played brides when you were kids?"

"Well, I'm not a little girl anymore so can we please not talk about this?"

"I'm only trying to help."

"I don't need that kind of help," she said with exasperation.

Her mother shook her head in resignation. "I don't know what you want."

"Neither do I, Mom. Neither do I," Krystal mumbled, but her mother had already gone back inside.

As Garret pulled his car into the small parking area behind 14 Valentine Place he noticed two figures on the steps. Even though it was dark, the door cast enough light for him to see they were women. It wasn't until he climbed out of his car and heard their voices that he realized one of them was Krystal.

From what was being said, it wasn't difficult to figure out that the other woman was her mother. Or that they were arguing. To his surprise, it was over the subject of weddings. When the screen door slammed shut, he knew one of them had gone inside.

As he rounded the corner of the house he saw that Krystal sat on the steps staring up at the sky.

"Are you keeping the crickets company?" he asked as he walked toward her.

She jumped to her feet with a tiny shriek. "Where did you come from?"

"I'm sorry. I didn't mean to startle you. I thought you heard me pull up." He jerked a thumb toward the parking lot.

"No, I didn't hear anything but my mother's screaming," she answered candidly.

"I wouldn't say she was screaming exactly."

She eyed him suspiciously. "Then you heard what she was saying?"

He shook his head. "Not really. Just the sound of voices—not what was actually being said."

"I think you're saying that to be polite."

"And if I am?"

"Thank you." She smiled at him and reached out to touch his hand. It was as if that night of the hospital ball had never happened and they were friends again.

But just as quickly as she reached out to touch him, she snatched her hand away. "I should go back inside. We had Dena's shower tonight."

The awkwardness was back and he hated its presence.

He guessed it was probably inevitable, considering everything that had happened. But he'd caught a glimpse of that spontaneous smile of hers and he wanted to see it again.

As she started for the door, he stopped her. "Krystal, wait."

When she glanced at him she wore a look of vulnerability and for one brief moment he was reminded of the way she'd looked that night when she'd come running out of Roy Stanton's apartment building.

"I'm hungry and I could use some company," he said quietly.

"I'm sure there's food left over from the shower if you want to come inside," she told him. "Some of the guests are still here."

"I brought my dinner," he said, lifting the delicatessen bag. "And that's not the kind of company I had in mind."

"I don't think Samantha's home yet."

"I didn't come to see Samantha," he told her, although it wasn't exactly true. They had arranged to meet for a late supper, but she'd been detained at the hospital. Instead of eating alone, he'd decided to stop by 14 Valentine Place. He was glad he did.

He walked over to the picnic table on the patio, hooked a leg over the bench and sat down. "I have enough for two if you want some."

"No, thanks."

"You could keep me company. I know I'm not exactly your favorite person lately, but I won't scream at you," he promised. When she didn't say anything he added, "You don't really want to go back inside, do you?"

She unfolded her arms and walked over to the picnic table and sat down.

"So who won the game?" he asked. She gave him a puzzled look and he added, "The headless paper dolls."

"Oh, that." A smile played at the corners of her mouth. "One of Quinn's sisters."

"I guess she would know what he looked like in swim trunks, wouldn't she?" he said with a half grin.

"Oh, she didn't get Quinn's right. No one did, which made Dena quite happy."

He glanced at the bright lights shining through the windows. "Is the party over then?"

"Mmm-hmm. Your mom and a few of the guests are still in the great room with Dena talking about the wedding."

"So was it a good shower?" he asked.

"It was great. I think everyone had a good time."

"What about you? Did you have fun?" He knew

that was like asking if the sky was blue. Krystal made her own fun wherever she went.

She smiled. "Yes. We had a few surprises for Dena that had everyone laughing."

That didn't surprise him. He unwrapped a sandwich and asked, "You sure I can't tempt you with one of these? I have an extra one."

She shook her head. "No, but you go ahead."

"What about an Evian?"

"Sure, if you have one."

He pulled a bottle of water from the bag and unscrewed the cap before handing it to her. "If I'd remembered the bridal shower was this evening I wouldn't have come over."

"Why? Do they give you the jitters or something?"

"Or something," he confessed with a half grin. "So what were you and your mother arguing about?"

"I thought you heard," she said with a lift of one beautiful eyebrow. She took a sip of water, then said, "Bridal showers put her in this mood where she wants to talk about weddings—and mine in particular, or I should say the lack of there being one in my immediate future."

"It must be something that comes with the territory of being a mom. They want to see their children married with children."

"Some moms. Leonie isn't like that."

He chuckled sarcastically. "That's what you think."

"She wants you to get married?"

"She hasn't come right out and said as much in so many words. I suspect she's a lot like your mom only much more subtle. I know she'd much rather see me married than have me go overseas with Doctors Without Borders."

"Are you still thinking about joining that program?"

He nodded. "I'll probably leave after the first of the year."

His answer startled her. "I didn't know that."

"I thought my mom would have told you. She's told practically everyone else. She's worried I'll end up in a war zone," he said lightly, although it was not anything to be joking about.

"Is that a possibility?"

"There's always the possibility of war somewhere and, unfortunately, those are the areas that need the medical relief."

She frowned. "I thought you said you wanted to vaccinate children in the impoverished regions."

"I do, but if doctors are needed in more urgent situations…"

"How long will you be gone?"

"Six months to a year."

"Ohmigosh, you're kidding!" She stared at him as if in shock.

He smiled, wanting to erase the worry from her face. "From the way you're looking at me, I could almost believe that you're going to be sorry to see me go."

"Of course I am. I don't want you to go if you're going into a war zone." This time there was no mistaking the distress in her voice.

She'd never been one to hide her emotions and it was obvious she was upset. He wanted to think it was because she cared about him. But he also knew she had a soft heart and there was a good chance she would have the same reaction to hearing that any one of her friends was about to embark on a difficult assignment.

She shuddered and said, "Can we talk about something else?"

"Sure." It was too beautiful a night to talk about anything she found upsetting. "Is it my imagination or do the stars look brighter than usual tonight?"

She propped her chin on her hand and stared up at the night sky. "There are a lot of them tonight, but it's hard to see them with so many lights in the city. It's one of the first things I noticed when I moved here. Back home if you were to sit out on a night like this you'd see gazillions of tiny white dots in the sky. Here you only see the bigger stars."

"That's one of the advantages of small-town living. Better stargazing," he noted.

She chuckled. "Probably the only advantage, but don't say that in front of my mom."

"She likes it in Fergus Falls?"

"She'd like nothing better than for me to return."

"You don't think that'll ever happen?"

She shrugged. "I suppose it could, but St. Paul feels more like home to me now. There's just so much more to do here. One of the reasons I left Fergus Falls was because I was bored."

She needed excitement in her life. He'd known that about her from the day they met. She was like a sponge, ready to soak up as many things as she possibly could. Maybe that's what attracted him initially. She was so very different from him.

She snapped her fingers in front of his face. "Are you there? Why do you always do that?"

"Do what?" he asked.

"Disappear inside your head. Why don't you just tell me what's on your mind?"

"You really want to know?" he asked.

"Yes."

Before he could do just that, a tall figure came out of the shadows calling her name.

She jumped to her feet. "Roy! What are you doing here?"

"You need to ask me that?" he answered her question with a question as he stood directly in front of her. "I've talked to your mother."

Krystal's eyes widened. She looked from Roy to Garret and then back to Roy. Then she grabbed Roy by the hand. "Come with me," she ordered, pulling him into the house.

Garret felt as if someone had just thrown a blanket over the stars. He wanted to follow them inside and say, "Are you nuts? Have you forgotten what this guy did to you?" But he knew he couldn't. Because the only thing worse than seeing her drag Roy into the house would be if he were to follow them and she'd tell *him* to leave.

Ever since the night of the hospital ball he'd wanted to believe that she was finished with Roy Stanton. Now he could see that he hadn't been wrong to believe that she'd only slept with him because she'd been so distraught over Roy cheating on her.

Suddenly the corned beef sandwich tasted awful. He jammed what was left of it into the bag and tossed it in the garbage on the way to his car.

CHAPTER FOUR

KRYSTAL'S HEART BEAT so fast she could feel it in her throat. Why would Roy come to see her unless he knew about the baby?

I'll be there to help you. Her mother's words echoed in her ears. Was this her idea of help? Calling Roy on her behalf? She realized that, like everyone else, her mother had assumed he was the father of her baby. She should have expected it. There'd been no opportunity for Krystal to tell her he wasn't.

As she dragged Roy down the hallway past the kitchen, he called out, "Hi, Mrs. Graham. How's it going?"

Her mother glanced up from the sink and smiled, looking quite pleased with herself. "Oh, hello, Roy. It's nice to see you."

It's nice to see you? Krystal almost laughed out loud. If only her mother knew the absurdity of the situation.

"Would you like some cake and coffee?" her mother asked.

Krystal thought that it was a good thing she didn't have a sharp object in her hand, because she might have used it on her mother. She wondered if anyone had used gestational insanity as a defense for assault.

"Roy and I are going for a walk," she announced, realizing it was the only thing she could do with him. She couldn't risk anyone overhearing what he might say to her and she certainly didn't want him in her room. She didn't want him anywhere near 14 Valentine Place tonight.

She dragged him through the hallway and out the private entrance to the backyard. As she looked toward the patio, she noticed that Garret was gone. A glance at the driveway told her his car was missing, too.

It was just as well. His absence meant one less stress factor.

"You know I really don't feel like going for a walk," Roy said as she pulled him toward the sidewalk. "I came over to talk to you, not walk."

"Well, in order to do one, you have to do the other," she snapped at him.

"Fine, but could we at least slow down? This isn't a race, is it?"

Until he called attention to her gait, she hadn't realized she was practically running. She slowed, hoping the flow of adrenaline would ease as well.

"So are you going to talk to me or aren't you?" he asked irritably when silence stretched between them.

"Not in the middle of the street I'm not. We're going to the park." She really didn't want to take him there, because it held too many memories from their past—of romantic strolls on moonlit nights and promises made beneath the stars. None of that mattered at the moment. Tonight it was just a place where they could talk in private. Fortunately it wasn't far away.

"All right, we're here. Let's get this over with," he said as soon as they reached the tennis courts at the end of the park.

They could have sat down on any of the vacant benches, but Krystal's emotions wouldn't allow her to sit. She folded her arms across her chest and faced him.

"I don't know why you came over, Roy, but you shouldn't have. I have nothing to say to you and I made it perfectly clear that there is no way in hell there will ever be anything between us again." Her heart still raced and she struggled to control the trembling that had started the moment she'd seen him in the backyard.

"I came because I don't need your mother calling me and giving me crap." He pointed his finger at her for emphasis, which only fueled the anger she'd been trying to keep at bay. Seeing him again brought back the memory of the night she'd entered his apartment and found him with a naked woman.

"And what crap would that be?" she demanded, refusing to be intimidated by him.

"Don't play games with me." Again he used his finger for emphasis. "I know what you're trying to pull on me and it's not going to work."

"I'm not trying to pull anything. Look, I don't know what my mother said to you, but I told you the last time I saw you, that all I want is for you to be out of my life. I meant it then and I mean it now," she said firmly.

"Are you pregnant?" He looked repulsed by the possibility.

"That's none of your business."

"It is when your mother calls me and tries to guilt me into doing the right thing," he replied angrily. His eyes narrowed. "You are pregnant, aren't you?"

"Yes."

Gone was the charm he'd always managed to fall back on whenever he found himself in a tight spot. There was nothing even remotely attractive about him at this moment. He used an expletive and kicked the ground with his shoe, sending a divot of grass sailing in the air.

"There's no way I'm being a father to a kid that isn't mine," he yelled at her.

"Good, because you are the last man on this earth that I would want to be a father to my baby. I'm going home." She started to walk away, but he stopped her with a hand on her arm.

"So who is the father? Is it somebody I know?"

Suddenly she knew the true reason he'd come to see her. He wasn't upset that her mother thought she was pregnant with his child. What really bothered him was the knowledge that she had had sex with another man.

"You have no right to ask that." She jerked away from his touch and again started walking toward home, but he stepped in front of her.

"I think I have every right. We were supposed to be getting married...or have you forgotten?"

"You're the one with the short memory," she shot back at him. "You had trouble remembering to be faithful to me, your girlfriend."

"I wasn't cheating on you. I was having sex. There's a difference. And I wouldn't have had to go elsewhere to get it if you wouldn't have got it into your head that we should wait to have sex again until after we were married."

She was getting sick of him thrusting his finger in her face as if she deserved to be scolded. Her own hand shot up and she pointed right back at him.

"Just stop! You have no right to blame me for your inability to keep your pants zipped. The only thing I'm guilty of is being stupid enough to think you were a man who deserved a second chance." She pushed him out of the way, determined he wasn't going to stop her progress.

He didn't try. She knew he was behind her as she made her way back to 14 Valentine Place. She could hear his footsteps. Just before she reached the house, he caught up with her.

"I'd appreciate it if you'd tell your mother I'm not the one who knocked you up." His tone remained hostile.

"I will. I'm sorry she called you," she told him, which was the truth. She still couldn't believe her mother had done such a thing.

He nodded, then walked over to his car and drove away. She didn't bother watching the taillights disappear down the street, but went inside where she found her mother in the kitchen with Leonie, finishing the last of the dishes.

"Is everything okay?" It was Leonie who asked the question.

"Yeah, everything's fine," she lied, forcing a smile to her face.

"Your mom said Roy was here."

She nodded. "Yes, but he shouldn't have come here. It was all a big mistake." She looked at her mother as she spoke the words.

Her mother shifted uneasily and said, "I should probably get going. It's a long drive home."

"You're going to stay overnight, aren't you?" Leonie asked. "You shouldn't be driving that distance at this late hour."

Her mother glanced at the clock. "I didn't realize it was so late. Maybe I should stay…if it's all right with you?" She looked at Krystal, her brows raised in appeal.

"Or you could use the spare bedroom on this floor," Leonie offered.

As much as Krystal would have liked to have had her room to herself, she didn't trust her mother out of her sight, not after what she'd done. "You can sleep on my futon, Mom."

"Why don't the two of you go upstairs?" Leonie suggested. "I can finish down here."

"Are you sure you don't mind?" Krystal asked, not wanting to leave her landlady with the remainder of the cleanup.

Leonie gave her a gentle shove toward the door. "Not at all. You go have some quiet time with your mom."

Krystal knew that once they were back in her room their time would be anything but quiet. She thanked her landlady and took her mother upstairs, where she confronted her about the phone call to Roy as soon as she'd closed the door.

"Do you know how awful that was for me tonight?" she said, facing her mother with her hands on her hips.

"I'm sorry it didn't go well with Roy," Linda said.

"Did you think it would?" Krystal asked in disbelief. "Why did you call him?"

"Because I know how bullheaded you can be and I thought that if I gave you a little shove in the right direction, the two of you could patch things up and get on with the important things in life."

"Important things like marriage you mean." She made a sound of frustration. "You had no right to butt into my life like that."

"I'm concerned about my grandchild."

"That doesn't give you the right to call up my old boyfriend and tell him I'm pregnant!" She was too angry to stand still so she went over to the closet to get linens for the futon and began making up the bed.

"I was only trying to help." Her mother moved to the opposite side of the mattress to help her. "I know you and Roy have had your differences, but I thought…"

"Differences?" Krystal interrupted her. "He's immature, irresponsible and incapable of being faithful."

"Well, it would have been nice if you would have thought about that before you slept with him," she said, shaking out the top sheet.

"I didn't sleep with him," she blurted out.

"What are you talking about?"

"He's not the father of my baby."

The revelation stilled her mother's actions and took the color out of her cheeks. Krystal continued to make up the bed, tucking the corner under the mattress. When she straightened, her mother hadn't moved.

When she finally found her voice, she said, "Well, if he isn't the father, who is?"

"Just a guy I know," Krystal said, returning to the closet for a pillow.

"Just a guy you know?" her mother repeated in disbelief. "You do something as intimate as make a baby with a man and you call him *just a guy?*"

"It's not what you think."

"Then why don't you tell me what it is? How long have you been dating this man?"

"We're not dating."

She grimaced. "Oh, please don't tell me he was a one-night stand. I didn't raise you to be that kind of girl."

"I'm not that kind of girl." Her voice rose with the denial. "I may date a lot of guys but I don't sleep around, Mom. I never have and I never will."

"He's not married, is he?"

"No."

"Thank goodness for that. Then there's still hope."

"Hope for what? That he'll want to marry me?"

"I don't think you realize how hard it is to find a husband when you're a single woman with a child."

Krystal knew it would be a waste of time to try to tell her she wasn't looking for one. "Mom, don't you think we've done enough arguing about this for one night?"

Her mother wasn't about to let the subject drop, however. "I just don't understand you. I did my best to teach you and Carly to be smart when it came to men. I don't know how many times I told you that if a man truly loves you, he puts a ring on your finger."

Krystal could have told her it was at least a thousand times. It was always the same broken record when it came to the lesson about love.

"You're young, you're beautiful.... I don't understand why you have such trouble finding a decent guy," her mother said in consternation.

"Trust me, Mom, they're not easy to find," she said on a note of resignation.

"Your sister didn't have any trouble finding one and she didn't have to leave Fergus Falls to do it."

She should have known that sooner or later Carly's name would be mentioned. Her sister had fulfilled their mother's dream—met a nice boy, married well and had a family. Now she had the big fancy house in Fergus Falls, in-laws who were well-known around town and the ideal life as far as her mother was concerned. Krystal, on the other hand, had done exactly what her mother had told her not to do—she'd followed in her mother's footsteps instead of learning from her mistakes.

She knew it was a good thing that someone knocked on her door, because in her current state she was dangerously close to saying something she'd regret. When she opened the door, she found Dena, still wearing the paper veil they'd made for her to wear at the shower.

"I know it's late, but I wanted to tell you thank you again for the best bridal shower a girl could have." She gave her an exuberant hug.

"You're so very welcome," Krystal responded.

"Is everything okay?"

She nodded but had to bite on her lip to choke back the emotions threatening to spill forth in the form of tears.

"I could use some girl talk. How about you?"

It was late and Krystal was tired, but she needed to talk to someone who wasn't going to judge her about her pregnancy. "I'd like that."

"Your room or mine?"

"Yours. Mom's staying the night and I think she wants to go to bed."

She nodded in understanding. "Should I make tea?"

"Not for me." She stuck her head back into her apartment to tell her mother she'd be over at Dena's, then pulled the door shut and gave Dena's arm a squeeze saying, "Thank you for rescuing me. I so need to talk to someone other than my mom."

"Things aren't going well?" she asked as she led her to her room.

"I love my mother, but I wish she wouldn't have chosen today as the day she was going to fix what was wrong in my life," she said, sinking down on to the love seat. She curled her feet up underneath and faced Dena, who sat down beside her.

"Oh-oh, it was that bad, was it?"

"It was worse." She stretched her arms up over her head and rotated her neck, hoping to ease the stiffness tension had created.

"Want to talk about it?"

She did, but she wasn't going to spoil the end of what had been a very happy evening for her friend. "You don't need to hear me whine about my mother. This is your day to be happy."

Dena reached across and touched her arm. "I may have wedding jitters, but I'm not a basket case yet. Besides, I want to know what happened when Roy came here."

"You know he was here tonight?"

She nodded. "I saw his car out front when I went outside to say goodbye to one of the shower guests."

Krystal sighed. "It was not a pretty scene, believe me."

"What did he say?"

She hesitated only a moment. After everything that had happened that day, she needed a friend now. She relayed the entire story, leaving out the part with Garret on the patio.

When she'd finished, Dena gave her another hug. "You poor thing. That's horrible!"

"It's unbelievable is what it is," Krystal said, shaking her head. "I guess there is one positive that came out of all of this. I'm finally rid of Roy."

Dena threw up her hands in a gesture of triumph and said, "Yes! And that is reason to celebrate." She jumped up and went over to her compact refrigerator where she pulled out a bottle of grape juice. When she'd filled two paper cups, she returned to the love seat.

"It's not wine, but it's the next best thing." She lifted her cup in midair for a toast. "To my dear friend

Krystal, who had a frog pretending to be a prince, but she was smart enough to see his warts and kick his butt back into the pond."

Krystal grinned, then took a sip of the juice. "Mmm. This tastes good. I'd like to propose a toast, too." She lifted her cup. "To my dear friend Dena, who never made me feel I was crazy for wanting to get back together with the frog after he came home from his military duty."

"You weren't crazy. You just had to be sure of your feelings and now you are."

Krystal drained the remainder of her juice and said, "I am." She shuddered. "Just thinking about that guy creeps me out. But enough talk about him. Let's talk about something fun. The wedding. It's getting so close! Aren't you excited?"

"I am but I'm also scared."

"Scared? About what?"

"I love the thought of being married to Quinn, but don't forget that besides getting a husband I'm getting two kids. What if I'm a lousy mother? I mean, I've never done it before. How do I know I can do it?"

She shrugged. "I don't know. I've been asking myself those same questions."

"We're in the same boat in that aspect, aren't we? We're both going to be new moms. The only difference is my kids are going to be seven and twelve. You're getting a newborn."

"And you already know Sara and Luke like you."

"Your baby's going to like you, too," she stated with no uncertainty. "You're going to be a great mom."

"Both of us will be," Krystal added with conviction. "We'll help each other out, right?"

"Of course. And what's really cool is that Sara will

be old enough to baby-sit, so if we want to go out for an iced latte we can. We'll have our own little new moms support group.''

While Dena rambled on, thinking up all sorts of fun things for them to do as mothers, Krystal could only stare at her in disbelief. Finally Dena asked, ''Why are you looking at me like that?''

''Because I was just thinking what a unique friend you are. I've told you Roy isn't the father of my baby, yet not once while we've been talking have you asked who is.''

She shrugged. ''I figured if you wanted to tell me you would.''

That was so like Dena. Always listening but never prying. If there was one thing she'd never be accused of doing, it would be gossiping.

''The reason I haven't told you is I've been trying not to complicate your life,'' Krystal told her.

Dena reached out to take her hand. ''It's not going to complicate my life. You know that anything you tell me won't leave this room.''

''I know that. That isn't the reason why I haven't told you.'' She took a deep breath and said, ''It's Garret.''

''Oh.'' If she was surprised, she hid it well. ''I take it you haven't told him yet?''

She shook her head. ''I was waiting until after the wedding. For obvious reasons.''

''Leonie,'' she said in understanding.

She nodded solemnly. ''And Samantha lives upstairs.''

Dena grimaced. ''And she's been seeing Garret.''

''It's going to be really awkward around here when everyone finds out.''

"No one will find out until you're ready to tell them," she assured her.

Krystal leaned over to give her another hug. "Thank you. I want so much for you to have the perfect wedding."

"Don't worry. Everything will be fine." Then she wrinkled her nose. "I just thought of something. I paired you and Garret for the bridal procession."

"That's okay."

"Are you sure?"

"Yes. We're still friends." Or we used to be, she should have added, but she really didn't want to go into the details of her relationship with Garret. And Dena, being the kind of friend she was, didn't ask.

Krystal was grateful when she changed the subject, asking her opinion on what hairstyles would work with the veil she'd chosen. There was no more talk of babies or boyfriends, and by the time Krystal returned to her room, she felt much better.

But as she climbed into bed, all the upsetting things that had happened to her during the day came into her mind. And one refused to be ignored. It was Garret telling her he was going to be gone for six months to a year in the Doctors Without Borders program. Visions of him in a war zone haunted her until she fell asleep.

As DENA'S WEDDING DAY approached and 14 Valentine Place became a beehive of activity, Krystal felt more confident that she'd made the right decision to wait to tell Garret she was pregnant. She saw how something as minor as a delay in Maddie and Dylan's travel plans could upset the harmony in the house. She wasn't about to risk creating an even bigger upheaval with her news.

To everyone's relief, Dena's third bridesmaid did arrive on the Friday before the wedding. She'd missed the final fitting for the bridesmaids and their dresses, but to Leonie's relief, her dress was a perfect fit. Everyone saw it as a sign the wedding would go off without a hitch.

"I am so lucky this fits," Maddie said as she pirouetted in front of Krystal wearing the plum-colored bridesmaid dress. "I thought for sure when I missed that fitting we were going to be scrambling to find a seamstress at the last minute."

"You're lucky you're here. If the weather hadn't improved, you could still be sitting at the airport in Paris," Krystal pointed out.

"Yes, and we might have missed the wedding entirely. You want me to zip you up?" she asked as she watched Krystal struggle to get the back closed on her dress.

"Thanks." She turned around, lifting her hair off the nape of her neck.

"It's a little snug," Maddie said as she hooked the zipper in place. "I thought you said you had yours altered."

"I did. It was too big in the shoulders."

"Well, now it's a little tight in the bodice." She came around to Krystal's front side to peer closely at the dress. She pinched a layer of fabric under her arm, then down the skirt. "It appears that it's just the bodice. I think you're going to have to leave the padded bra at home."

Krystal didn't tell her that she wasn't wearing a padded bra. The fullness in the bodice was due to her swollen breasts, another of the changes her body had undergone during her early pregnancy.

"It doesn't feel tight," she told her, although it wasn't quite the truth.

"No? Well, then don't worry about it. I'm sure none of the men will care," Maddie said with a knowing lift of her brows. "You look lovely."

"So do you. It's a great dress. Don't you just love it?"

"I do. I was a little worried when I saw the picture, but now that I'm here—" she pivoted in front of the full-length mirror "—I can see that Dena did a great job of picking a dress that minimizes the tummy area, although nothing's going to hide this I'm afraid." She rested her hand on her slightly swollen stomach.

"Nothing should. You look beautiful," Krystal told her because it was the truth.

"I look pregnant." Maddie turned to the side. "I'm pretty big for twenty-two weeks, don't you think?"

"Mmm-hmm." Krystal wasn't sure what to say. It had been a shock to see Maddie walk through the front door of 14 Valentine Place wearing maternity clothes, because Krystal knew that in two months' time she would be wearing the same size and looking just as pregnant as her friend.

"At first the doctor thought it might be twins, but it's only one. Leonie told me all of the boys were over nine pounds, which means I'll probably have a big baby. I guess that's the price I have to pay for falling in love with a Donovan."

Krystal knew it was an opportunity to tell her friend that she was paying the price, too, but she hesitated because Maddie, besides being her friend, was also Garret's sister-in-law. Even though Krystal trusted her to keep her secret, she didn't want to put her good friend in the position of knowing something of importance and not being able to share it with the rest of her family. Krystal also knew that Maddie told Dylan everything and as much as she wanted to believe he wouldn't say anything to Garret, she simply didn't think it would be wise to tell any of the Donovans unless she was telling all of them.

"You're glowing, Maddie. You must be happy," Krystal remarked as Maddie stood in front of the mirror.

"I am happy. Dylan and I didn't plan to start a family so soon after we got married, but now that I'm pregnant, it just feels so right," she said.

"You're going to make wonderful parents. I wish you weren't going to be so far away when the baby's born. I miss you."

Maddie reached for her hand and gave it a squeeze. "Oh, I miss you, too. France is wonderful, but it's not home. It would feel more like home, however, if my friends would visit," she said with an appeal in her eyes.

"Oh, you know I'd love to, but..."

"If it's money stopping you from coming over, Dylan has a ridiculous amount of frequent flyer points."

She held up her hand. "It isn't that. This just wouldn't be a good time for me."

"Oh, come on. You're the one who always wants to travel someplace new and exciting. Paris is definitely exciting. And if you come before I get much bigger, Dylan and I can take you to the most fabulous places—"

She stopped suddenly and said, "Quick. Give me your hand." She took Krystal's palm and placed it on her stomach. "The baby's kicking. Can you feel it?"

Krystal shook her head because at first she didn't notice anything, but then she felt a tiny flutter. "Ohmigosh! I think I did!"

"There it is again. Feel it?"

Krystal giggled gleefully. "That is so neat!"

"I know. You should feel what it's like on my end." She rolled her eyes. "This little guy is either going to be a soccer star or a dancer. His feet never stop."

"Guy?" Krystal looked at her inquisitively. "Are you hoping for a boy?"

"It is a boy," she announced proudly.

"You found out?"

She nodded. "They did an ultrasound at twenty weeks, but don't say anything to Leonie. We haven't told her yet."

She shook her head. "Of course I won't. She's going to be so excited."

"I think she wanted a girl, but she'll just have to wait for her first granddaughter." She reached for her purse. "I have pictures in my bag. Want to see?"

Krystal nodded and Maddie pulled out an envelope. "It's amazing how much of the baby's anatomy you can identify." She named the different body parts as she pointed to them with her finger.

Krystal gazed in amazement at the grainy printouts. It was hard to believe that something very similar was forming inside her. "It's really a little person, isn't it?" she said as much for her own benefit as Maddie's.

"Look at the tiny little hands and feet! When I see these pictures, I get this lump in my throat and mist in my eyes."

Krystal understood why. "It's just so incredible to think that…" She didn't finish her sentence, because if she had she would have told Maddie that in two months she'd know if she was carrying a boy or a girl.

There was a knock on the door followed by Dylan's

voice. "Hey, don't take too much time in there. We have a wedding rehearsal to get to."

"We'll be down in a few minutes," Maddie called out, then said to Krystal, "We'll have to talk later. There's so much I want to tell you."

"The same goes for me. I've missed you," Krystal told her, her eyes filling with unshed tears.

"I've missed you, too. I wish I could have been here for Dena's shower. How is she holding up?" Maddie asked as she tucked the photos back into their envelope.

"She was fine until this morning," Krystal answered. "It's actually quite funny. You know how she's always trying to look as if she has everything under control...well today, she's the total opposite. She's running around like a chicken with her head cut off."

"That doesn't sound like the Dena I know," Maddie commented. "Back in college she was the one who kept me grounded."

"I know what you mean. We've become really good friends. I'm so glad you recommended her to Leonie."

"You become good friends with everyone who lives here."

"Yes, which makes it really hard when they move away. At least when you left Dena moved in across the hall. I don't know what I'm going to do if I don't like the next person who takes her place."

"That won't happen, because you know Leonie is very careful when it comes to choosing her tenants," Maddie told her.

"I don't think she's looked for a replacement for Dena—she's been too busy helping with the wedding plans.'' She sighed. ''Guess I'll just have to be alone for a while.''

''You're not alone. Isn't Samantha Penrose upstairs?''

''Oh, yeah. I forgot about her. I don't really know her.''

''She hasn't been down for any girl talk?''

''Uh-uh. I hardly see her around here at all.''

''She's a doctor and if she's anything like Garret, she works all the time,'' Maddie surmised.

''I think she's a lot like Garret. That's probably why they get along,'' Krystal pointed out.

''I was surprised when Leonie told me she'd rented a room to her. What's the deal with her and Garret anyway? Are they really back together?''

She shrugged. ''I don't know. You'd have to ask him.''

Maddie stared at her, her hands on her hips. ''Since when do you not know what's going on at 14 Valentine Place?''

She turned away so Maddie wouldn't see her face when she answered. If there was one thing she knew she couldn't do, it was lie to Maddie. They'd lived together too long and had become too close of friends.

''I told you why. I haven't seen her. Or Garret for that matter. And Leonie's been so caught up with the wedding....'' She trailed off, not wanting to say too much about Samantha.

''I'm looking forward to meeting her.''

''I thought you knew her. She and Garret dated in college.''

Maddie shook her head. ''They broke up before I moved to St. Paul. I remember Garret talking about her, though.''

Krystal wanted to ask her what he'd said about her,

but Dylan pounded on the door for the second time, reminding them they needed to hurry. Maddie disappeared with her husband, leaving Krystal to change out of the bridesmaid dress. Before slipping on the two-piece skirt and jacket she was wearing to the rehearsal, Krystal stood in front of the mirror in her bra and panties. Turning sideways, she tried to imagine Maddie's gently swelling tummy on her body. Then she placed her hand on her stomach, searching for some sign there was a baby kicking inside. There wasn't any.

Hearing Maddie so lovingly include Dylan's name when she talked about the baby made Krystal wish that she wasn't going through her pregnancy alone. She, too, had questions and concerns she wanted to share with the father of her baby. Only she couldn't. At least not yet.

Soon she would tell Garret he was going to be a father and then what? She wondered. His reaction was something she'd thought about often and each time she'd hoped that, after his initial shock, he would tell her he wanted to be a part of the baby's life. Until the night they'd conceived a child, they had been friends. Surely they could maintain a friendly relationship for the sake of their child.

She closed her eyes, not wanting to think about it. But she had to think about it. Because in a very short time there would be no more hiding the truth.

KRYSTAL KNEW DENA had planned for her to be escorted down the aisle by Garret. What she didn't expect was that she'd be seated next to him at the groom's dinner following the rehearsal. She had hoped to sit next to Maddie, but she found herself sandwiched between Dylan and Garret, and feeling very uneasy about it.

If she could have pleaded a headache and gone home after the rehearsal, she would have, but she knew Dena would suspect the reason she'd left. She'd spent the past six weeks trying to keep from letting her situation spoil Dena's happy occasion. She could get through a few more hours.

So she put on a happy face and acted as if she was enjoying herself. It wasn't as hard as she thought it would be. She was, after all, a people person and had no trouble making conversation. The difficult part was eating.

"Aren't you hungry?" Garret asked, glancing at her plate where most of her dinner sat untouched.

"I think I'm too excited to eat," she told him, not wanting to admit the true reason for her lack of an appetite. She usually became nauseous about this time every evening. Tonight was no exception.

He looked at the truffles next to her plate. "I've never known you to pass on chocolate."

Normally she didn't, but she knew that inside the chocolate confections was a boysenberry cream that killed any temptation she might have had. "There's a first for everything, I guess," she said with a weak smile. "Would you like them?"

He grinned. "It would be a shame to let them go to waste."

She shoved the plate in his direction. "Enjoy."

"Thanks." Before he could eat them, his five-year-old nephew went running past. Garret reached out to slow him down, grabbing him around his waist and lifting him onto his knee.

"Hey there, Mickey! Whatcha got, buddy?"

"Trucks," he said, proudly displaying two Hot

Wheels cars in his hand. One was a red pickup and the other was a yellow dump truck.

"Hey, they're pretty cool," Garret said.

"Do you like trucks?" he asked his uncle.

"I sure do. Can I try it?"

Mickey handed him the red pickup and Garret set it on the white linen tablecloth, moving it around his plate and glass and making zooming noises.

Mickey followed his example, pushing the tiny dump truck with his small fingers.

"We need to make a parking garage." Garret told him, then took his napkin and draped it over his water glass. He then pushed the red pickup under it.

More zooming sounds came out of Mickey's lips as he wheeled his tiny truck around the plate and under the linen tent. Then he spotted the uneaten truffles and reached for one. Garret's hand stopped his.

"Let's ask your mom first," he said, then glanced across the table at Jennifer Donovan for approval. "Do you care if Mickey eats another chocolate?"

"No, but he's going to make a mess of your clothes. Why don't you send him back over here," she answered, motioning to the chair next to hers.

"No, I want to sit by Uncle Garret," Mickey protested.

"He's okay," Garret said.

"He's pretty messy when it comes to eating chocolate," Jennifer warned.

"I don't mind." He gave his nephew the candy.

As his mother predicted, Mickey soon had chocolate on his hands and face. Krystal watched Garret take the napkin from the water goblet and wipe the boy's cheeks. The five-year-old protested, but only because he was using the makeshift garage to do the job.

"Uncle Garret! What about our cars?" he shrieked.

Krystal offered him her napkin. "Use mine. I'm finished eating." She watched the two of them play with the miniature trucks, noticing how patient Garret was with the young boy as they made roads using the silverware.

Gradually the dinner party began to break up. Guests left the table and began mingling and Mickey was sent back over to his parents.

Krystal thought about the scene she'd just witnessed. She'd always known Garret thought highly of family. All of Leonie's sons did. Only now she realized how important that was. In five years time it could be her son sitting on his knee.

When he flipped a penny on to her plate, she gave him a puzzled look. He said, "That's for your thoughts. You looked lost in them. I figured they must be good."

She didn't want to tell him that she'd been thinking he'd make a good father so she said, "You're really good with kids. You should be a pediatrician."

"I've thought about it, but I like family practice," he told her.

Dylan came over to stand beside him. "Hey, I have a question for you, little brother. It's about Maddie's pregnancy."

Krystal knew that was her cue to leave. She excused herself and joined Maddie and Leonie, who were discussing the plan for the morning. While they talked, her glance kept straying to the two brothers she'd just left.

As they stood next to each other it was easy to see the similarities. They had the same strong jaw with a hint of five-o'clock shadow, the same cheeks that dimpled when they smiled and the same brown eyes that held just a hint of mischief. Dylan's were less serious looking than Garret's, but they could play the same kind of havoc with a woman's heartbeat. She wasn't sure why she'd always thought Dylan was the best-looking of the four Donovan brothers. Garret wasn't hot in the sense that his brother was, but he had something that set him apart from the others.

He wasn't as broad in the shoulders as Dylan, but he was just as tall. Dylan definitely had more bulk to his frame, but Krystal knew that beneath Garret's loose-fitting jacket and slacks was a firm body. Heat spread through her as she remembered what he'd looked like lying next to her in bed, naked.

Until that night she'd always thought of him as being reserved and had expected that when he took a woman to bed for the first time he'd be a bit shy. But there had been nothing inhibited about his actions that night. Once she'd made it clear to him that she wanted him, he'd made love to her with an intensity that had had her begging for more. He'd been strong yet tender. In control yet unselfish. She had felt a sense of empowerment that she could unleash such passion in a man.

Just thinking about it made her tremble inside. Never had any man made her feel so desirable. "You don't know how long I've wanted to do this," he'd said, then called her a fantasy come true.

A fantasy. It was the one word that had ironically brought her back to reality. Maddie used to tell her she thought Garret had a crush on her, but she'd never paid any attention. She'd been too busy looking for love elsewhere.

Love. If only what she and Garret had shared had been love. It had felt so good and so right to be in his arms, yet she knew that they'd been together for the wrong reasons. She'd pretended he loved her in order to ease the pain of Roy's betrayal. He'd had a chance to make a fantasy a reality and hadn't passed on it.

They'd both agreed it had been a mistake. They'd parted and gone their separate ways, unable to return to what they once had—friendship. As she stood staring at him, she wondered if he ever thought about that night.

As if he could read her mind, he glanced at her. For one brief moment she thought she saw a glimpse of the man who had gazed so lovingly at her that night in May.

"Krystal, what do you think?" Maddie's voice broke into her thoughts and forced her to pull her eyes away from Garret's.

"I'm sorry. I didn't hear what you said."

"Quinn wants to take all of the wedding party to the reception. Leonie and I think just the two of them should ride in the limo."

"I agree with you. They ought to be alone," she answered.

"Of course they should," Leonie seconded. "I can ride with Shane and Jennifer and this way Krystal can go with you and Dylan," she said to her daughter-in-law.

"Why can't you ride with us?" Krystal wanted to know.

"Our rental car only holds five," Maddie explained. "Garret's coming with us, too."

"And Samantha," Leonie added.

Samantha. So he was bringing her to the wedding. Krystal quickly masked her disappointment, not wanting either Leonie or Maddie to see it.

"Why doesn't Leonie ride with you and I'll drive myself," she suggested brightly as if nothing was wrong.

"You are *not* driving yourself," Maddie insisted.

"While you two figure it out, I'm going to check on something," Leonie said, then disappeared.

"It's silly for you to drive alone when you could ride with us," Maddie said as soon as her mother-in-law was gone.

"And feel like a fifth wheel with you four? No thank you," Krystal stated in no uncertain terms.

Maddie flung her arm around her shoulder. "You could never be a fifth wheel with us. Besides, I don't think Samantha is actually Garret's date. Dena invited her to the wedding. She does live at 14 Valentine Place."

The last thing Krystal wanted was to be stuck in the back seat of a car with Garret and Samantha. Just thinking about the entire day tomorrow gave her a headache. With the exception of Sara and Luke, the junior bridesmaid and ring bearer, every other member of the bridal party was a part of a couple. She would be the only odd one out.

To her relief, Maddie said, "We can figure all this out tomorrow. One way or another, we'll all get to the church and the reception."

"Yes, we can. And as much fun as this groom's dinner is, we need to get our bride back to 14 Valentine Place so she can get her beauty rest," Krystal added.

"Good idea." Maddie looked in Dylan's direction. Without saying a word, he came toward her. He'd sensed she wanted to leave and had responded to the single glance she'd given him.

They knew each other so well, so intimately that they didn't need words to communicate with each other. Krystal wondered if she'd ever have that kind of a relationship with a man.

Her mother's words echoed in her ears. *Do you know how hard it is for a single woman with a child to find a husband?*

She couldn't think about that right now. She wouldn't think about it, especially not with Garret coming toward her. She glanced around, thinking he might be making his way toward someone else, but there was no one else nearby.

"Are you sure you're feeling okay?" he asked when he reached her.

She wished his voice didn't sound so impersonal. She wanted to hear in his voice the same tone she heard in Dylan's when he asked Maddie if she was feeling all right.

"Yeah, I'm fine," she replied. He looked uncomfortable and she asked, "Is anything wrong?"

"No." He rubbed his jaw, then said, "I just want you to know that I'm going to do whatever I can to make sure it won't be awkward tomorrow...you and I being paired together."

"Oh, me, too," she told him, wishing there was no need for them to even be bringing up the subject.

"It shouldn't be awkward. We've been friends for a long time."

"Yeah, we have," she agreed with a weak smile.

"Are you bringing a date to the wedding?" he asked.

"No. Are you?" She knew she shouldn't have asked, but she needed to know if he really was seeing Samantha again.

Krystal never heard his answer, because Dena interrupted them. "Sorry, Garret, but I need this woman," she said, looping her arm through Krystal's with an apologetic grin. "The car's leaving. You two can talk tomorrow."

Tomorrow. Krystal wished it never had to come.

CHAPTER FIVE

AS PERSONAL ATTENDANT to the bride, Leonie appointed herself in charge of the bridesmaids and made it her duty to insure everyone was on time. She collected each and every one on Saturday morning and took them to the beauty salon, where Krystal had arranged makeup and hair appointments for the bridal party. After a light lunch catered by one of Leonie's friends, they headed for the church.

"Oh my gosh, it's hot," Krystal complained as she stepped out of the air-conditioned car into the bright sunshine.

"Happy is the bride the sun shines on," Leonie recited cheerfully.

"If that's true, then Dena is going to be one happy lady," Maddie noted, shading her eyes with her hand.

"Please tell me the church is air-conditioned," Krystal said on a moan as she lifted the large garment bag containing her bridesmaid dress from the back of the car.

"It must be. It didn't feel warm in there last night at rehearsal," Lisa Bailey remarked.

"No, but yesterday it wasn't this hot, either." Krystal could feel perspiration beading on her skin as she slammed the side door shut. "If I don't get inside soon my makeup is going to melt."

As they all made their way to the church entrance,

Maddie tugged on Krystal's elbow. "You seem a little on edge. Is everything okay?"

"Don't worry about me. I'll be all right," she answered, although today nothing felt right and she hated pretending it was, especially with Maddie.

When she stopped at a drinking fountain just inside the door, Maddie waited for her while the others went on ahead. "Are you sure you're okay? You usually love weddings, but if I didn't know better I'd say you don't want to be at this one."

Krystal should have known that Maddie would pick up on her mood. They'd been friends for a long time and not even distance could erase the intuitive bond that existed between them.

"I'm really happy for Dena and Quinn. It's just that…" She paused, wondering if she should simply be honest and tell her she was feeling lousy because she was pregnant. Then Leonie called out to them from down the hall and she knew couldn't. Not yet. So she said, "You know how my stomach gets when I'm nervous." It wasn't a lie. Anyone who'd lived at 14 Valentine Place knew she often had tummy troubles when she was anxious.

Maddie bought the explanation. "I thought maybe that was why you didn't come down for breakfast today. I have some antacids in my purse if you think they'll help."

"No, it's all right. I'll be fine."

But she wasn't fine and Leonie noticed a short while later when she helped her hook the clasp on her necklace. "You look a little pale, dear. I know you don't like to eat when you're nervous, but you really should have a bite of something," Leonie advised. "Why don't you have a piece of fruit?" She motioned to a small insulated cooler she'd packed with beverages and snacks.

Krystal nodded but didn't act on her suggestion.

Talk turned to the wedding ceremony and Krystal's queasy stomach was relegated to the same category as Dena's pacing—accepted as part of the prewedding ritual. Leonie fussed over the bridesmaids, smoothing wrinkles and pinning up errant curls.

Despite taking some of Maddie's antacid tablets, Krystal continued to have an unsettled stomach. It wasn't her only complaint. Her feet had swollen, making her specially dyed shoes uncomfortable. She did her best not to let her discomfort show, but Maddie noticed.

"You should have some fruit. It'll perk you up. Plus, it's delicious." She popped a fresh strawberry in her mouth. "I ought to know. I've eaten enough of it. You would not believe my appetite with this baby. I barely finish one meal and I'm planning the next."

Krystal couldn't imagine feeling that way. Lately she'd had to force herself to eat and then it was only accomplished out of sheer willpower because she knew that in order to have a healthy pregnancy, she needed nutritious foods.

"I thought you said you had morning sickness," Krystal remarked.

"At first I did. It was awful. Felt sick all day long. But then right before my fifth month…" She snapped her fingers. "Just like that it was gone. I've never felt as good as I do now."

Krystal hoped that meant she was getting close to being over her bout with the malady. Right now she'd give just about anything for it to go away for one day. She wondered if Maddie was right about the fruit and grabbed a small container of sliced cantaloupe from the cooler. To her surprise, it tasted good.

When she'd finished Maddie asked, ''Feeling any better?''

''A little,'' she told her honestly. She'd learned that the best remedy for a queasy stomach was to lie down, but the bride's room had no cots or lounges. There were, however, padded bench seats in the hallway.

Telling Maddie she was going to take a walk, she slipped out into the corridor. It was empty, quiet and much cooler than the dressing room. She stretched out on a vinyl padded bench, her feet dangling over one end. With her eyes closed, she practiced a relaxation technique she'd learned at a one-day seminar for working women, letting her focus travel through her body. She was on her hips when a male voice broke her concentration.

''Had a late night, did you?''

She opened her eyes to see Garret standing over her. ''Oh! Hi.''

''Hi yourself. I thought maybe I was going to have to kiss you to wake you.''

She knew it was said in a teasing manner for there was a smile on his face, but at that moment it was exactly what she wished he would do. Kiss her. She remembered how good those lips could feel on hers.

She quickly lowered her eyes so he wouldn't see what she was thinking and said, ''I wasn't sleeping. I was meditating.'' She sat up, smoothing down the skirt of her dress. ''This waiting can get to be a little nerve-wracking.''

''The girls are jittery, are they?''

''Probably not any more so than the boys,'' she retorted. He offered her his hand and she took it. ''Thanks.''

"You look—" he paused as his eyes roved over her figure. "—fantastic."

She couldn't stop the blush that covered her cheeks. "Thank you." She looked him over and said with a teasing smile, "You don't look half bad yourself. Reminds me of the night of the hospital ball." As soon as she'd said the words, she regretted them. What neither of them needed was a reference to what had happened between them. She tried to make light of it by saying, "We were all dressed up, you in a tux, me in my 'night on the town' blue dress."

She wished they weren't in a corridor of the church with only minutes before Dena's wedding, because it could have been an opening for her to tell him the truth about what had happened that night.

Then he said, "We agreed we weren't going to talk about that night."

She felt like a fool. "We're not talking about it. Forget I mentioned it," she said abruptly, then started back.

"Krystal, wait." He grabbed her by the arm. "I'm sorry. I shouldn't have said that." He ran a hand over the back of his neck. "God, I hate what that night has done to us."

Her heart missed a beat. "What do you mean?"

"You know what I mean. We used to be friends."

She breathed a sigh of relief. For a moment she thought he'd somehow figured out she was pregnant. "We're still friends. You said we were last night."

"It doesn't feel like we are to me. It's more like we're acquaintances being pleasant to each other because it's expected of us."

She looked away, unsure what she should say. He hadn't said anything she didn't feel. Sex had ruined their friendship. She'd heard other women say sleeping with a guy you only regarded as a friend was a mistake. Now she knew for herself how true it was. Maybe some friends could continue on as if nothing had happened. It was obvious she and Garret couldn't.

"I'm sorry that night ever happened, Krystal, but it did and there's nothing we can do about it now except try to forget." There was a resignation in his voice that made her cringe inwardly.

He regretted sleeping with her. No, he didn't just regret it. He wished it had never happened. She hadn't lived up to his fantasy obviously. The thought cut through her, causing her throat to tighten with emotion. She didn't want to feel hurt, but she did.

"I guess fantasies are just never worth the price you have to pay for them, are they?" Her voice faltered with a combination of hurt and anger.

Before he could respond Shane's voice called out, "Hey, you two! It's time!"

Garret turned as his brother came striding toward them.

"You'd better get back in there." Shane jerked a thumb in the direction of the groomsmen's dressing room. "Quinn's so nervous I'm worried he's going to hyperventilate."

Krystal felt the same way. She watched Shane throw an arm around Garret's shoulder and drag him away. He didn't protest, giving her reason to believe he was relieved to be away from her. He'd said what he wanted to say. He'd told her he wished he could forget they'd ever slept together.

Krystal wanted to turn and run out the door as fast as her legs would carry her. Only she couldn't. She dropped down onto the padded bench seat and hung her head in her hands wishing she had never told Dena she'd be a bridesmaid. How was she ever going to get through the rest of the day?

The sound of heels clicking on the tile had her lifting her head to see Maddie coming toward her.

"You're still not feeling well, are you?" She sat down beside her.

She shook her head, trying to swallow back the emotion. "I shouldn't have told Dena I'd be in the wedding." A lone tear trickled down her cheek.

Maddie wrapped her arm around her. "Oh, don't cry, Krys. You want me to tell Dena you're sick? She'll understand. I know she will."

She was so very tempted to say yes, but then Sara, the junior bridesmaid, was at their side saying, "Ohmigosh! Dena is so freaking out because you two aren't in there. Come!" She waved with her hand. "The wedding coordinator is lining everyone up to start the processional. Hurry!"

"What do you want to do?" Maddie asked.

Krystal took a deep breath and willed her composure to return. "I think I can make it."

"Are you sure?"

"Yes." As she rose she wobbled on her feet. Seeing the look of panic on Maddie's face she said, "Relax. It's the shoes. My feet are killing me."

"Why don't you change them? I'm sure Dena wouldn't mind," Maddie suggested.

"No. I'm not going to be the only one in odd-colored shoes," she stated in no uncertain terms. "I'll make it."

"I think she'd rather see you with a different pair of shoes, then hobbling in those," Maddie pointed out.

"I'm not going to hobble. See." She demonstrated by taking a few steps without any difficulty.

When they reached the apse, Dena was already in

place, her father at her side. Krystal caught a glimpse of the inside of the church. It was full, as was to be expected considering Quinn was a professional hockey player. She also noticed that the large fans suspended from the ceiling were turning. She took a deep breath, willing her body to relax as she slipped between Maddie and Sara.

Just before the processional began, Maddie whispered over her shoulder, "Last chance to back out."

Krystal shook her head. She'd get through this day with sheer willpower because she wanted it to be special for Dena. She turned around and gave the bride a thumbs-up sign and a smile, then clasped her bouquet firmly. She waited until Sara was a third of the way down the aisle before stepping onto the white carpet.

True to the word she gave Maddie, she walked steadily even though her feet ached. At the altar she continued to gaze straight ahead, reaching for Garret's arm without actually looking at him. She felt him stiffen and hoped nobody noticed how uneasy they both were as they walked to their spots at the altar.

Krystal knew from rehearsal that all of the bridesmaids would be on Dena's left and the groomsmen on Quinn's right. Although Garret was her escort, the only time she needed to be next to him was during the recessional when they'd walk back down the aisle arm in arm.

As she stood waiting for Dena to make her grand entrance, she glanced out at the crowd. It was no wonder the church felt stuffy. It was packed with people, many of whom were fanning themselves with wedding programs. At the start of Mendelssohn's refrain, everyone rose to welcome the bride.

Warm air undulated with the crowd's movement. Krystal tried not to think about how stuffy it was in-

Maddie. I'm going to tell Leonie...soon, but until I do, I need you to not say anything.''

She reached for her hands and gave them a squeeze. "You know you can trust me to keep your confidence.''

The door swung open again and this time Krystal recognized the woman's face. It was one of Quinn's sisters announcing that the dancing would soon begin and all bridesmaids were wanted in the ballroom.

"Tell her we'll be right there,'' Maddie instructed her, and the woman disappeared out the door again. "We'd better go.''

Krystal nodded, dabbing at the moisture in her eyes. "Thank goodness for waterproof mascara, huh?''

Maddie grinned and wiped her eyes, too. "I just can't believe we're both having babies!'' As Krystal bent to pick up her shoes she asked, "Are your feet going to be okay?''

"Yeah. I'm not even going to try to put on these shoes. I'll dance in my stockings.'' As they walked out the door, Krystal placed her hand on Maddie's arm. "I'm sorry I couldn't tell you sooner. I wanted to, but...''

Maddie gave her another quick hug. "It's all right. I understand.''

As Krystal knew she would. "Thanks. I'm thinking of leaving early. You don't think Dena will mind, do you?''

"Maybe I should go home with you. We could say I wasn't feeling well and you were going home to keep me company. No one would question my reasons for leaving.''

Krystal shook her head. "Dylan would insist on going with you and then there'd be two bridesmaids missing. I'll be just fine. You don't need to worry about me.''

"But I do worry. Do you want Dylan to give you a ride home?"

"No, I'm going to call Shannon." And with another deep breath she headed back to the ballroom.

GARRET KNEW THAT everyone in his family—especially his mother—thought Samantha Penrose was a good match for him. He understood why. Even he had to admit they had a lot in common. They were both dedicated doctors, wanting to make a difference in the world.

What his family didn't understand was that Samantha—like him—wasn't looking for a mate. She'd made it perfectly clear that she'd be willing to pick up where they left off three years ago. At one time he would have jumped at the opportunity. But not now, which was why he was relieved when she was called back to the hospital that night.

"We're thinking about stopping for coffee," Dylan said as the last of the wedding guests filed out of the reception hall. "Want to join us?"

The us referred to Maddie and Leonie, since Shane and Jennifer had taken Mickey home and put him to bed earlier in the evening. Garret was tired himself, but he wanted to spend time with his brother and Maddie so he accepted their offer.

"Why not just come back to the house?" Leonie suggested. "We can get pastries on the way at that new twenty-four-hour deli over on Snelling."

"That'll work for me. I left my car at Mom's this morning," he told everyone.

"Yeah, and this way if Samantha gets back, you

can pop upstairs and see her,'' Dylan said with a sly grin and a nudge in his brother's rib cage.

"Or she can join us for coffee. We'd love to get to know her better,'' Maddie said.

Samantha, however, wasn't home when they got back to the house, but Garret noticed Krystal's light was on in her second-floor window. She'd left the party several hours earlier saying she was tired, yet she hadn't gone to bed.

"It's too bad Jason wasn't able to come home for the wedding,'' Leonie said as the four of them sat at the round wooden table. "I do believe that was one of the most beautiful weddings I have ever seen.''

"Mom, you say that about every wedding you attend,'' Garret reminded her with an affectionate grin.

"I do not. This one was special.''

"I agree,'' Dylan said, "but I'm not sure our baby brother would have appreciated it. He wasn't too fond of having to come home from California for Maddie's and my wedding,'' Dylan reminded her.

"When you're twenty, weddings are not on your list of important social events,'' Garret added.

"I think he would have had a good time had he been home,'' Maddie commented. "I know I had a wonderful time. What about you, Garret? Did you have fun?''

He grinned. "Let's just say it wasn't as bad as I thought it was going to be.''

"Bad?'' Leonie tapped his wrist lightly in reprimand. "How could you even use that word about such a lovely party?''

"Because it was a party,'' Dylan said with a chuckle. "You know he hates any gathering where there are more than four people—not counting family, of course,'' he added with a grin.

Garret raised his coffee cup in salute. "True."

"You're like your father that way. He hated weddings.''

"I don't hate them. I just feel more comfortable when there aren't a couple of hundred people crowding around me.''

"There were actually five hundred at the wedding,'' his mother pointed out. "That's what made it fun. All the energy and excitement of people celebrating Dena and Quinn's marriage.''

"You really love going to those things, don't you?'' Garret noted.

"Yes, and so do a lot of others,'' his mother stated. "You noticed how many people groaned when the band announced the last number.''

"And what a way to end a celebration,'' Maddie noted. "Doing the conga.''

"It's too bad Krystal wasn't there,'' Leonie mused. "She loves a good conga line.''

The mention of Krystal's name had Garret thinking about the way she looked when she'd been sick after the wedding ceremony. Fragile and vulnerable. When Maddie had told him that she'd gone home because she wasn't feeling well, he'd wanted to phone her to see if she was all right, but he knew she wouldn't welcome such a call. She'd made it perfectly clear earlier in the day what she thought of his concern for her well-being.

"I'm a little worried about her,'' his mother said. "It's not like her to leave any party early.''

"She's fine,'' Maddie insisted. "I think she was just tired.''

"She's been tired a lot lately. I hope she's not run-down. I'd hate to see her catch one of those viruses going around. There are so many right now. It happens every year at this time. Kids go back to school and germs spread," his mother continued, her brow creased with concern. "I wonder if I should check on her."

"Do you want me to go up?" Maddie offered.

Dylan got up from his chair and came around to place his hands on her shoulders. "You, my sweet, lovely pregnant wife, should be in bed. I'm sure Krystal is fine and is more than likely sound asleep. You can talk to her in the morning. Right now, I'm taking you back to the hotel and putting you to bed."

"I should get going, too," Garret said rising to his feet, trying not to think about Krystal and how tanta-lizing she'd looked in her purple dress. "I'll walk you to the car."

They'd all parked in the back. Dylan had just opened the door for Maddie and tucked her inside the rental car when he patted his pockets. "Oops, forgot my keys inside." He looked at Garret and said, "Watch my girl while I run back in and get them."

Garret nodded and glanced back at the house, once again noticing the light on in Krystal's window. Mad-die saw the direction of his gaze and said, "Is that a professional concern or friendly concern in your eyes?"

"Both."

"She told me you were with her when she got sick at the church."

"Yes, but she wasn't happy I was. She didn't want anyone to know about it—not even me, a doctor."

"No, I don't imagine she would. No woman wants anyone to see her in that condition."

"I'm also her friend."

"Yes, thank goodness you are. For some reason she didn't feel as if she could tell me about the baby. I guess she didn't want to spoil Dena's big day."

Garret frowned. Baby? Krystal?

"I think she thought she could get through the day without any problem," Maddie continued. "I can relate to that. Morning sickness is so unpredictable. You can be sick one minute and feel fine the next."

Morning sickness? The reason Krystal had been sick at church was because she was pregnant? He was too stunned to say anything, not that it mattered. Maddie kept talking.

"I know they teach you about that stuff in school, Garret, but unless you're a woman and you've suffered from it, you have no idea how terrible it can be. You feel so miserable." His expression must have revealed his shock for she suddenly gasped. "Oh, my gosh! You didn't know, did you?" He didn't need to answer her question. "Oh, please don't tell her I told you. I thought since you were with her that she would have told you…"

"Are you sure…" he began, but Maddie cut him off.

"Shh. Here comes Dylan and he doesn't know yet," Maddie warned him just seconds before he came into view bouncing a set of keys in his hands.

"Hey, I got 'em." He patted Garret on the arm. "We gotta go. We'll see you tomorrow morning for brunch, right?"

"Er…yeah, if I can make it," he said absently, his

mind still trying to comprehend what Maddie had just told him. Krystal was pregnant?

Maddie tossed a goodbye in his direction, doors slammed shut, and the car pulled away. Garret didn't move. He simply stood there staring up at Krystal's window.

It all made sense—now. How come he hadn't seen the signs himself? He was a doctor for crying out loud.

Maybe because she'd worked very hard at not letting him see any of the symptoms. He tried to think back to what she'd worn the last few times he'd seen her. Silky-type cargo pants that were baggy. A dress that hung loose over her slender frame.

He wondered just how pregnant she was. It was something he was going to find out. Instead of getting in his car, he went back inside 14 Valentine Place.

CHAPTER SIX

WHEN GARRET LET HIMSELF back into the house he found his mother at the sink rinsing out the coffee cups.

"What are you doing back? Don't tell me you forgot your keys, too?" she asked.

"No, I'm going upstairs. I want to leave a message for Samantha." He told the white lie because he couldn't tell her the truth. Right now he wasn't sure he knew the truth. "Don't worry about me, Mom. I'll let myself out. You go on to bed."

"Okay, dear. Good night," she called as he headed for the stairs.

When he came to the second-floor landing he stopped. He could see the sliver of light beneath Krystal's door. He raised his fingers to the wood and rapped.

She didn't answer right away and he knocked again, this time with more force. The door flew open and there she stood, mouth open, wearing nothing but a pale blue nightgown. Her hair was mussed, her eyes half-shut. As usual, she looked beautiful. And also as usual, his body reacted.

"Were you asleep?" he asked.

"Of course I was asleep." She glanced over her shoulder to the clock. "It's two o'clock in the morning."

"I saw your light from downstairs."

"I must have fallen asleep with it on. What's happened? Is something wrong with Leonie?" Panic replaced the sleepy look in her eyes.

"No, Mom's fine," he reassured her.

"Then what is it?" She obviously was confused as to why he would be at her door in the middle of the night.

"I need to come in."

"Sure." She stepped aside and he walked past her.

It had been a while since he'd been in her room, but it looked the same. It reminded him of a sexy boudoir with its large brass bed draped in peach chiffon as the focal point. Satin pillows lay scattered across the floor and the bed linens were in a tangle. The one light that was on had a peach-colored scarf draped over the shade giving everything a rosy glow, and the room smelled the way she did—of a floral fragrance that had just a hint of wildness to it.

"Do you want to sit down?" She gestured toward the futon.

"No, I'm not staying long."

"If you came here to check on me, it's not necessary," she said. "I'm not sick."

"I know. You're pregnant."

That stunned her into silence. She looked at him the way his patients did when he had a syringe in his hand, her face growing paler by the minute. With the thin cotton nightgown the only thing covering her body, he could see the gentle swell of her belly. Aware of his eyes on her, she reached for her robe and pulled it on.

"It's too late. I've already seen it," he said as she tied the sash.

He waited for her to say something, but nothing came out of her mouth. For the first time since he'd known her, she appeared to be at a loss for words.

"It's true, isn't it?" he said.

She moistened her lips with her tongue, then said, "Yes. I'm sorry."

He frowned. "For what? You don't need to apologize to me, Krystal."

"I feel I do. I feel this is all my fault. If I hadn't practically begged you to take me bed, we wouldn't be in this—"

"Wait a minute!" he cut her off. "Are you saying that I'm the father?"

Her eyes darkened and her voice rose. "Of course it's your baby. Nobody else could be the father." When he didn't say anything, she cried, "You think it's Roy's?"

"You were back together…" He didn't finish when he saw the look on her face, which wasn't much different from the one that had been there when she'd been sick in the bathroom at the church.

"For three days!"

He ran a hand across his forehead. This was getting him nowhere.

"Think," a small voice inside him whispered, but it was hard to do when he felt as if he'd just stepped off the planet and was falling into a black hole in space.

"I don't understand how this could have happened. We used protection." He stated the thought foremost in his head.

She shrugged. "It must have failed. Condoms aren't the most reliable form of birth control."

"Weren't you on the pill?"

"No, I was not," she stated with a hint of indignation. "I didn't plan to go to bed with you, in case you've forgotten."

How could he forget? She reminded him every

chance she had. "I am aware of that but I thought—"
He stopped abruptly, realizing he'd never asked her
about the pill. He'd assumed she was on it and they
would have double protection.

"You thought what? That I take it regularly so
whenever I pick up a guy I can sleep with him?" Her
cheeks colored. "I wasn't planning to have sex with
anybody that night. Not you or Roy. For your information, Garret, I don't go to bed with every man who
buys me dinner and pays me compliments." He could
hear the tears in her voice and it made him feel like a
first-class jerk.

"I didn't say you did," he said quietly.

"You didn't have to say it. It's there in your attitude," she accused him on a muffled sob.

The only attitude he had right now was one of disbelief. Ever since he'd been a child he'd mapped out
what he wanted for his life. Become a doctor, make a
difference in the world. Having a child with a one-
night stand had never been in his plan.

"How do you think I feel? I'm the one who did the
good deed here. I went out on that date with you as a
favor and I'm the one who ends up pregnant," she
reminded him. "And now you stand there and treat
me like I'm cheap." She burst into tears.

He raked a hand over his head. "For God's sake, I
don't think you're cheap, Krystal. I'm trying to understand how this happened."

"What's there to understand? We had sex. I got
pregnant."

Yes, that about summed it up. He'd gone and done
exactly what his father had warned him not to do when
he was a teenager. He'd gotten a girl pregnant. Only
Krystal was no girl—she was a woman and he was a

man. They were two adults who should have known better.

But he'd wanted her. Ever since the first day he'd met her he'd fantasized as to what it would be like to be her lover. The night of the hospital ball he'd been given a chance to fulfill that fantasy and he'd taken it. It hadn't mattered that she was only with him because she'd been hurt by the man she loved. It had been a night of passion for pleasure's sake only. A night they both agreed they would forget ever happened.

Only now there would be a permanent reminder. No matter how emotional she was, he needed to be rational. "Okay. What's done is done. Let's not dwell on that. Can we try to discuss this calmly?"

She nodded and he mentally calculated how long it had been since the hospital ball. "So you're what? Fifteen, sixteen weeks?"

"Sixteen," she confirmed.

He tried to look at her as if she were his patient, but he couldn't. She wasn't someone who'd come to the clinic to see him. She was the woman who'd conceived his child.

"Are you sure about the conception date?"

That raised her hackles again. "Do you think I'm lying to you?"

"No, I don't," he said on a note of frustration. "Would you stop reading something into my words that isn't there?"

He hated how adversarial their relationship had become in such a short time. "I'm trying to think but it's difficult to do with you throwing accusations at me."

"I'm sorry," she said on a sniffle.

"I'm in shock here. You've had some time to get used to the idea. I've had about ten minutes."

"I'm sorry," she repeated on another sniffle.

"It's all right," he said, raising his hands. "I would appreciate it if you could try not to cry quite so much. I know this is a difficult situation for you, but you getting so emotional that we can't have a rational discussion isn't doing us any good, either."

"It's my hor-hormones," she said on a hiccup. "They're wacko."

Seeing her looking so vulnerable made him soften his tone. "I know they are." He led her over to the bed where he sat her down. "Just sit there quietly for a minute while I think, okay?"

She nodded and didn't say a word. All he heard was an occasional sniffle.

His insides were churning, his body begging him to run. It's what he usually did to relieve stress—take a run either at the gym or on the street. He paced the narrow confines of her apartment.

He should have known she couldn't sit quietly for very long. "I'm sorry I didn't tell you before now."

"Why didn't you tell me?"

"I didn't want to spoil Dena's wedding. You can imagine what this kind of news would have done to the atmosphere in this house. I wanted it to be a happy time for her."

"We could have kept it between us."

She nodded and bit down on her upper lip. "Maybe I didn't want you to be your usual analytical self and present all my options to me."

"There is only one option, right?"

She nodded. "I'm having this baby."

It was what he wanted to hear. What he'd expected to hear from her. "Who knows you're pregnant?"

"No one in your family except Maddie."

He didn't think it was necessary to reveal that Maddie had accidentally told him.

"What about your family?" he asked.

She nodded. "Carly and my mom both know. Oh, and Dena and Quinn found out by accident and I told Shannon."

All of them knew before he did. It didn't make him happy.

"Other than the morning sickness, have you had any problems?"

"Mmm-hmm. My feet are swelling, my back aches, and look at my skin." She thrust her chin up so that he could get a closer look at her face. "I have acne."

He moved closer to her to get a better look. "That's not acne. It's a couple of pimples."

"They look awful. Luckily Shannon is a makeup artist and could cover them for the wedding. The worst part though is that I'm emotional."

"You're always emotional."

"Not like this."

"No, never quite as bad as this," he agreed. He paced some more, his mind trying to absorb what she'd told him. With two words his well-planned, orderly life had been thrown off course and he wasn't sure it would ever be set straight again.

"Now what happens?" she asked.

"I don't know," he answered the only way he could. "This is the last thing I ever expected would happen to me."

"I know. I feel the same way."

He wanted to go over and take her in his arms and hold her, but something stopped him. Maybe it was the knowledge that sympathy wasn't the sole motivation for wanting to be close to her. Ever since they'd made love he'd been having trouble forgetting how good it had been between them. Knowing that she was carrying his child only made her more desirable.

"It's late," he said on a sigh. "I'd better go."

She nodded, her arms wrapped around her midsection. "I am truly sorry that whole night backfired on us, Garret. I only wanted to help a friend."

He didn't need to be reminded of why she'd gone out with him. Or why she went to bed with him. She couldn't have Roy so she'd settled for him, and he, in seeking his fantasy, hadn't hesitated to take advantage of the situation. The irony of it all was enough to make him want to grab a stiff drink.

"None of that matters now, Krystal." He walked over to the door, pausing before he opened it to say, "I'll call you when I've had time to process all of this."

She simply nodded and showed him the door.

KRYSTAL AWOKE THE following morning and stared at the ceiling. Before she even lifted her head she reached for the soda crackers next to her bed. She didn't need them, however. No queasy tummy, just hunger. She carefully climbed out of bed and padded about her room. Still nothing.

She closed her eyes and said a brief prayer of thanks. Lately she had no clue as to when or where she'd have an attack of morning sickness. She wondered if she dared hope that her bout with it was coming to an end. It would certainly make life a lot easier.

Not that she expected her troubles would disappear with the absence of morning sickness. It was trivial compared to some of the issues facing her. Like what was going to happen now that Garret knew she was pregnant.

A knock on her door raised the hairs on the back

of her neck. Her first thought was that Leonie had
heard she was pregnant and had come to confront her
about it. She glanced at the clock and saw it was after
ten. She knew Leonie had arranged to meet her children for brunch this morning. The house should be
empty.

The knocking became louder and steadier. Krystal
could feel her heart pounding in her chest. She took a
deep breath and pulled the door open. "Carly!" She
stared at her sister in disbelief. She looked as if she'd
been up all night and had left the house in a hurry.
Next to her was four-year-old Emily, who didn't look
much better. Her hair hadn't been combed and both
looked as if they'd slept in their clothes. Behind them
were two of the biggest suitcases Krystal had ever
seen.

"What are you doing here?" A sinking feeling in
her stomach warned her she wasn't going to like the
answer.

"You said I could always come to you in a time of
need." There was no emotion in her sister's voice. She
looked as if she could collapse any moment, her face
pale, her eyes rimmed with dark circles.

"Of course you can. Come on inside." She smiled
at Emily and ruffled the little girl's hair as she said
hello. Then she gave each of them a gentle shove,
urging them to step inside the apartment while she
dragged the suitcases in behind her.

As soon as they were all inside and the door was
closed, she said,

"If I didn't know you were so happy with Joe I'd
think you'd left him."

"I did leave him," Carly said quietly.

The sinking feeling in Krystal's stomach plunged
all the way to her toes. "But you love him. So does

Emily.'' She glanced at her niece, who stood clutching a soft furry pig close to her chest.

''But he doesn't love me.''

''Of course he does. Look, if you've had a fight…'' she began but her sister interrupted her.

''It wasn't a fight. He doesn't want me anymore.'' Her voice was a hollow echo of its usual cheery tone. ''It's over. Everything. Our marriage…my life…'' she said despondently, paying no attention to the fact that Emily was wide-eyed and taking in every word she said.

''You look awfully tired. Why don't I make the futon into a bed and you can lie down for a while,'' Krystal suggested, putting her hand on her arm.

She shook her head. ''It's no good. I can't sleep. I have to think.''

''Carly, you need rest.''

''What I need is Joe but I can't have him,'' she said on a frantic whisper, then burst into tears, flinging herself facedown on the futon. It was the worst crying Krystal had ever heard from her sister. Before she could console her, Emily let out a wail and began to cry at the top of her lungs, too.

Krystal scooped the four-year-old into her arms and comforted her. ''Shh. It's okay, Emily. Don't cry. Your mommy's going to be okay.''

The little girl hiccuped. ''N-No, she's not. She hates my daddy.''

Krystal carried her over to her bed and set her down. ''She doesn't hate your daddy. She's just angry at him, but everything's going to be okay. Now can you sit here for a few minutes and let me talk to your mommy?''

The little girl shook her head and bawled even louder. ''I want to go h-home.''

"I know you do and you will, but first everybody has to stop crying…including your mommy. I'm going to help her do that, but I need you to be a big girl and put on a happy face. Can you do that for me?"

She nodded but continued to cry.

Krystal walked over to the portable TV and turned it on. "Look. You can watch a movie. I have *Shrek*. You like *Shrek*, right?" She put a DVD in the player.

The little girl nodded but continued to cry.

"What if I told you I'd paint your fingernails if you could sit quietly for a few minutes." She held up her hands. "Wouldn't you like to have pretty polish on them?"

Krystal could see she was interested. "Do you have purple?" Emily asked on a hiccup.

"Yes, and it has sparkles in it. It's really pretty. Does your mom ever paint your toenails?" When she shook her head, Krystal went on, "I can do both your fingers and your toes, but only if you have a smile on your face. What do you think?"

The weakest of smiles slowly appeared, accompanied by several sniffles.

Krystal kissed her on the forehead. "Beautiful. Now you hold on to that smile and I'll see if I can make your mommy feel better, okay?"

She went over to the futon and sat down beside her sister. "Carly, you've got to pull yourself together. You're upsetting Emily," she said in a gentle but firm tone.

Her sister continued to sob. "I can't help it. It hurts so bad."

"I'm sure it does, but this isn't just about you. It's about Emily, too." She deliberately kept her voice low as she talked. "You're frightening her. You don't want to do that, do you? Try to keep your voice down.''

As if suddenly aware of the emotional impact she was having on her daughter, Carly sat up, swiping at her tearstained face with the backs of her hands. ''I don't know what I'm going to do,'' she said softly. ''He doesn't want me, Krys.''

''I think you're wrong, Carly. Joe's crazy about you. He always has been.''

She shook her head. ''He wants someone else.''

Anger toward her brother-in-law erupted inside Krystal. ''Are you sure about that?''

She nodded miserably. ''He's been cheating on me. He admitted it.''

Krystal felt sick and it had nothing to do with being pregnant. She didn't understand how her brother-in-law could be unfaithful to her sister. They had always seemed so happy together.

''What a no-good, low-down…'' She almost uttered an expletive until she remembered her niece was sitting not more than ten feet away. ''How could he do such a thing?''

''It's my fault. I should have watched my weight more carefully. I knew fat was a turnoff for him.''

The notion that her sister felt responsible for his sordid behavior sparked Krystal's anger. ''For Pete's sake, Carly, you are not fat! And even if you were, that doesn't give him the right to cheat on you. He's your husband and he took a vow to be faithful.''

''Every man wants a wife he can be proud of.'' Her voice had a defeated tone Krystal had never heard before. Usually her sister was the steady, confident one in the family. It was one of the reasons why, even though Krystal was older, their roles had reversed, with Carly acting like the big sister.

"There's no reason why Joe shouldn't be proud of you," Krystal insisted. "Carly, you are a lovely person and you're a good wife and mother. I'm not going to let you take the blame for this," she said on a fierce whisper.

She might as well have been talking to the wall. It didn't matter what she said, her sister had already accepted the blame for her husband falling in love with another woman.

"He wanted me to take golf lessons, but I didn't think it would be any fun," she said in this tiny voice that sounded nothing like the Carly she knew.

"What does golf have to do with anything?" Krystal demanded.

"*She* golfs. And she's skinny."

"You've seen her?"

Carly bit down on her lower lip and nodded. As her eyes pooled with tears, she looked up at Krystal and asked, "What am I going to do?"

Krystal hugged her. "The first thing you're going to do is get some rest. You need sleep."

"Mommy, are you crying again?" Emily's little voice could be heard above the sound of the TV.

Carly managed to swallow back the tears, but she couldn't stop the trembling in her shoulders. "Mommy's okay, sweetie," she called out in a broken voice. She forced a smile that Krystal thought was the most pathetic excuse for a grin that she'd ever seen, but Emily didn't seem to mind.

She climbed down from the bed and came running over to throw herself at her mother. "Can we go home now, Mommy?"

"Not just yet," Carly said gently, meeting Krystal's gaze over the small blond head.

"But I'm hungry," the four-year-old whined.

Krystal reached for a box of tissues and shoved it on to her sister's lap. "Mop up and we'll go downstairs. I could use some breakfast, too."

Carly looked at her daughter. "Emily, you already ate breakfast."

"She can have more." Krystal looked at her niece and asked, "What do you like to eat?"

"Froot Loops."

Krystal frowned. "Oh, we don't have any Froot Loops. But I can make you pancakes. Would you like that?"

"Yes, please," the tiny voice answered. "Can Mommy come, too?"

"Mommy's not going to go with you," Carly answered, then looked at Krystal. "I don't want to see anybody. I look a mess."

"You don't need to worry. The Donovans all went to brunch this morning," Krystal assured her. "We'll have the kitchen to ourselves."

Carly shook her head. "It doesn't matter. I'm not hungry and I couldn't eat anything even if I tried."

No, Krystal didn't suppose she could. Seeing how pale and exhausted her sister was, she decided not to press the issue. "All right. You stay up here and get some rest. We won't be long. Promise."

She knew it was a promise that wouldn't be difficult to keep. Krystal wanted to get in and get out of the kitchen before any of the Donovans returned. She shivered as she thought about their family gathering together, wondering if Garret was telling them the news this very minute.

It was an unsettling thought. One that was so unsettling she found her appetite had vanished by the time she'd made the pancakes. She fed Emily and hurried back upstairs.

GARRET WAS RESTLESS. The others had noticed and commented on it, but he'd allowed them to believe the reason he'd left the table four times was to check in on a patient of his in the hospital. The truth was he'd gone outside to pace the parking lot. He did his best thinking when he was alone and he definitely needed to think.

He wouldn't have come to the family brunch if it wasn't for the fact that Dylan and Maddie would only be visiting a short while before they returned to France. He would have preferred to eat a stale piece of toast in the privacy of his own apartment where he could pace the floor and try to figure out what the best course of action was regarding Krystal.

Every time he thought about her his insides became all jumbled. He still couldn't believe she was carrying his child, yet he knew it was true. Krystal was not the kind of woman to lie about such a thing. And if she were going to lie about the paternity of the baby, she would have said it belonged to Roy. He was, after all, the man of her dreams. The one she'd been trying to forget the night she'd slept with Garret.

"You're awfully quiet," Maddie broke into his thoughts. "You're not just a little bit hungover, are you?" she asked with a twinkle in her eye.

"No, you saw how little I had to drink last night," he answered.

"Then it must be those phone calls you made to the hospital. You're worried about a patient, aren't you?"

Before he could answer, Dylan leaned closer and said, "Maybe he wasn't calling the hospital because of a patient. Could be he was speaking to one lady doctor who has his stomach all tied up in knots?''

Maddie elbowed her husband. ''Stop teasing.'' To Garret she said, ''Tell me more about this Doctors Without Borders program. Have you heard when you'll be leaving?''

''I'm not sure.'' It was one of the things that was on hold at the moment—as well as the rest of his life. If he left in January to go overseas to work, it meant he'd be gone when Krystal had her baby. He frowned.

''Not soon enough for you, eh, bro?'' Dylan misread the gesture. ''I bet it's soon enough for Mom, though.''

Leonie heard his comment and said, ''It's only natural for mothers to want their children close by. But you, Dylan, know better than any of your brothers that I never interfere with your career goals.''

Dylan lifted his coffee cup in salute. ''You're the best, Mom.''

An echo of ''hear, hear,'' could be heard as the other family members agreed.

''Shane's the only one of us who hasn't spread his wings and flown off to distant parts,'' Dylan remarked.

''No, I leave that to my brothers. Me, I'm happy right here in good old Minnesota with this little guy,'' he said, wrapping his arms around his son. ''You're smart, Garret, to go after what you want. You might as well travel and do the kind of work that interests you. Once you marry and have a family, you won't have the choices you have now.''

Garret felt as if his choices had already become restricted. When Leonie and Maddie excused themselves to go to the ladies' room, five-year-old Mickey announced he needed to use the facilities, too. Shane took him by the hand leaving Dylan and Garret alone at the table.

"One day that'll be me," Dylan said as he watched their brother and nephew walk away hand in hand. "I still can't believe I'm going to be a father."

"You're happy about it, aren't you?" Garret asked.

Dylan chuckled. "Isn't it obvious?"

Garret smiled. "Just checking." He was glad his brother had brought up the subject of fatherhood, because it gave them the opportunity to talk. "Did you and Maddie plan to have kids so soon after you were married?"

"No, and to be honest, at first I felt a little cheated. I thought we would have a couple of years with it being just the two of us. Then wham! We're married one month and she gets pregnant."

Garret could understand that sentiment—it was what had kept him tossing and turning last night. He too felt cheated. He'd missed out on the chance of falling in love with a woman before discovering he was going to be a father.

"I should have known better though," Dylan continued. "The same thing happened to Shane and Jennifer." He wagged his finger at Garret. "So be forewarned. When that time comes and you meet the right woman, it could be wham!"

Garret nodded and looked away, not wanting to give him any indication the warning came too late. He took a sip of his coffee, then asked, "So what got you past that feeling-cheated stage?"

"Seeing how happy Maddie was," Dylan answered. "She told me the minute she found out. Plus the knowledge that the baby inside her is a part of me. It's my son." He shook his head in amazement. "I'm telling you, Garret, it's an incredible feeling. I can't explain it. I guess you're just going to have to experience it yourself someday to know what I'm talking about.''

Garret almost told him about Krystal. He thought about it, but before he could actually do it, Dylan was reaching into his pocket and pulling out an envelope. He handed it to him.

"It's an ultrasound of the baby, but I guess I don't need to tell you that, do I?'' he said with a proud grin.

"Actually, this printout is called the sonogram,'' Garret corrected him. "Ultrasound is the procedure.''

"Can you see? It's a boy!'' Dylan boasted.

Garret smiled as he gazed at the printout. "Yup. Looks like a Donovan to me. Big head, big feet.''

"You've probably seen hundreds of these, but it's the first one I've ever seen,'' he said, looking at it once more before tucking it back into his pocket. "Technology is amazing, isn't it?''

Garret nodded in agreement. "You're going to make a good dad, Dylan,'' he said sincerely.

"Thanks. It means a lot to me to hear you say that. I know we haven't always seen eye to eye on things.''

Garret shrugged. "Does that surprise you? We're brothers.''

"We're a lot alike,'' he said, tucking the sonogram back into his pocket.

"You think so?''

"Yup. You're very protective of the people you care about. That's why you were so upset with me when Dad and I weren't getting along.''

It was the one time in their family history where there had actually been a rift that had caused heartache. Garret was glad it was in the past. "I wasn't trying to protect Dad,'' he felt obliged to say.

"No, you were trying to protect Mom. So was I.''

Garret leaned back, thinking about his father, wondering what he'd say if he were still alive. What advice would he give him regarding Krystal? "I miss Dad."

"So do I. He did some things I didn't like, some things I'll never understand, but he was still my father. And I'm sad that I don't have the chance to share this time of my life with him. Remember how excited he was when Mickey was born?" His eyes clouded at the memory. "He was a grandpa for only a short time, but he loved it."

"Yeah, he did," Garret concurred with a sigh. He eyed his brother thoughtfully, then said, "Marriage has changed you, Dylan."

"Why? Because I realized that Mom was right?"

"About what?"

"Remember when we were kids and one of us would get mad at Dad, we inevitably would say, Dad just doesn't get it. She'd always tell us, Oh, he gets it all right. And one day, when you're a father, you'll understand just how much he gets it. I think I'm beginning to understand. Fatherhood changes a man's life."

Garret agreed with him silently. It had been less than twelve hours since Krystal had told him about her pregnancy and already his life had changed. Only right now it didn't seem to be the positive change it was for his brother.

Again he was tempted to tell Dylan about Krystal, but he couldn't. Not yet. Not when he wasn't sure what he was going to do. Or what she was going to do for that matter.

It was something he hadn't given much consideration until now. He'd spent most of his time thinking about the impact this baby would have on his life. Now he realized he hadn't given any thought as to what it would do to hers. Like him, she had decisions to make.

"Listen to me, rambling on about fatherhood like this. I'm probably boring the socks off a single guy like you," Dylan said with a brotherly pat on his shoulder.

Garret shook his head. "No, not at all," he said honestly.

"I'm just so excited about this baby," he told him. "I'll tell you what. When the day comes and you're in my shoes, I promise I'll let you talk my ear off."

Again Garret was tempted to tell him that day had come, but Maddie was coming toward them. "Bet I can guess what you two are talking about," she said.

"I had to show him the picture." Dylan hugged her before she sat back down, his hand on her slightly bulging stomach.

It was such a loving gesture Garret couldn't help but be envious. Little did Dylan know that Garret *was* walking in his shoes. The problem was, he couldn't fill them. He didn't have a happy marriage, or a loving wife. He didn't even live with the mother of his child. Maddie had told Dylan the minute she suspected she was pregnant. Krystal had known about her pregnancy for months before she even told him.

No, he would not be walking in Dylan's shoes. He was going to have a pair all to himself. He only hoped he knew what to do with them.

CHAPTER SEVEN

As soon as Emily had finished eating her breakfast, Krystal took her back upstairs. Carly wasn't asleep, but was on her cell phone. From the look on her face and the tone of her voice, Krystal knew she wanted privacy and suggested she finish her conversation in the hall.

While she was gone, Krystal made good on her promise to Emily to paint her fingernails and toenails. When that was accomplished, she braided the little girl's long blond hair, then read her a story. As she suspected, her niece fell asleep before she'd turned but a couple of pages.

It wasn't much later that Carly came back into the room wearing the same weary, downtrodden look she'd had when she'd arrived on her doorstep that morning.

"Are you okay?" Krystal asked.

She nodded. "That was Mom, in case you couldn't tell. She gave me the usual 'you don't solve problems by running away from them' speech."

"She ought to know." Krystal knew it was a catty remark, but she couldn't help herself.

"Yeah. How many times did we move because of some guy she no longer wanted in her life?" She dropped down on to the futon. "I feel sick."

Krystal sat beside her. "You're exhausted. I wish you'd try to get some sleep."

"I can't sleep. I keep seeing him…with her." She shivered, then rubbed her hands on her arms. "Everyone in town knows about it. I'll never be able to face anyone ever again…not even Sofie."

Sofie was her best friend. She also was Joe's cousin. "It's probably not as bad as you think." Krystal tried to be optimistic.

"Yes, it is." She wrapped her arms around herself. "I don't care what Mom says. I'm never going back, Krys. I can't."

Krystal knew at this point it wouldn't do much good to tell her sister it was unrealistic to think she could run away from the situation forever. Instead, she said, "What about your house?"

"I don't want it. It's his anyway."

"He built it for you."

"Doesn't matter. I don't want it anymore. He can keep it." There was no emotion in her voice, just a flat resignation that told Krystal how deeply hurt her sister was.

"You don't need to make that decision now. How you feel today might not be how you feel tomorrow, and you have to remember that even if you don't reconcile with Joe, you're going to need a place to live," she stated pragmatically.

Carly didn't appreciate her attempt to be rational. "Look, if you don't want me here, just say so. I'll leave."

"I do want you here. You're my sister and I love you and I want to help you in any way I can. All I'm saying is that at some point, you're going to have to sit down with Joe and get this all straightened out." She worked at keeping her voice even, not wanting this to disintegrate into an emotional argument.

"Maybe you didn't hear me. It is straight as far as

Joe is concerned. He doesn't want me for a wife. He wants Miss Bathing Suit. There's nothing left to think about.'' Carly's voice rose in frustration.

Krystal raised her hands in surrender. ''All right. I'm sorry. I didn't mean to imply you hadn't thought this through. But I have to tell you, Carly, that it doesn't seem right to me that he's the one who cheats on you, yet you're the one who moves out. Do you know how many times I've heard you say that house is your dream home?''

''That was before he brought *her* there.''

''He didn't…'' She trailed off in disgust.

Carly nodded. ''That weekend Emily and I went with Mom to visit Aunt Lois? She was there at the house, eating in my kitchen, taking a bath in my whirlpool tub, and sleeping with my husband in my bed!'' Again the tears ran down her cheeks.

''Why, that big zero! Who does he think he is?'' Anger coursed through her. ''You should have kicked his butt to the curb, Carly. He doesn't deserve you or Emily.''

Carly looked at her with woeful eyes. ''He told me he built the house for me. He said it was a gift of love, that it would be the house where all our dreams came true. Then he turns around and does *that*…with *her*.''

Seeing the pain of betrayal on her sister's face made Krystal want to smack her brother-in-law. Carly was far from perfect, but she was a good wife to Joe and a good mother to Emily. She didn't deserve to suffer such a humiliation. Krystal wrapped her arms around her sister and tried to comfort her.

''Oh, Carly, I'm sorry. No wonder you're so upset. That is unforgivable.''

''That's what I told Mom. She thinks I should just go back home, but I can't forgive him, Krys.''

The Harlequin Reader Service® — Here's how it works:

Accepting your 2 free books and gift places you under no obligation to buy anything. You may keep the books and gift and return the shipping statement marked "cancel." If you do not cancel, about a month later we'll send you 6 additional books and bill you just $4.47 each in the U.S., or $4.99 each in Canada, plus 25¢ shipping & handling per book and applicable taxes if any.* That's the complete price and — compared to cover prices of $5.25 each in the U.S. and $6.25 each in Canada — it's quite a bargain! You may cancel at any time, but if you choose to continue, every month we'll send you 6 more books, which you may either purchase at the discount price or return to us and cancel your subscription.

*Terms and prices subject to change without notice. Sales tax applicable in N.Y. Canadian residents will be charged applicable provincial taxes and GST.

If offer card is missing write to: The Harlequin Reader Service, 3010 Walden Ave., P.O. Box 1867, Buffalo, NY 14240-1867

NO POSTAGE
NECESSARY
IF MAILED
IN THE
UNITED STATES

BUSINESS REPLY MAIL

FIRST-CLASS MAIL   PERMIT NO. 717-003   BUFFALO, NY

POSTAGE WILL BE PAID BY ADDRESSEE

HARLEQUIN READER SERVICE
3010 WALDEN AVE
PO BOX 1867
BUFFALO NY 14240-9952

Do You Have the LUCKY KEY?

PLAY THE Lucky Key Game

and you can get

FREE BOOKS and a FREE GIFT!

Scratch the gold areas with a coin. Then check below to see the books and gift you can get!

YES!
I have scratched off the gold areas. Please send me the 2 FREE BOOKS and GIFT for which I qualify. I understand I am under no obligation to purchase any books, as explained on the back of this card.

336 HDL DVAK

135 HDL DVAZ

FIRST NAME

LAST NAME

ADDRESS

APT.#

CITY

STATE/PROV.

ZIP/POSTAL CODE

2 free books plus a free gift

1 free book

2 free books

Try Again!

Visit us online at www.eHarlequin.com

DETACH AND MAIL CARD TODAY!

(H-SR-10/03)

© 2002 HARLEQUIN ENTERPRISES LTD. ® and ™ are trademarks owned by Harlequin Enterprises Ltd.

"I don't blame you."

"Then you don't think I'm wrong for leaving?"

"No! How could you be wrong for walking out on someone who's done that to you?"

"Mom said all men make mistakes and that before I do anything I'll regret, I should think about Emily," she said between sobs. "She needs a father."

"She also needs to see her mother treated with respect," Krystal pointed out.

Just then Carly's cell phone rang. Glancing at the caller ID, she whispered, "It's him."

For one moment Krystal saw a spark of hope in her sister's eyes. It was enough to tell her that no matter what Carly said, she still cared for Joe.

Again Carly went out into the hall for privacy, but this call was significantly shorter than the one she'd had with their mother. When she returned, the hope that had momentarily brightened her eyes was gone.

"He only called because he wanted to talk to Emily," she said, tossing her cell phone on to the futon. "I told him she was sleeping, but I don't think he believed me." She groaned in frustration. "I wish I could run far away where he'd never be able to see her again."

"Mom's right about one thing, Carly. He is Emily's father and, no matter what happens between the two of you, that's not going to change."

"I don't want him in her life," she said bitterly.

Krystal didn't think it was a good time to remind Carly of Joe's responsibilities toward his daughter. Her sister was too distraught to have any perspective on Emily and Joe's relationship.

"I don't blame you for feeling that way. It's only normal for you to be angry right now. He's done a terrible thing and I know you only want what's best for Emily.''

Carly looked up at her with gratitude in her eyes. ''I knew you'd understand. You don't want Garret in your baby's life, either, do you?''

She shifted uncomfortably. ''Carly, I never said I wasn't going to tell Garret I'm pregnant.''

''If you were smart, you wouldn't,'' she advised her.

She didn't tell her that it was too late. Garret already knew. Instead she moved the conversation back to her sister's situation. ''Did Joe give you any money when you left?''

''He doesn't have any.''

''What do you mean he doesn't have any? His parents own half of Fergus Falls.''

''I know, but they stopped giving him money a long time ago. They knew it was ending up in the casino.''

''He has a gambling problem?'' Krystal frowned. ''How long has this been going on?''

Carly shrugged. ''Since he got bored being with me, I guess. I'm a boring person, you know.'' Self-pity laced her words.

''You are not boring. And even if you were, it wouldn't give him the right to gamble away your household money. How bad is your financial situation?''

''Bad enough.''

''You do have some money, right?''

''Yeah, yeah, I have some.'' She got up and began to pace the floor, rubbing her forehead with her fingers. ''I can't believe he had that woman at the house when he was talking to me.''

''Carly, would you forget about the other woman? You need to think about what you're going to do. How

much money do you have right now?'' She tried to
steer the conversation back to the practical.

She shrugged. ''I don't know. A couple of thousand,
I guess. There should be some money in my savings
account.''

''Don't you know?''

She shook her head. ''Joe was the one who took
care of the bills.''

''Obviously, he didn't take care of them very well
if he's broke,'' Krystal said with disdain.

''Can we not talk about him?'' Carly pleaded.

Krystal sighed. She knew they would not have a
rational conversation at this point. Krystal knew it was
up to her to get things under control.

''We need to talk about you and Emily. You need
a place to stay until you figure out what you're going
to do,'' she told her sister.

Carly interpreted that statement as a sign that she
wasn't welcome as Krystal's houseguest. ''I knew you
didn't want me here.''

''I do want you here, but look at this place.'' She
waved her arm in the air. ''It's not big enough for
three people.'' Although her room was quite large for
an efficiency-size apartment, she had no kitchen and
she had to share a bath with the other second-floor
tenant.

''All right, all right, I get the message,'' Carly said
impatiently, jumping to her feet. ''I'll get out of your
way and you won't have to be bothered by me.''

Krystal groaned. ''Will you stop?'' She reached for
her sister's hand. ''How many times do I have to tell
you I want you here?'' She let out a long sigh of
frustration. ''If you would let me finish what I have
to say, I'd tell you that I am not going to send you
home or to Mom's. I'm going to ask Leonie if you

can use the apartment across the hall. It's about the same size as this one." It was not a request Krystal wanted to make—not after what she'd told Garret last night, but she didn't see any other option at the moment.

A ray of optimism brightened her sister's face. "You think she'll say yes?"

"I'm not sure what Leonie will say," she answered honestly, knowing her relationship with her landlady could have changed dramatically since yesterday. She didn't tell Carly that but said, "We're not supposed to have children in this building, but she's made exceptions in the past so she might now."

"Do you want me to come with you?"

Krystal glanced at her niece asleep on the bed. "No. You stay here with Emily." As she headed toward the door, she said, "Wish me luck. I'm going to need it." And for more reasons than one, she added silently.

WITH EACH STEP KRYSTAL TOOK down the stairs, her anxiety increased. She knew Leonie was home because she could hear voices. The sound wasn't coming from the kitchen, however, but the great room.

As she stepped into the entry, she saw that most of the Donovans were gathered there. All heads turned in her direction at the sound of her footsteps. Conversation ceased and from the way everyone stared at her, Krystal thought it could only be for one reason. Garret had told them she was pregnant with his child.

"Good morning…or I guess I should say good afternoon," Leonie greeted her. "How are you feeling?"

"I'm fine. Thanks," she replied, wishing she wasn't the center of attention.

"When you left the wedding last night I was worried you were coming down with the flu that's going around.'' Her landlady eyed her in a motherly way.

She shook her head. "No, no flu."

Krystal's eyes met Garret's in an unspoken question. They gave her no indication what he was thinking. She quickly glanced at Maddie and saw sympathy and understanding.

"Come join in the celebration," Dylan said. It was then that Krystal noticed the open bottle of champagne.

"What are you celebrating?" she asked cautiously.

"Donovan babies," he said with a grin.

Babies. Plural with an *s*. Krystal conveyed her panic to Maddie with a glance.

"We hope there will be more than one coming in the near future. Shane told us he and Jennifer would like to have another baby."

Krystal didn't realize she was holding her breath until she let it out in a rush. "That's great!" she finally managed to squeak out.

Shane looked at Maddie. "Thank you for not saying we're *trying* to get pregnant or else I never would have heard the end of it from this guy," he said, jerking a thumb in Dylan's direction.

"It was only yesterday that I was telling Garret the Donovan men have never had to work hard at that particular project," he said with a grin.

Maddie playfully punched him on the arm. "You shush."

"Hey—it's a good kind of work, isn't it?" Dylan added. "All kidding aside—" he lifted his champagne flute "—I'm looking forward to the third Donovan grandbaby. This way our little guy will have another boy cousin to keep him company."

"Or a little girl cousin," Leonie spoke up.

"We all know Mom would like a granddaughter," Shane said with an affectionate grin aimed at his mother.

"Well, I've had four boys, so it wouldn't surprise me if I had four grandsons," Leonie told them all with a shrug of her shoulders.

Krystal knew her face was red and hoped no one else noticed. She tried not to look at Garret, but she couldn't help casting a glance his way. His face had the same unreadable mask it always had. She didn't know how he could keep his emotions hidden. Worried that she wouldn't be as successful at hiding hers, she said, "I'm going to leave and let you have your family moment together."

"Don't be silly," Leonie said, pulling her by the elbow into the room. "You're like one of the family, isn't she?" she said to no one in particular and a chorus of yeses answered. "You must celebrate with us."

"I'd like to, but I have company. My sister's here. Actually, she's the reason I came down here. Leonie, I need to speak with you for a few moments—if you don't mind?"

"Of course, dear. Why don't we go into the kitchen?"

Dear. She hardly felt worthy of the affectionate title. She followed her landlady, listening to her chatter happily about how wonderful the wedding had been.

When they were alone, she asked, "What is it you need to talk to me about?"

Krystal gave her an abbreviated version of what Carly had told her, ending with, "So she really could use a place to stay until she figures out what she's going to do."

"You want her to take Dena's room?"

"If it wouldn't be too much of an inconvenience for you."

"It's not an inconvenience at all," Leonie insisted. "I haven't had time to find a new tenant. Tell Carly she's welcome to use the room."

"She'll pay you…" she began, but Leonie cut her off.

"There's no need for her to pay. Once she's back on her feet we'll talk about it. Dena moved everything out of that room except the bed. I'll send up some fresh linens and she may need some hangers for the closet."

Her generous spirit only made Krystal feel more uneasy about her own situation. "Thank you. That's very kind of you."

Leonie brushed aside her compliment. "It's what family does in a time of need. They take care of one another."

Krystal gave her a smile of gratitude, then went back upstairs. She could only hope Leonie would feel the same once she learned Krystal was expecting Garret's baby.

KRYSTAL SPENT THE remainder of Sunday taking care of Emily. While Carly slept, she took her niece to the park, where they flew a kite and had a picnic lunch. Being with four-year-old Emily made her realize that, for the past few months, she'd been focusing on how difficult her life had become because of her pregnancy. Stress and uncertainty had overshadowed the fact that one day she would be blessed with the greatest gift a woman could have—a child.

Playing with Emily and watching her mimic her mother's behavior made Krystal hope she was carrying a girl. "A son is your son till he takes his wife, but a daughter's your daughter all of her life." How many times had she heard her mother say those words? She wasn't sure they were true. After all, Leonie had four sons and they were all very close to her, yet Krystal found herself hoping for a daughter.

Normally Krystal ate her meals in the kitchen, but on this particular Sunday evening she decided it would be much easier to order pizza and eat in her room. Carly slept most of the day, getting up to take a couple of bites from a slice, then returning to the futon.

Krystal marveled at how resilient kids could be. Emily, with all the innocence of a typical four-year-old, hopped and sang as Krystal brushed her teeth and got her ready for bed.

As Leonie had promised, she'd sent up fresh linens to Dena's old room. She'd also put a vase of fresh-cut flowers on the small bedside table and a message of welcome.

"If there's anything else you need, please let me know." It was signed, "Love, Leonie."

"She's very kind, isn't she?" Carly said when she read the note.

"Yes, she is."

"Have you told her about…" her sister began but Krystal cut her off, not wanting her to mention the baby in front of Emily.

"No, and it's important that she hears it from Garret. You understand?"

Carly gave her a cross look. "Of course. What do you think I'm going to do? Blab?"

Krystal wasn't sure what Carly would do in her present emotional state. She didn't bear much resemblance to the sister she knew. "I hope you don't."

Carly just rolled her eyes. "I'm tired. I'm going to

bed,'' she said, pulling back the covers. "Get in, Emily.''

The little girl looked around. "I don't want to sleep in here.''

"Why not? There's nothing wrong with this room,'' her mother said.

Big eyes surveyed the nearly empty apartment. "It's scary.''

Krystal could see Carly didn't have much patience. "It won't be. I'm going to be in bed with you.''

The little girl looked as if she were going to cry. "Why can't we go home?''

"Because we can't,'' Carly said wearily.

"Maybe Emily wants to sleep with me?'' Krystal suggested. "Would you like that?'' she asked her niece.

The little head nodded, her lower lip still pushed out.

"What do you think?'' Krystal looked to Carly for approval.

Carly looked as if she wanted to protest but was simply too worn-out to say anything. "Go ahead. Most of her stuffed animals are in there anyway.''

So Emily took Krystal's hand and headed across the hall where the four-year-old climbed up onto the bed, positioning her plush pig on one side of her and her bunny rabbit on the other.

"Are you going to pull the shade?'' she asked, pointing toward the window.

"Sure am.'' Krystal walked over to the window. As she reached for the shade pull, she glanced outside and saw Samantha standing next to Garret's car.

She quickly lowered the shade, not wanting to stare at them. She wondered if he had told her about the baby.

As she climbed into bed, she tried not to think about Garret and Samantha. What he did or didn't say to Samantha was none of her business. Right now she had more important things to worry about. Like helping her sister and Emily get through the next few days.

She glanced at her niece. "There. Is that better?"

Emily nodded. "Are you coming to bed now, too?"

Normally Krystal would have said no, but she was exhausted. Emotionally and physically. She took off her robe and slid in next to her niece. She was about to turn off the light when Emily sat forward.

"Can you leave the light on for a little bit?"

"I'll tell you what," Krystal said climbing back out of bed. "How about if I plug in a night-light for you? I have one I think you'll like." She dug through a drawer until she found a tiny light in the shape of a rose. She plugged it in next to the bed. "There. How's that?"

"I like it," Emily said, then lay back down against the pillow.

After more hugs and good-night kisses, she thought maybe her niece would finally go to sleep. First, however, she had to say her prayers. Krystal listened while Emily went down her list of people to bless, which included her aunt. It was the last line, however, that weighed heavily on her mind long after she'd fallen asleep.

She said, "And please make Mommy and Daddy stop fighting."

THE NEXT FEW DAYS Krystal felt as if she were walking through a minefield, waiting for any one of the several explosive situations in her life to detonate. She waited for Garret to call or come see her, but he didn't. She waited for Leonie to confront her about the baby, but she didn't. She waited for her mother to come riding in on her high horse because Carly was still at her place, but so far she hadn't. About the only place Krystal could feel any sense of comfort at all was at the salon, where at least listening to other people's stories took her mind off her own problems.

She had told her boss of her pregnancy, but none of her co-workers, with the exception of Shannon, knew she was having a baby. Since it was nearly impossible to fit into any of her clothes, it was only a matter of time before everyone knew. She took advantage of the large bib-front aprons provided by the salon, wearing them with the hope they would hide her weight gain. It also helped that the heat wave had broken and fall had arrived, bringing cooler temperatures and a reason for her to wear dusters and sweaters.

If it wasn't for the fact that Leonie was a client at the salon, she would have made her pregnancy public knowledge by now. What she didn't want, however, was for her landlady to hear from someone else that she was pregnant, which was why, when she saw that Leonie had scheduled an appointment for later that week, she called Garret.

As she suspected, he was unavailable, which meant she had to leave her name and number and wait for him to return her call. To her surprise it wasn't a long wait. She was in the middle of cutting a client's hair when the receptionist announced over the loudspeaker that she had a call on line three.

Krystal excused herself and hurried into the employee lounge. She pressed the button next to the blinking light. "This is Krystal."

"It's Garret."

She swallowed to ease the dryness in her mouth.

"I…" she began. "I need to know what you're planning to do."

"Krystal, I don't know what I'm going to do. It's only been three days since you told me."

"I mean about your mother. I feel guilty keeping this from her."

She heard him sigh and imagined him raking his hand over the back of his neck, the way he always did when he was stressed. "I know. I feel the same way and I'm going to tell her soon."

"She's coming in on Friday to get her hair done. It wouldn't be good if she heard the news from someone other than you or me."

"No, you're right." Again there was a sigh. "I'll take care of it before then. Is that it?"

She wanted to say, *No, that's not it. In about five months we're going to be parents and I don't have a clue as to how you feel about it.*

But she couldn't tell him that right now. He was an overworked doctor with a long list of patients demanding his time, and she had a client with one side of her hair shorter than the other waiting for her to finish the job.

"Yeah, that's all I wanted." She tried to make her voice as impersonal as his, but knew she failed.

"All right then, we'll talk soon," he told her and, before she could utter another word, he'd hung up.

Soon? When is soon? she wondered. She thought it might be that evening. When she arrived home, she saw his car outside 14 Valentine Place. Butterflies danced in her stomach at the thought of him inside with his mother. She used the tenants' entrance to the house rather than walk through the main dining area.

When she reached the second floor, she found Emily on the flight of stairs leading to the third floor.

"I'm playing with my Slinky. Mommy bought it for me today. Watch." She climbed several risers then let the metal spring toy flop down, giggling as it tumbled from stair to stair.

"Where's your mommy?"

She pointed to Krystal's room. "In there. Want to play with me?"

"In a minute, sweetie. First let me talk to your mommy, okay?" She went into her apartment and found Carly inside reading a magazine.

"Why is Emily playing on the stairs?"

"She has a Slinky. Where else would she play with it?"

"This is a boardinghouse that's not supposed to have any children living here."

"So? Leonie doesn't mind. She told me it was okay."

"And Samantha?"

"She said it was okay, too."

"You asked her?"

She nodded. "If you don't believe me, you could have asked her yourself. You just missed her. She left a couple of minutes ago. Does she know about…" Her glance moved down to Krystal's stomach.

"I don't know but I'm wishing you didn't," she snapped.

"I told you I wouldn't say anything and I haven't."

Krystal knew stress was causing her to be short with her sister. "I'm going to change my clothes and then we'll go get some supper. There's a good coffee shop over on Grand that has a kids' menu."

"I don't feel much like going out. Can't we just eat downstairs?"

"We could but Maddie and Dylan are still here. They're probably having dinner with Leonie."

"No, they aren't. They all went out to eat."

It seemed that her sister knew more about what was going on in the house than she did. "Anything else you want to report happened while I was gone?" she asked dryly.

"Mom called, like, three times."

"She didn't say she was coming to visit, did she?"

Carly shook her head.

That was one land mine she could sidestep for today anyway. "Are you sure I can't talk you into going out for something to eat? We could go to the cinema café. There's an animated feature playing there that Emily would enjoy. We could get a bite to eat."

"I don't feel much like sitting through a movie."

"You don't feel much like doing anything, Carly. Why not do it for Emily?" Krystal urged her.

Just when she thought she'd have to take her niece by herself, Carly agreed. The evening turned out to be a better experience than Krystal expected. The film may have been rated G for kids but much of its humor was intended for adults. For the first time in three days her sister actually laughed.

When they got back to the house, however, her mood turned sullen once again, when Emily asked if she could call her daddy and tell him about the movie. Carly told her daughter her cell phone needed to be recharged before they made any more calls. Krystal's offer to use her phone drew a nasty look from her sister, but she didn't try to stop Emily from calling her father.

To Emily's dismay and Carly's relief, Joe wasn't home. Emily left a message in her tiny voice, which had Krystal looking at Carly in sympathy.

Long after they'd all gone to bed, Krystal was still awake. Not only was she restless, she was hungry. For the first time since she'd been pregnant she had a craving. It was for the root-beer-flavored Popsicles she'd purchased for Emily. She tried to ignore it, but all she could think about was sucking on that ice-cold treat.

She glanced at the clock. It was after midnight. Normally Leonie would be in bed at this hour, but with Dylan and Maddie visiting, there was a good possibility she might still be awake. The question was, did Krystal want to risk running into her?

The craving refused to go away and she gently slid out from beneath the covers, not wanting to disturb Emily, who still refused to sleep with her mother across the hall. She pulled her robe from the closet and headed for the kitchen. The house was quiet as she made her way down to the first floor, the only light the glow of a lamp that was always lit in the hallway.

On tiptoe Krystal padded into the kitchen. She didn't turn on any lights, simply went straight for the refrigerator. She stood with the freezer compartment open, searching for the Popsicles when the overhead light came on. Startled, she let out a gasp.

"You're caught."

It was Dylan dressed in a pair of khakis and a polo shirt. Krystal looked behind him, expecting to find Maddie, but she wasn't there.

"I didn't expect to find you raiding the refrigerator," he said.

"I'm hungry. I thought you and Maddie would have gone back to the hotel by now."

"You know how Mom is. She likes to stay up late and talk. What are you after?"

"Popsicles." She pulled one from its box and held it up.

"Maddie wants some yogurt. I thought she'd be

sending me out for pizza or ice cream, but she craves yogurt.'' He shook his head in disbelief.

''At least it's a healthy craving.''

He opened the lower part of the refrigerator. ''And Mom has some here in the house. I could have been out pounding the pavement looking for an all-night diner if she had asked for a pastrami on rye.''

She smiled at him. ''You're a good man, Dylan Donovan. Not many men would go out past midnight to satisfy a wife's cravings.''

''Not many men have a wife like Maddie.''

''I'm glad to hear that marriage agrees with you.''

He grinned. ''Garret tells me I'm like a smoker who's quit the habit. Now that I'm smoke free, I want everybody else to be.''

''You think everyone should get married?''

''Not everyone, but my brother could use a good woman.''

''And does he agree with you?'' She couldn't resist asking.

''Net yet, but I still have a few days left to work on him,'' he said with a wink. ''You know Garret. Work always has been his number-one priority and with this Doctors Without Borders assignment he's accepted, he isn't making it any easier.''

They were interrupted by the appearance of Leonie. ''I came to see what was keeping you,'' she said to Dylan as she entered the kitchen.

''I take it Maddie's looking for her snack,'' he said, holding up the yogurt carton.

''Yes, and I need one more cup of coffee. I'll be with you in a minute,'' she told her son before he left. Then she turned to Krystal. ''Couldn't sleep?'' she asked as she refilled her coffee mug.

''I was a bit restless,'' Krystal admitted.

"You're worried about Carly, aren't you?" She unwrapped a sugar substitute and poured it into her coffee. "I'm sorry we haven't had much time to talk lately. There's been so much activity going on around here."

"I've been really busy, too. I haven't even had much time to spend with Maddie."

"She and Dylan are so happy." She sighed. "It does a mother's heart good…you know what I mean?"

Krystal nodded. "They're a good match."

"I've been lucky. My two elder sons have married lovely women. Now if I could get Garret married, I'd have only Jason to worry about."

"I thought Garret was going overseas."

She took a sip of coffee, then said, "He is. That's why he needs someone who understands his dedication to his profession. Someone who'd be willing to wait for him while he's gone."

Krystal swallowed with difficulty. She knew by the tone of Leonie's voice that she had someone in mind. Samantha.

"You sound like you're taking a professional interest in his personal life," she remarked.

Leonie raised one hand. "I plead guilty. I know I said I would never interfere in my sons' personal lives, but Garret is the one of the four I think needs a little nudge."

"And in which direction do you want to nudge him?" she asked.

"Samantha's perfect for him. She's smart. She's independent. She has a good sense of humor." She used her fingers to enumerate her many good qualities. "And most importantly, she understands his world."

Leonie wasn't saying anything Krystal hadn't already said to herself. As much as she hated to admit it, Samantha Penrose was a much better match for Garret than she would ever be. It was not something she wanted to tell her landlady, however.

Unfortunately, Leonie asked her opinion. "You've had some time to get to know her. Don't you think she's a good match for Garret?"

She took a lick of her Popsicle to get rid of her dry mouth. "It doesn't really matter what I think, does it? I mean, isn't Garret the one who should be deciding?"

Leonie reached over to give her a hug. "You are absolutely right, but you can't blame a mom for trying, can you?" she said with an endearing grin. "Besides, I have a feeling he may not need a push when it comes to settling down and having a family."

Krystal didn't want to ask the question, but it refused to stay unanswered. "What makes you say that?"

"Dylan told me he and Garret had a man-to-man talk the other day about marriage and children. One thing I have been pretty accurate on is recognizing when a man is looking for someone to spend his life with and I do believe Garret is ready."

And there was Samantha, just waiting to pounce, Krystal thought. She didn't want to think about Garret…or Samantha. She looked at the clock and said, "Oh! I didn't realize how late it is. I'd better get to bed." She forced a smile, mumbled something about wishing Garret all the best and then said good-night.

"Good night, dear," Leonie said in her usual sweet voice. "And try not to worry. Carly will get through the bad times."

Maybe Carly would, but the question was, would she? Until now she'd been thinking about the baby in terms of it belonging exclusively to her and Garret.

Her conversation with Leonie had reminded her of the possibility that he could marry and bring another woman into the equation. And Samantha could be that woman. She could become a stepmother to her child.

Krystal couldn't let that happen. She wouldn't let it happen. Unfortunately, it wasn't her call to make. It was up to Garret. And he hadn't told her anything about what he'd been thinking.

Was it any wonder she couldn't sleep?

CHAPTER EIGHT

KRYSTAL ENDED UP getting very little sleep that night. The following morning she felt tired and blue. Her mood worsened when she discovered she had nothing left in her closet that fit her pregnant body. She borrowed a pair of slacks from her sister, who wore a larger size than she did, and headed for the salon.

The first thing she did when she arrived was find her friend Shannon. "Did you mean it when you said I could borrow some of your maternity clothes?"

"Of course I meant it, but I'm not sure they're going to fit you. You're welcome to come over and try them on though."

"I'd better do it soon. Look." She lifted her shirt to reveal two large safety pins holding her slacks closed.

"I'm surprised you made it this long. I was in maternity clothes by the end of my third month. Why don't we go shopping after work? There's a new place over on Grand Avenue that specializes in clothing for the expectant mother."

Krystal grimaced. "I suppose I don't really have a choice, do I?"

Shannon gave her a sympathetic shake of her head. "I'll call the sitter and tell her I'm going to be a little late."

"Thanks. I could use some time with a friend."

"Are things getting you down?"

She told her about her conversation with Leonie the night before and her worry that Garret might marry someone like Samantha.

"Are they dating exclusively?"

She honestly didn't know. "I'm not sure, but it doesn't really matter, does it? I mean, if Samantha isn't the one, there will probably be another woman like her who captures his heart."

"That doesn't mean he'll ignore his obligation to his son or daughter."

"That's not what's worrying me. What if he gets married and decides that he and his wife should be the baby's full-time parents?"

"What you need to do is to talk about this with Garret. Tell him your concerns," Shannon urged her.

They were concerns that kept her on edge all day long. When she met Shannon after work the first thing her friend said to her was, "Don't frown. It causes wrinkles."

"In that case by the time this baby arrives I'll be a prune."

Shannon squeezed her arm. "Oh, it's not that bad."

Krystal didn't see how it could get much worse. Shannon attempted to cheer her up on the short walk to the clothing store, but her efforts were wasted.

When Krystal stepped inside the shop full of maternity clothes and accessories, she groaned. "I don't want to be doing this." She attempted to turn around and leave, but Shannon wouldn't let her.

She put her hands on Krystal's shoulders and pushed her toward the rack of matching tops and slacks. "You don't have a choice in the matter. You need clothes for work." Shannon dove into the rack, pushing aside hangers, critically eyeing the garments before pulling out a dark green pantsuit. "This is cute. You can't even tell it's maternity."

Krystal pulled open the jacket and grimaced at the sight of the elastic insert in the front of the slacks. "What do you call this?"

"Comfortable," Shannon answered. She pulled out several more items, then said, "Go try them on."

Krystal hesitated until Shannon gave her a gentle shove. "Go."

"Here. Hold my purse for me," she said, then went into the curtained dressing room. When she had the first of the outfits in place, she stepped back out into the store to get Shannon's opinion.

"I'm never going to fill this out," she said, tugging on the elastic insert in the pants.

"Trust me, you will. That jacket would be a good choice because it will go with practically anything. Green's always been a great color on you because of your hair."

She glanced at the price tag. "It's affordable, too. It's a possibility." She went back into the dressing room, pulling the curtain shut behind her, stripped off the clothes and tried on several more outfits. Shannon suggested she give them all to the salesclerk and decide when she was finished which ones she could afford.

It was while she was in the middle of changing that she heard the electronic Mexican hat dance song ringing on her phone.

"That's your cell, Krys," Shannon called out from the other side of the curtain.

"It's in my purse. Will you get it for me?" she asked, poking her arm through a slit in the curtain. Shannon placed the phone in her palm and Krystal pulled it into the dressing room and flipped it open.

When she saw it was Garret calling, her heart began to race.

"Hello."

"It's Garret. I'm at the salon," he told her. "Mom thought you worked until six today but they said you'd already gone home for the day. I noticed your car's still in the parking lot."

"Yeah. I'm with Shannon. We're shopping."

"We really need to talk and I don't have much time. How far away are you?"

"Not far. I'm in a clothing shop over on Grand."

"I'll come there then, unless you want to come back here."

Neither option sounded particularly exciting at the moment. She stared at her reflection in the mirror. Dressed in only her bra and underpants, she could see the changes pregnancy had caused. Her body was getting wider, more rounded. Although she was alone in the changing room, she felt exposed and vulnerable.

"Krystal, which would be better? Should I come to you or do you want to come to me? We need to talk," he said for the second time, his voice urgent.

"You can come here, but I'll need about fifteen minutes."

"All right. I'll wait for you outside. Just tell me the name of the store."

"It's Motherhood Fashions," she told him. "Just go over to Grand Avenue and take a right. You can't miss it."

He said, "I'll be there shortly" and hung up.

She stuck her head outside the dressing-room curtain. "That was Garret. I guess I'm going to find out what he plans to do."

"Maybe Leonie's wrong about him and Samantha."

"She's a romance coach. She's seldom wrong about these things."

"Yes, but it's different when it's your own kids. You lose your objectivity."

"Maybe." As she struggled to get back into Carly's slacks. Shannon's arm shot through the curtain. Dangling from her fingers were bras and underpants.

"I don't need underwear," Krystal told her.

"Trust me, in a few weeks' time, you will."

"But those are huge. You have the wrong size."

"No, I don't." She wiggled them in front of her. "Do you want them or not?"

She sighed. "I guess." When she couldn't get the pin closed to hook Carly's slacks, she called out, "Bring me a pair of jeans from out there, will you?"

Shannon did as she was requested. Krystal was in the middle of pulling them on when her friend announced, "Garret's out front."

Krystal fumbled with the buttons on her blouse as her heart skipped a beat. "Will you do me a favor and tell him I'll be out as soon as I've paid for this stuff? And tell the clerk I'm going to wear this pair of jeans home." She ripped off the tag and handed it to Shannon.

Krystal finished buttoning her shirt, then pulled on the coat-length sweater she had worn to work, appreciating that it covered the elastic insert on the maternity jeans. She took a brush from her purse and ran it through her hair, then powdered her cheeks and applied a lip gloss.

When she stepped outside the dressing room, Shannon asked, "Do you want me to wait for you?" Her eyes went to the sales counter where Garret stood staring in her direction.

She shook her head. "No, you go home to Josh. I'll call you later, okay?"

Shannon nodded and slung a "see ya, Garret" in his direction as she left. Krystal walked over to the sales counter and handed the clerk her charge card.

"It's already taken care of," she told her, smiling in Garret's direction.

Krystal's mouth dropped open. "You paid for my clothes?"

"Yes, he did." The clerk handed him the bundle of clothes wrapped in plastic, then gave a smaller bag to Krystal. A look passed between the very attractive salesclerk and Garret. For a brief moment, Garret's smile reminded Krystal of the way Dylan grinned at women. Dylan the flirt. Had Garret been flirting with the salesclerk?

As he walked away she realized that he wasn't even aware of the effect his smile had on women. The salesclerk said, "Have a nice day now," in a tone Krystal was certain she never used on women.

"Why did you pay for my things?" Krystal asked him as they left the store.

"Because I wanted to," he answered simply, then paused to hold the door open for her.

"I wish you wouldn't have. It makes me feel obligated."

"Why? I'm the reason you need these clothes," he pointed out. He walked over to the car and opened the rear door. He laid the bundle on the back seat then slammed the door shut again. "I'm on my dinner break. You don't mind if we go someplace where I can grab a quick bite to eat, do you?"

She shook her head. "There's a Chinese place on the next block that has a buffet."

"It'll do," he told her. "Should we walk or drive?"

"We'd better walk. Parking's limited."

As they started up the street, he asked her if she was hungry.

"A little," she answered, which was quite an understatement. She was starving. Her appetite had definitely picked up the past couple of days.

"How are you feeling today?"

She shrugged. "Okay."

They walked the rest of the way in near silence, with the exception of small talk about the weather. It wasn't until they were seated in the restaurant that he brought up the reason for them being together.

"I'm sorry this had to be so last-minute, but my schedule's been impossible lately. I'm glad you were able to meet with me because the sooner we get this taken care of, the better."

She assumed *this* meant what they were going to do about the baby. The arrival of a waiter postponed their discussion. They each ordered tea and were told they could visit the buffet whenever they were ready. It was obvious he was ready. He stood and held her chair for her. If there was one thing Leonie had done, it was to teach her sons manners. Garret's were impeccable.

They made their selections at the buffet, then returned to the table. He looked at her plate, which was barely half-full. "You should be eating more than that."

"I'm trying to eat more often and have smaller meals. It's supposed to help with the morning sickness."

"You're still bothered by it?"

"Not as often, but it hasn't disappeared completely."

"It should just about have run its course."

"So everyone tells me. I've also heard that some women have it their entire pregnancy."

"Some do."

He ate his dinner as he did most things in life—very deliberately. As his hands moved from his utensils to his napkin to his teacup, she noticed how beautiful they were. Most of the guys she dated had rough, callused hands with thick fingers. His hands were large but they were smooth and graceful. She remembered what they'd felt like on her skin and a warmth spread through her.

She looked down at her food, wishing she was anywhere but here in this restaurant waiting for the man across from her to tell her what his plans were for their unborn child. She knew he had to have given it considerable thought, otherwise he wouldn't be here with her. She also knew that when he was ready, he'd tell her what was on his mind.

She remembered when she moved into 14 Valentine Place, and attended her first house party given by her landlady. Maddie had told her about spending a summer with the Donovans when she'd been a teen and how it was Garret who'd made her feel welcome.

At the time Krystal couldn't understand why Maddie regarded him as her favorite among the brothers. He didn't say more than two sentences to her the entire evening. Actually, she didn't think he'd said more than two sentences to anybody except Maddie.

Later that night, when Krystal had remarked on how different he was from the rest of the family, Maddie had said, "Don't let his quietness fool you. He's brilliant and he's a great guy once you get to know him." At the time Krystal wasn't looking for brainy men who seldom spoke. But as she'd gotten to know him, she'd realized that what Maddie had said was true. Although he seldom told you what was on his mind, you knew it was always churning with thought.

Right now she wished she knew what thoughts were running through his head. With each minute of silence that passed, she became more anxious. Maybe he thought it was more important to eat first and talk later, but she was tired of waiting for him to find the right moment to speak. She needed to know what his plans were and she needed to know now.

"You said you don't have much time," she reminded him.

He looked up at her. "I never have much time."

"Then don't you think we should talk about the baby? That is why we're here, isn't it?"

"Yes." He set down his fork and gave her his undivided attention. That was another thing she'd discovered about him. He always made her feel as if everything she said was important.

"I've been doing a lot of thinking on the subject," he began.

"I figured you were. It's been five days."

"Decisions of this importance aren't arrived at overnight, are they?" It was a rhetorical question for which he expected no answer. "It's a situation I never expected to find myself in."

"Me neither."

"First I want to apologize to you. I'm sorry that my actions have led to this. I should have used better judgment."

"Garret, you don't need to apologize. It was just as much my fault as it was yours."

"I guess it really doesn't matter whose fault it was. It doesn't change the fact that we're now in a situation where the decisions we make will affect the life of another person." He stared into her eyes as he talked and she could see a strength that she found comforting. "I want to do the right thing, Krystal."

"So do I."

"Legally I have responsibilities toward this baby and you know I'm not the kind of man who would ever try to deny those responsibilities. But I don't want my obligations to only be financial."

She swallowed back the dryness in her mouth. "What do you want them to be?"

"You know my family background." She nodded and he continued. "There was no divorce, no blending of families. My brothers and I had two parents there for us every day."

"You were lucky. That isn't always the reality for kids nowadays."

"But I want it to be the reality for my kids."

This is it, she thought. Leonie was right. He was considering settling down and who would be more appropriate for him than Samantha? Her hands tightened around her napkin.

"I want my children to be raised in a two-parent family the way I was. I want them to go to bed each night knowing that their mom and dad are in the same house and will be there for them no matter what happens. Don't you agree it would be better for this baby to have two parents who live together instead of being shuffled back and forth between single-parent homes?"

"Yes, but…" She wanted to tell him what was on her mind, but emotion clogged her throat. Yes, she knew that he would make a good father and even though she didn't know Samantha all that well, she didn't think she needed to fear that she'd be a bad mother to her child. Together the two of them would be able to give her baby a very good life. They certainly had the financial means. But the thought of relinquishing full-time custody of her child…it was too painful to even consider.

"I want to be a full-time father," he continued. "To have my son or daughter with me every day, not only on weekends or whatever time some judge determines I'm allowed to visit. People have married for reasons not nearly so important."

She took a drink of water to get rid of the dryness in her mouth. "Then you're definitely considering getting married?"

"I've never believed that cohabitating is a good idea and in this case it would involve not only two adults but a child as well." He shook his head. "It would send the wrong message. I've given this a lot of thought and marriage seems like the only solution."

"For you, maybe. But what about me? What about what I want?" She struggled to maintain her composure, not wanting her emotions to lead her astray, but at the moment her insides were trembling.

"What do you want?" he asked.

She took a deep breath, then as calmly as possible said, "I'm not sure, but I know I don't want Samantha Penrose raising my child."

He frowned. "Samantha? What does she have to do with this?"

"You said marriage appeared to be the only solution…" She suddenly realized she'd been listening through a filter shaped by Leonie's perception.

"I'm not planning to marry Samantha," he told her, his brown eyes darkening as they stared at her intently. "What makes you think I am?"

"You've been seeing her."

"We work together and we've gone out a few times, but I'm not going to marry her."

"Then who—" She stared at him in disbelief. "You want *us* to get married?"

"We are the baby's parents."

"Yes, but…" His suggestion caught her totally off guard. Never would she have suspected he'd offer marriage to her as a solution to their baby dilemma. "But we're not in love."

"Not everyone marries for love, Krystal."

"Maybe not, but it's important to me."

"As important as giving your baby a father? You said you wouldn't want Samantha to raise your child. Well, I don't want another man to raise mine, either, and I especially don't want someone like Roy Stanton doing the job."

"You can be sure I am never going to marry Roy," she stated in no uncertain terms.

He raised one eyebrow. "Can I?"

"Yes! I'm not in love with him!"

"Then there is no reason why we shouldn't marry…unless there's someone else in your life?"

"No. I just don't see how we can get married considering the circumstances," she told him.

"Our circumstance should be what convinces you marriage would be the best thing," he argued.

At a loss for words, she could only stare at him.

"We've been friends for a long time," he told her, leaning forward and holding her gaze with his own. "And there's some chemistry between us, Krystal. Otherwise that night after the hospital ball wouldn't have happened."

She very rarely blushed in front of men, but this was one moment when she couldn't prevent the red that warmed her face. "Then you expect…" She stared down at her plate.

"Only if it feels right between us."

She kept her eyes downcast and nodded.

"I think it could work for us. You know my family...they all love you... Mom already thinks of you like a daughter."

"Those are not reasons to get married."

"No, but that baby you're carrying is." An alarm sounded and she realized that it was his watch. He clicked it off and said, "I'm sorry, but I have to get back to the hospital." He motioned toward her half-eaten plate. "Do you want a box for that?"

She shook her head. "It's all right."

He signaled for the waiter and paid the check, then escorted her to the car. They drove the short distance to the salon in silence. At her car, he transferred the bundle of maternity clothes from his car to hers, then opened her door for her and waited for her to get in.

"Think about what I said, will you?"

She nodded and he added, "I'll stop by this weekend for your answer. No matter what you decide, we need to talk to my mother. It's probably easier on both of us if we do it together, don't you agree?"

It was one of the few things he'd said today with which she did agree. "Thank you for dinner...and for the clothes."

"It's the least I can do," he told her, then tapped on her window. When she rolled it down he said, "Drive safely, won't you?" She nodded and he went back to his car and drove away. Krystal watched the taillights disappear down the street, then reached for her cell phone and frantically dialed Shannon's number. She needed her best friend.

Only her best friend wasn't there. All she heard was her recorded voice-mail message asking her to leave her name and number.

"Shannon, it's me. You're not going to believe what's happened. Call me."

WHEN SHE ARRIVED at 14 Valentine Place, Krystal discovered that she had a visitor. Her mother's car sat in the parking lot. Just what she didn't need tonight of all nights. She groaned, closed her eyes and rested her head on the steering wheel, wishing she didn't have to go inside.

The next thing she knew a woman's voice was calling to her. "Are you all right?"

Samantha had opened her car door and was leaning in, giving her a very thorough appraisal.

Krystal lifted her head. "Yes, I'm fine."

She looked as if she didn't believe her but didn't pursue the line of questioning. "You shouldn't be driving if you're tired."

"I'm not tired and I'm not driving," she told her. "I'm just sitting here thinking."

Samantha didn't waste any more words. She simply nodded and said, "If you're sure you're okay, I'll go inside."

"I'm fine. Thank you."

She walked away and Krystal wondered what she thought. Did she know that she was pregnant? Garret had said they were friends, leaving her to wonder just how much Samantha Penrose did know about her relationship with him.

Krystal climbed out of the car, dragging her maternity clothes with her. She went through the private entrance, not wanting to run into any of the Donovans. When she reached her room, the door was open. As she expected, her mother was inside sitting on the futon flipping through the pages of a fashion magazine. Emily was asleep on the bed.

"Oh, you're finally home. We wondered what happened to you. The salon said you left at five-thirty," Linda said in a soft voice.

"Yes, but Shannon and I went shopping." She left out the part about having dinner with Garret. "Why didn't you tell me you were coming?"

"I thought you'd tell me not to come."

Krystal sighed. "I'd never do that."

"No, but Carly would. I was hoping she would have come to her senses and gone back to Joe by now."

Krystal took a deep breath and counted to ten. She didn't want to have words with her mother over Carly's situation. "She needs time to think things through," she told her, hanging her garments in the closet.

"Well, I'm worried about her."

"I am, too, but she is an adult and we have to respect that she has to do what she thinks is best for her."

"In her confused state I'm not sure she knows what's best," her mother said, setting the magazine aside.

"Maybe not, but if she makes a mistake, she'll figure out a way to fix it, I'm sure."

"Kryssie, the longer she stays away from Joe, the less likely it is they're going to get back together."

Krystal raked a hand through her hair. "Mom, we've been over this a dozen times on the phone. If Joe doesn't want the marriage to continue, there's nothing Carly can do."

"She can fight for her man," her mother stated vehemently.

"Maybe she doesn't think he's worth fighting for."

Linda made a sound of disgust. "Do you know how many women would love to be Mrs. Joe Benson?"

"Obviously too many, which is why he thinks he can go to bed with whomever he pleases and whenever he pleases."

"He had one affair," her mother corrected her.

"He was supposed to have none. Doesn't it bother you that he cheated on your daughter?"

"Of course it does, but I also know that marriages survive infidelity. They have a child together." She glanced at the sleeping Emily.

"I know. For her sake I'd hate to see them divorce, too."

"But you think their marriage is over, don't you?"

"I don't know, Mom," she answered honestly. "All I know is two people who I thought had everything going for them are now separated and contemplating divorce."

"They seemed to be so much in love, didn't they?" Linda said wistfully.

Krystal nodded soberly. "I remember their wedding day, standing next to Carly at the altar, watching the way they looked at each other. I thought they were two of the luckiest people in the world. So in love, so happy to be starting a marriage together."

"I thought the same thing. When I saw the looks on their faces as they came down that wedding aisle, I said to myself, 'I may have failed miserably in the love department, but my baby girl got it right.'" She shook her head. "I guess sometimes love isn't enough."

That caused Krystal to jerk her head up. "Why isn't it?"

Her mother shrugged. "If I knew the answer to that, there'd be a lot fewer divorces." She chuckled. "Maybe that's the mistake we all make. We fall in love and we get married thinking love is all we need."

"It might not be all that we need, but it has to be there to make the marriage work," Krystal stated, more for her own reflection than her mother's.

To her surprise, Linda didn't agree. "I'm not so sure."

"How can you say that?"

"Because I have friends who didn't marry for love and they have happy marriages. If I hadn't been so idealistic, I could be in such a marriage right now."

Krystal frowned. "What are you talking about?"

"You were barely three. I was seeing this man named George. He was crazy about me, but I didn't have the kind of feelings for him that I'd had for your father. I liked him. He was a good man, but it wasn't that all-consuming, intense physical kind of emotion that happens when you fall in love. He told me it didn't matter, that in time a better kind of love would grow between us, one based on friendship, mutual respect, his love for my children." She sighed. "I didn't think it would work, so I said no."

"And you regret it?"

Linda simply looked at her and said, "Yeah, I really do."

"It might not have lasted," Krystal said.

"No, you're right. It might not have, but I'll never know. I do know that the man I did love with my whole body and soul didn't stay, either."

"You're talking about my father, aren't you?"

As usual, whenever the subject came up, she was quick to close the door on it. "There's not much point in talking about him. I didn't drive all the way down here to discuss water over the dam."

"Why did you come?"

"Because I'm worried about you and your sister.

You seldom call. How am I supposed to know if you're all right?''

"We're both fine.''

"I don't know how you can say that when your sister's marriage is falling apart and you're expecting a baby with no marriage prospects in sight," she said irritably.

Krystal could have corrected the latter statement but chose not to bring Garret's name into the conversation. "Some people might think we're both lucky. Marriage isn't for everybody. You did just fine without a husband. Carly and I will, too.''

Linda sighed in exasperation. "We'd better change the subject or we'll end up fighting again. Are you hungry? Have you had dinner?''

"Yes, I stopped and had a bite before I came home. I hope Carly fed you. By the way, where is she? Did she go to bed already?''

"No, she went to drop her car off at the garage. It wouldn't start this morning and she thought she was going to have to have it towed, but then Leonie asked one of her sons to take a look at it and apparently he got it going for her.''

Krystal could just imagine Dylan being asked to help out. "Oh, I wish she hadn't done that.''

"Why not? He was able to get it running and save her the expense of a towing fee. He followed her to the garage just to make sure she wouldn't have more trouble with it stalling on her.''

"Still it was an imposition on Dylan's time.''

"Dylan? I thought Carly said it was Shane who helped her.''

"Shane?" Krystal frowned. "I'm surprised he was around.''

"It's a good thing he was." Linda glanced at the

clock radio next to Krystal's bed. "I thought she'd be back by now."

"What time did she leave?"

"About an hour ago. I'm not sure how far away the service station is though."

"If it's the same one I use it's only about twenty minutes from here."

"Then she should be back shortly," her mother said, and changed the subject. "So tell me how you're feeling? Have you felt the baby kick yet?"

She shook her head.

"With both you and Carly, I felt life around the fifth month. I'm surprised you've made it this far without having to wear maternity clothes."

Krystal opened her sweater to expose the jeans. "I just got them."

"Ah." Linda eyed Krystal's still-slender figure. "Are you eating properly?"

"Yeah, of course."

"What about the father. Does he know yet?"

So they were back to that square. "As a matter of fact he does."

Her mother regarded her suspiciously. "And?"

"Nothing's changed, Mom, if that's what you're getting at. And if you don't mind, I'd rather not talk about me and the baby. Tell me what's new in your life. Are you still taking those ceramic classes?"

To Krystal's relief, her mother took the hint and went on to talk about life in Fergus Falls. When an hour had passed and there was still no sign of Carly, Krystal said, "I wonder what could be keeping her?"

"Maybe she waited for them to fix the car."

"I thought that was the point of Shane following her over there…so he could give her a lift home."

"Call her on her cell phone."

Krystal tried but could only connect to her voice mail. After leaving a message, she said to her mother, "Are you planning to stay the night?"

"It would be nice to spend some time with Emily."

Tonight, Krystal didn't feel like having another guest. She needed time alone to think about Garret's proposal. Not that her mother leaving would give her any privacy. She glanced at her niece asleep in her bed.

"You can sleep on the futon," she heard herself say.

"Are you sure you don't mind? I don't want to get in your way."

She shook her head. "You won't get in my way, Mom. I'm just going to take a shower and go to bed anyway. I'm really tired and I need sleep."

"Yes, you do. I remember what it was like at your stage of pregnancy. Maybe I should go downstairs to wait for Carly."

"Someone should probably sit with Emily until I get out of the shower," Krystal suggested. "If you're hungry, I could get something delivered from the deli."

"No, I'm fine."

"You can make yourself a cup of coffee." She motioned to the small cart on wheels in the corner where she kept a hot plate and a one-cup coffeemaker for those times she didn't want to go downstairs to cook.

"That sounds good." Linda gave Krystal a gentle shove. "You go take that shower and don't worry about me."

But Krystal did worry about her mother. And she worried about Carly who still hadn't returned. But most of all she worried about Garret and what she was going to do about his proposal of marriage.

CHAPTER NINE

"DID YOU HEAR ABOUT Gladys Lingenfelser?" the salon receptionist asked Krystal the following morning when she arrived at work.

"No, what about her?"

"She had a stroke. They moved her to the nursing home yesterday."

Tears misted Krystal's eyes. "That is so sad. Thanks for telling me."

"I figured you'd want to know."

Krystal nodded and headed for the employee lounge, dabbing at her eyes with a tissue. It always upset her to hear that misfortune had struck one of her elderly clients. Being pregnant only made her emotional response more dramatic.

Gladys Lingenfelser was in her thoughts often that day, so much so that by the time she'd finished working, she'd made up her mind to go visit her. After calling Carly to say she wouldn't be home for dinner, she stopped in at the flower section of the grocery store and bought an African violet and a package of gingersnaps, then headed over to the nursing home.

Her distress was eased somewhat when she saw Gladys sitting up in bed. Although she needed help eating her dinner, she was able to talk and seemed in good spirits considering the circumstances. Gladys smiled when she saw the violet and told Krystal she was the nicest hairdresser she'd ever had in all of her eighty-seven years. Krystal promised to stop by on Tuesday when she came to wash and style the hair of several of the other residents.

After a short visit with Gladys, Krystal headed over to see another of her favorite clients. Expecting she wouldn't be in her room, she went straight to the recreation center, where she spotted the white-haired woman playing bingo.

"Win anything?" Krystal asked as she slid on to a chair.

Dolly Anderson grinned from ear to ear when she saw her. "Kryssie! What are you doing here on a Saturday night? You should be out with one of your boyfriends instead of visiting old ladies."

"I don't have a boyfriend and you're not old."

"Oh yes I am," she said with a wag of her finger. "And what do you mean you don't have a boyfriend?"

She spread her hands in frustration. "What can I say? I went from having too many to having none."

"Sounds to me like your romance train has stalled."

"I think it's derailed. Permanently," Krystal told her.

Dolly laughed.

Krystal took one of the round plastic disks and placed it on her bingo card. "He called B-twelve."

Dolly waved her hand. "It doesn't matter. If you win it just means you get to pick the movie for tonight. I've seen all the ones they have."

Krystal reached into her tote and pulled out the box of gingersnaps. "I brought you something."

"Well, aren't you just the sweetest thing," Dolly gushed, gazing at the cookies as if they were a pot of gold.

"How's your hip?"

"Oh, it could be better, but it hasn't kept me from taking care of my garden. The harvest is almost over."

Krystal nodded. "Thank you for those wonderful tomatoes. They were delicious."

"You are most welcome. If I were still in my house, you'd have so much more, including a pumpkin."

Krystal placed another marker on the bingo card. "Look. You have four corners."

Dolly's hand shot up. "Bingo" she called out in a shaky voice.

Krystal applauded enthusiastically. "Good job."

"You brought me luck."

As soon as the numbers had been confirmed, Dolly was given a coupon good for one free movie rental and Krystal said, "There. Now you get to choose the movie for tonight."

"Want to stay and watch with me since your romance train is stalled?"

Krystal thought about it. She could go home and listen to Carly and her mother, or she could watch a movie with Dolly. She chose the movie.

"Good," Dolly said with a satisfied grin. "I know just the one I want to watch. It's one of your favorites, too. Might put you in the mood to get back on the romance train."

Krystal doubted it, but she didn't tell Dolly that. She just smiled and helped the older woman to her feet.

GARRET GLANCED AT HIS WATCH. His mother had said dinner was at seven-thirty and it was now ten-fifteen. He couldn't even say he was late. He'd missed it completely. Not that his mother would be upset. She understood what it meant to be a doctor and knew that his schedule was as unpredictable as the Minnesota weather.

But he had several reasons he didn't want to miss this dinner. It was Dylan and Maddie's last night in town before they went back to France. There were things he hadn't said to his brother, things he should have said. He checked his watch again, hoping he would get that opportunity.

He had hoped that by tonight Krystal would have made a decision regarding his marriage proposal, because he could get everything out in the open. He knew, however, that whether or not she accepted it, he needed to tell his family about her pregnancy.

He'd already decided tonight was to be the night. He'd wanted to discuss it with Krystal first but had been unable to reach her all day. His only choice had been to leave her a voice-mail message telling her he planned to make the announcement this evening.

As he stepped into the house, he heard voices coming from the great room. He hung his raincoat on a hook. From the hallway he could see Dylan and Shane were at one end, Maddie and his mother at the other. Krystal was nowhere in sight. Disappointment seeped through him. He'd hoped that she'd be there.

"Sorry I missed dinner," he said as he made his entrance into the great room.

His mother got up to give him a hug. "Better late than never. Are you hungry? I saved you a plate. All I have to do is put it in the microwave." She looked at him as if he were ten again and needing her attention.

"Thanks, Mom, but you sit. I'll do it later. Right now I'd rather spend some time with Dylan and Maddie," he said, looking at his brother.

"We can do that in the kitchen. We haven't had dessert," Maddie told him. She gave her husband's arm a tug. "Come. We're going to eat your mother's apple pie. Let's move the party there."

"Isn't the party missing a couple of people?" Garret asked Maddie as she ushered everyone out of the great room.

"Jennifer stayed home with Mickey because he has a cold," she answered.

"What about Krystal? I thought she was coming for dinner."

"Oh, she's around. I think she went upstairs to check on Carly and Emily."

"She's coming back down, isn't she?"

"She'd better. We haven't said our goodbyes." Maddie changed the subject, asking him about his work at the hospital while his mother fussed over getting him something to eat. He wished she would simply sit down and that Krystal would return so he could make his announcement.

But his mother continued to move about the kitchen and Krystal didn't appear. Garret grew more uneasy.

Finally he heard footsteps on the stairs and Maddie said, "There's Krystal now."

He looked toward the doorway and saw her come in wearing a two-piece gray slack set that Garret remembered seeing in the selection of maternity clothes the clerk had rung up for him. It was the only time he'd ever seen her in gray. Usually her clothes were bright and colorful and fun. This outfit made her look demure—so very unlike Krystal.

"Oh good, you're back." Maddie was the first one to speak to her. "I was worried we weren't going to get to say our goodbyes."

"That would never happen," Krystal said, coming into the kitchen.

"Is Emily okay?" Maddie asked.

She nodded. "Actually, tonight's the first night she's slept with Carly. She's been sleeping with me in my bed."

Krystal's eyes met his, revealing an uncertainty he had come to expect whenever he looked at her lately. Her red hair framed her pale cheeks and immediately he wondered how she was feeling. As if she could read his mind, she gave him a weak smile of reassurance. His heart missed a beat. She had a vulnerable look that made him want to protect her.

Dylan pulled out a chair for her, placing her directly across from Garret. "Would you like a piece of apple pie?" he asked her.

"Ah…no…no pie for me, thanks," she answered, and Dylan turned his attention to helping Maddie serve dessert. When Shane excused himself to make a phone call, it left only Garret and Krystal seated at the table.

"Did you get my phone message?" he asked.

She nodded.

"Then you're okay with me being here tonight?"

"Not really," she admitted, shifting uneasily. She lowered her voice to a whisper and asked, "Are you sure you want to do this now?"

He nodded. "It needs to be done. Trust me. I know my family. They'll understand."

If he could get everyone to sit back down at the table, that is. The way Krystal's eyes kept darting back and forth, he could see she was just as uneasy waiting for everyone to return to the table. He took a couple of bites of the leftover pot roast his mother had re-heated for him, then shoved his plate aside.

"I'm really glad everyone—or almost everyone—is here," he began. "I have some news I want to share with the family."

He saw his mother's eyes twinkle as she nudged Maddie. "Does it concern your trip overseas?"

He took a deep breath. "Actually, I've decided not to take part in the Doctors Without Borders program."

There was a silence as all eyes stared at him in bewilderment.

"But why not?" His mother asked the question he knew all of them were thinking.

"Well, my plans have changed." He didn't want to look at Krystal, but he couldn't help himself. She sat with her hands squeezed so tightly together he could see the whites of her knuckles.

"I don't suppose there's a woman involved in these changed plans," Dylan said with a sly grin.

"Actually, there is," Garret admitted. From the look of agonizing anxiety on Krystal's face, Garret knew he needed to get to the point. "The reason I'm not going to accept the responsibility of working in the Doctors Without Borders program is because I have a more important responsibility to take care of here. I'm going to be a father."

Stunned silence greeted his words and then his mother said, "Oh, my goodness! Samantha is pregnant?"

He rolled his eyes. "No, Mom, not Samantha," he snapped impatiently.

"Then who?" His mother's voice was almost a whisper.

Before he could tell her, Krystal spoke. "It's me, Leonie. I'm pregnant with Garret's baby."

This time the silence was deafening. He wished someone would say something. Anything. He was grateful when Dylan jumped to his feet and offered him a handshake and then a hug saying, "Congratulations, little brother.'' Shane did the same thing, but his mother said nothing.

She sat with a look of bewilderment on her face, staring at Krystal. ''You slept with my son?'' she finally said.

''I'm sorry,'' Krystal's apology crackled with unshed tears.

''Mom, don't blame Krystal. I'm equally responsible,'' Garret said, but it was as if his mother didn't hear him.

''I treated you like a daughter,'' Leonie said to her in a voice that wobbled uncharacteristically.

Maddie came to Krystal's defense. ''Leonie, Krystal is like a daughter to you and she's like a sister to me. This doesn't change that.''

Then his mother turned to Maddie and asked in an accusing tone, ''Did you know about this?''

Krystal jumped to her feet. ''If you're going to be upset with anyone, it should be me, Leonie,'' she said, her body trembling. ''And this is exactly why I was afraid to tell any of you—I knew this would happen.'' Then she burst into tears and ran out of the room.

Maddie called out after her and would have followed her, but Garret stopped her.

''I'll go.'' Before he left, however, he turned to his mother and said, ''You didn't react this way when Dylan told you he was going to be a father.''

''You can't expect me not to be shocked, Garret,'' she told him.

''No, but I did expect you to be fair,'' he said before turning to leave the room. He climbed the stairs to the second floor. When he reached the landing, Krystal's door was closed. He knocked lightly, saying, ''Krystal, it's me.''

She opened the door and he saw her tearstained cheeks. "She hates me," she said on a hiccup.

"No, she doesn't." He pulled her into his arms. It seemed like the natural thing to do. It was also the first time she'd been in his arms since the night of the hospital ball. She felt warm and soft and she clung to him, quietly sobbing into his chest.

"I'm sorry," she finally said, straightening. "I'm superemotional because of the hormone thing." She motioned for him to come inside, then closed the door behind him.

"My mother could have reacted a little less emotionally herself."

She hiccuped. "At least she didn't slap me, like my mother did."

"Your mother slapped you?"

She nodded. "It's hard for mothers to hear that kind of news." She reached for a tissue to blow her nose.

"That doesn't give them the right to behave the way they did. We're adults, Krystal, not some fifteen-year-old kids who need supervision."

She dropped down on to the futon. "Apparently we needed it that night."

"No, what we needed was better birth control protection."

She looked at him briefly, then buried her head in her hands. "Don't remind me."

He pulled her hands away from her face. "You can't hide from the facts, Krystal. Don't you think it's about time you stopped beating yourself up for something that you can't change?"

"You sound as if you're okay with all of this," she said, allowing him to pull her into the crook of his arm.

"I've accepted that I'm going to become a fa-

ther…if that's what you mean." Her hair smelled like
oranges and her body was warm as it rested against
his. "We can't go back and change what's already
happened, so we might as well go forward, right?"

"It isn't that easy."

"I didn't say it was going to be easy." She sighed
and he wished he knew what she was thinking. "I'm
sorry I didn't tell my mother ahead of time in private.
It would have given her time to get over the initial
shock. Maddie's right. She does think of you like a
daughter."

"Well, at least she did at one time."

"And she will again. She's just not thinking clearly
right now. I'm sure that I'm the last of her four sons
she expected to be in this position."

"She wouldn't be so upset if it were Samantha who
was pregnant. She thinks she's a good match for you
and she's right." She shook her head. "It's just plain
stupid to think that you and I could make a marriage
work."

He didn't like the sound of that. "That sounds like
a rejection of my marriage proposal."

She cast a sideways glance at him. "I'm sorry, but
I just don't see how it would work. I mean, I know
that marriages based on friendship can work. I have
plenty of clients who married for that very reason."

"So why wouldn't ours work?"

She shrugged. "I don't know. Maybe it would. Do
we have to decide this tonight?"

He shook his head. "No, we don't. The important
thing is we told my family."

"Yeah. And you saw the way your mom reacted.
So now what do we do?"

"Give her some time."

"That's easy for you to say. I'm the one who lives

in her house.'' She leaned her head back and closed her eyes. ''What a mess I made of things.''

''You didn't do it alone,'' he said, pulling her closer to him. ''I did my part.'' He liked the way she felt in his arms. It made him feel as if they were a team in this mess. He also liked the way she touched him when she talked, even though it was that aspect of her personality that was partly responsible for their situation.

Suddenly her eyes flew open and she reached for him, her hand grabbing his leg. ''Oh my gosh.''

''What is it?''

''I think the baby kicked.'' She grabbed his hand and placed it on her tummy. ''Right here.''

They sat in silence, waiting for some sign that it had been the baby that had moved.

''There. Did you feel it?'' she asked him, a look of wonder on her face.

When he shook his head, she lifted the gray fabric and placed his hand under it. His palm met silky-smooth underwear.

''Try right there,'' she said, excitement lighting up her already beautiful eyes.

He soon discovered she was right. He felt the tiniest of movements beneath his fingertips. His eyes met hers and he smiled. ''You're right. She kicked.''

''She? How do you know it isn't a he?''

Because all he could think about was having a daughter who looked exactly like her. But he didn't tell her that. ''I don't, but we'll know soon enough. You must be scheduled for an ultrasound.''

She nodded. ''Next week. I heard they can't always tell the sex though.''

''That's true,'' he confirmed. ''I'd like to be there with you.''

''During the ultrasound?''

"Yes, that won't bother you, will it?"

"No." There was a knock on the door, startling her. She pushed his hand away and got up to see who it was.

"Can I come in?" he heard Maddie's voice say. "I'd like to talk to you and Garret."

Krystal let her in and as soon as the door was opened they went into each other's arms. "I'm sorry. I tried to help, but I'm afraid I only made things worse," Maddie said.

As soon as she'd finished hugging Krystal, she turned to Garret and wrapped her arms around him, too. "This can't be easy for you, either."

"We could have handled it differently," Garret admitted.

"He's right," Krystal seconded. "I should have told everyone a long time ago."

"None of that matters," Maddie said with her familiar smile of understanding. She reached out to touch Krystal's arm. "Hey—everything will work out. I only wish I could be here to help you. I hate the thought of you going through this alone."

"She's not alone. She has me." Garret said. He could see the unasked question in his sister-in-law's eyes. "Why don't I let Krystal tell you what her plans are. I should probably go downstairs." He looked at Krystal and asked, "Are you going to be okay?"

"Yeah, thanks."

"Call me if you need anything," he told her.

Maddie reached for his arm to give him another hug. "You're a good man, Garret. If that husband of mine gives you any trouble, let me know."

"Dylan's the least of my worries," he said, then reluctantly went back downstairs to the kitchen. As he expected, his mother sat at the table with his brothers.

The way the three of them stared at him when he entered the room, he knew they'd been discussing only one thing.

"All right, get it off your chests. I can see you're dying to ask me how it happened," he said, plopping himself down on a chair.

"How did it happen? You're a doctor for crying out loud," his mother said, obviously still upset with the news.

"I didn't realize that doctors were exempt from unplanned pregnancies," he answered.

"I think she means you should have known better," Dylan said in an aside that his mother heard.

"You *should* have known better," she repeated. "And what about Samantha?"

"What about her?" he countered.

"Were you just using her as a smoke screen to hide your affair with Krystal?" his mother wanted to know.

"There is no affair with Krystal," he stated emphatically. "And you ought to know me well enough to know that I don't use people."

"Yes, I do know you, which is why I'm having trouble understanding how something like this could have happened," his mother went on.

"It just did, so can we drop the fact that it did and move on to what's going to happen next?"

"I think that would be smart," Dylan stated.

"How far along is she in her pregnancy?" Leonie asked.

"The baby's due in February," he replied.

Again his mother's mouth dropped open. "How long have you known she was pregnant?"

"About a week."

"So she kept it from you, too?"

He ignored that question. "Mom, I know this isn't

what you expected from me, but it's happened and I can't change it. Now you can either choose to be happy that you're having another grandchild or you can spend your time finding fault with me and Krystal. I mean, I am going to be a dad. Wouldn't you rather spend your time giving me advice on that subject?''

She smiled then and reached across to cover his hand. ''You're going to make a wonderful father...just like your brothers.''

''I'm going to try, Mom, and Krystal will be a good mother. You ought to know that.''

She sighed. ''Yes, I do know that,'' she admitted quietly. ''Have you discussed how you're going to raise this child?''

''Yeah, we have, but nothing's settled yet, except we both know that we want to do the right thing.''

''The right thing...what do you consider the right thing?'' she asked cautiously.

''I'm a Donovan, Mom.''

''Then you mean marriage.''

''I want my child to have the kind of home I had,'' he admitted.

''Then you need to marry for love, not convenience,'' she advised him.

''Mom, you said you'd never wear your romance coach hat with us boys,'' Shane reminded her.

''I'm not trying to give him advice. I just want him to think very carefully before he makes a decision as important as marriage. It's a commitment that should be based on love, not convenience.''

''That sounds like advice, Mom,'' Dylan rebuked her gently.

She gave Garret an apologetic smile. ''I just want what's best for you.''

''I know you do, Mom, but you have to trust me to

do the right thing," Garret told her. "I created the problem and I'll find a solution to it."

"He's always been the brains in the family," Dylan said with affection.

"I can handle this, Mom. You don't have to worry about me."

Her face remained skeptical.

Later that evening, after goodbyes had been said, Garret walked with Shane out to their cars. He was surprised when his brother said, "You know, as much as I hate to admit it, Mom has a point. You don't have to get married to do the right thing by Krystal."

"Whose side are you on anyway?"

"Yours. Always yours, but what if the marriage doesn't work out?"

"I'll make it work."

"Yeah, that's what I said, too."

Garret frowned. "What are you talking about? You and Jennifer announced last week that you're thinking about having another baby."

"It turns out that I was a bit premature with that idea. She doesn't really want another child. I found that out this evening before I came over here. She's been taking the pill and I didn't even know it."

"What's going on?"

He shrugged. "Who knows? Maybe we're just going through a rough spell." He leaned up against his truck. "All marriages do."

"Are you saying your marriage is in trouble?" Garret could hardly believe it could be true.

"We don't spend enough time together, that's all. Ever since she went back to school, it's been that way."

"So make time for each other."

He shrugged. "That's easier said than done."

"I've got next weekend off. You want me to take Mickey so you two can go away for a couple of days?"

He shook his head. "It's not going to happen. She's got classes every weekend."

"What about a nice dinner then?"

"I'll let you know." He clapped him on the arm. "Thanks for the offer."

"Thank you for sticking up for me in there." He jerked his head toward the house.

"You kind of threw us a curve ball. None of us realized you and Krystal were seeing each other."

"We're not." A car passed through the alley and he realized that the things he wanted to discuss with his brother were better said someplace other than in his mother's backyard. "Look. How about if we stop at Al's and I'll tell you all about it?"

KRYSTAL AWOKE to find Emily at her bedside saying, "I get to go to Sunday school today."

Krystal propped herself up on one arm as her sister appeared in the doorway. "You're going to church?"

"Yes. I'm not sure when we'll go back to Fergus Falls and Emily's used to going to Sunday school," Carly answered. "Leonie suggested we go to the one where Shane and Jennifer take Mickey."

"Is Mickey going to be at Sunday school?" Emily asked.

"She knows Mickey?"

"They've played together a couple of times when Shane's been over visiting his mother," Carly said, then held out her hand for her daughter. "Come on, Emily. We don't want to be late."

"Can Aunt Krystal come?"

"I don't think she feels well." Carly looked at Krystal and asked, "Do you?"

Krystal had the distinct impression she didn't want her going to church with them, which was silly. What difference would it make—unless she thought Krystal would make them late.

"No, I'd better stay here," she told Emily. "I'm not feeling very good."

Carly nodded, saying, "We'll close the door on our way out."

Emily blew her a kiss. "Hope you feel better."

Krystal pretended she caught the kiss, then blew one back. "See you later." She lay back against the pillows, thinking that it had been a long week—a week during which she'd managed to avoid seeing her landlady. Garret had suggested she give Leonie some time to come to terms with what had happened.

Upon reflection, she thought it was a bad idea. For Garret it might work to do a lot of thinking, but all it had done was to create more anxiety in her. The time had come for the two of them to clear the air. If Leonie wasn't going to come to her, Krystal would go to her.

She climbed out of bed and was about to head for the shower when there was a knock on the door. She called out, "Come in," and Leonie stepped into her room.

"Is it too early for me to be here?" she asked.

"No, not at all." She reached for her robe and slipped it on as she climbed out of bed. "Actually, I was just thinking about coming down to see you."

She didn't miss the way Leonie's eyes traveled to her stomach. She knew she'd caught a glimpse of just how pregnant she was before she'd covered up with the robe.

"I bet you miss Maddie and Dylan." Krystal knew

it was a dumb statement, but it was an awkward situation and she felt she had to say something. Anything.

"Yes, I do." Leonie didn't move from her spot in front of the door.

"I hope they had a smooth flight back." She focused her attention on tying her robe, avoiding Leonie's eyes.

There was an awkward silence and Krystal knew she couldn't avoid the reason her landlady was in her room. "I'm sorry I didn't tell you I was pregnant."

"You've always been able to tell me anything."

"Yes, but this was different."

"I suppose you're right," she said thoughtfully. "Have you made any decisions?"

"You know that Garret thinks we should get married."

"Oh yes, he told me that. How do you feel about it?"

Krystal could see she was doing her best to remain detached, to act as if she were coaching one of her clients.

"I'm really confused right now...about a lot of things," she admitted.

"Krystal, you know that I have an agreement with all my tenants. I don't give unsolicited advice on anyone's love life."

But Krystal had a feeling she was going to make an exception and she was right.

"You're like a daughter to me and I don't want to see you make a mistake."

Krystal didn't doubt for one minute that the advice was given with the best of intentions. She knew Leonie too well to suspect she had any other motive.

"Maybe it wouldn't be a mistake," she said quietly.

"Are you in love with Garret?"

"No."

"Then it would be a mistake."

She wasn't saying anything Krystal hadn't already said to herself. How could she marry Garret when she didn't love him with her whole heart and soul?

"Babies need two parents," she stated with conviction.

"And this one will have two wonderful, good people as its parents. Whether or not you're married to Garret, your child will be a Donovan and he'll be a part of this family. You both will be part of our family. You know Garret. Can you imagine him having it any other way?"

She couldn't, but she also knew that eventually Garret would probably marry. If not Samantha, then someone like her. Probably another doctor who Leonie would consider to be another good match like Samantha.

Krystal tried not to feel hurt, but a pain rifled through her. How quickly their relationship had changed. Leonie had treated her like a daughter, yet when it came right down to it, she didn't want her in the family. Krystal wanted to tell her how much it hurt her to hear those words, but she couldn't.

She bit down on her lip and fought for control of her emotions. "I only want to do what's best for the baby."

"I know you do, that's why I'm here. I wouldn't be your friend if I didn't try to help you through this situation."

Krystal realized their definition of help was not one and the same.

"I'm not trying to tell you what to do, Krystal. I just want you to think carefully about all of your options. Don't rush to make any hasty decisions. You have some time to think things through.''

Krystal nodded, not trusting herself to speak.

''I want you to know that I will support whatever decision you make.''

Krystal wondered how true those words were. Would she welcome her into the family even if she and Garret went against her advice?

''Thanks, Leonie. That means a lot to me,'' she managed to say.

''If there's anything I can do to help you, I want you to let me know.'' She opened her arms and Krystal went into them. ''Let's make today a new beginning, all right?''

''Okay,'' Krystal agreed, and gave her a smile as she left.

But as soon as the door had closed behind Leonie, tears fell down Krystal's cheeks. She didn't like that their relationship had changed. It was as if Leonie didn't have a clue as to how terrified she was being a single woman about to have a child. She wanted things to be the way they used to be, where Leonie had been her friend, her confidante, her mother.

Krystal crumpled on to her bed in a heap of self-pity, feeling very much alone. No one understood what she was going through. Not her mother, who thought that above all, getting married should be a priority. Not Leonie, who thought it would be in everyone's best interest if she didn't marry Garret. Not Carly, who was so wrapped up in her own marital problems that she couldn't expend any emotional energy on her sister. And certainly not Garret.

Or did he? Maybe it was time she found out.

CHAPTER TEN

GARRET WAS A LIGHT SLEEPER and woke immediately when the phone rang. "Yes."

"It's me—Krystal."

She wouldn't have needed to identify herself. He could never forget her voice and on the phone it had an even sexier sound than it did in person. It was one of the things that had attracted him to her the first time they met. He pushed himself up on one elbow.

"Good morning."

"It's nearly afternoon," she told him.

He glanced at the clock. "You're right. It is."

"You were sleeping. I'm sorry."

"No, it's all right."

"I shouldn't have disturbed you. You were probably up half the night with a patient."

"No, I wasn't." It was true. The reason he had trouble sleeping was that he had been unable to stop thinking about her. "I'm glad you called."

"Really?" She sounded doubtful.

"Yes, really." He sighed. "If we're going to have a child together, we need to work at being comfortable together, don't you agree?"

"We never used to have to work at that," she reminded him.

"No, we didn't."

"I miss the way things were between us. We used

to talk…and laugh…'' He could hear the sigh in her voice.

''I miss that, too,''

''That's one of the reasons why I called. I thought that if we spent some time together and we made it a rule that we weren't going to talk about the baby, then maybe we could become friends again.''

''I'd like that.''

''You would? Good. Maybe we could do something today…if you're not busy?''

She wanted to spend time with him. It was a tantalizing thought. ''No…no, I'm not busy,'' he answered, relieved that he hadn't scheduled anything for his day off. ''Have you had breakfast…or maybe I should say lunch?''

''I can do either one. Name the restaurant and I'll meet you there.''

He knew she made the suggestion to avoid another confrontation with his mother. ''There's a café right around the corner from me that's good. Why don't you come to my place and we'll go from here?''

''I can do that, although I must warn you my estrogen levels are high. Are you sure you want to take the risk?''

He chuckled. ''I think I can handle it.''

''All right. I think I'll be okay as long as we stick to the rules.''

''Rules?''

''No baby talk.''

Which he knew meant she didn't want to talk about his marriage proposal, either. ''Okay. Give me about thirty minutes to shower and take care of a couple of things, will you?''

The couple of things involved the state of his apartment. It was its usual disorganized mess and he groaned at the thought he had only thirty minutes to get it in order. He moved as quickly as he could, picking up clothes, straightening tabletops, stuffing glasses and cups into the dishwasher.

She hadn't been there since the night of the hospital ball when they'd had little time for anything except satisfying their hunger for each other. As usual, his body reacted to the memories and he went straight to the shower for relief.

She arrived forty-five minutes later and apologized for being late. "I had trouble getting my hair to behave. Being pregnant has made it extremely unruly," she said, pointing to her red tresses, which did look a bit unruly to him. They went in every which direction, but he had a hunch it was an effect she'd created.

She wore a light jacket, which she kept on while giving his place a quick survey. "It looks different from when I was last here."

"Yes, well, we didn't spend much time in this room, did we?" If he thought he could get her to blush, he was wrong. To his surprise, she lifted one eyebrow provocatively and smiled.

"I don't think I've ever had my clothes off that fast." There was a sparkle in her eye telling him that she, too, remembered how oblivious they'd been to everything but each other. Then she spread her arm in a gesture that encompassed the entire room. "This definitely looks like you."

"Why do you say that?"

"There are books everywhere." She picked up one that was on the top of the stack next to his favorite chair and read the title aloud. *"The First Nine Months?"* Then she sifted through the rest of the pile. "I think you have all the bases covered when it comes to babies."

"It's new territory for me."

"Me, too." She rolled her eyes. "Oops, already broke the rule." She pulled a face, then looked around and spotted his chess set carved out of wood. She fingered several of the pieces saying, "A game for thinkers. Maddie says you're really good at it."

"What? Thinking or playing chess?"

She grinned. "Both."

"Maddie plays a pretty mean game of chess herself. What about you?"

She shook her head. "I never learned how."

"I could teach you," he offered.

She wrinkled her nose. "I don't think so."

"It might be good for the baby," he said in a tempting tone.

"Why do you say that?"

"You know how they say reading to the baby in utero stimulates the brain? Well maybe hearing her mom and dad discussing chess moves will give her an edge intellectually. As you said, this is a game for thinkers."

"But what if I'm horrible at it?"

"You won't be."

"You sound pretty sure about that."

He shrugged. "Just a hunch I have."

"We're doing it again," she told him.

"Doing what?"

"Breaking the rule."

He gave her a weak smile. "Sorry. But as long as it's broken, let me add very quickly that I've arranged to be at your doctor appointment next week. You did say you didn't mind if I was there, right?"

"No, I want you to come. We'll find out whether you're right."

Puzzled, he asked, "About what?"

"Always referring to the baby as a girl."

"That's because it is a girl."

"We'll see," she said with a playful grin.

Then her stomach growled and he said, "We need to get you something to eat. Should we walk or drive?"

"Walk. I need the exercise."

It was a beautiful autumn day with temperatures unseasonably warm—so warm the restaurant's patio was open for dining. He was pleased when she said she'd like to sit outside. Although they sat in the shade of an umbrella, when she tipped her head a certain way her red hair caught the sunlight.

She'd always been stunningly beautiful, drawing the attention of many male eyes. Today was no different. He didn't miss the looks of envy that came his way when they'd walked in together. She was by far the most beautiful woman he'd ever escorted anywhere and, like the night of the hospital ball, he found himself wishing that she wasn't with him out of a sense of duty.

Then he had to stop himself. He didn't need a beautiful wife. He needed a woman who loved him.

When he glanced across the patio he noticed Samantha at one of the tables. She wasn't alone. She sat next to a man he recognized as a lab technician from the hospital.

Krystal noticed something had distracted him and asked, "What's wrong? Is your mother here or something?"

He shook his head. "It's nothing."

She dropped her napkin on purpose so she could turn around and see what it was that had captured his attention. When she sat back up she said, "That's hardly nothing. It's your girlfriend with another guy. We can leave if you want.''

"There's no need to leave. She's not my girlfriend.''

"Because of me. I'm sorry.''

"You don't need to apologize, Krystal.''

"Yes, I do. If I hadn't…if this hadn't happened, you'd be with her right now. It just seems like a cruel twist of fate. I mean, the reason we went to the ball together was for you to get her attention and then you did and now this…'' She shook her head in regret. "How can I not feel bad about that?'' A tear escaped, trickling down her cheek.

He reached across the table to stop it with his finger. "You don't need to cry for me, Krystal.''

"I can't help it,'' she said on a broken voice. "It's so sad.''

"What's sad is you crying over nothing. The reason Samantha and I aren't together has nothing to do with you or the baby.'' Although that wasn't quite the truth. He'd often found himself thinking about Krystal when he was with Samantha. He signaled for the waiter. "We'd like our food to go,'' he told him when he appeared, then said to Krystal, "We'll eat at my place. It'll be much more comfortable for both of us.''

"I don't know why I bother with eye makeup,'' she said as she dabbed at her eyes with a tissue.

"I don't know why you do, either. You certainly don't need it.''

"Yes, I do. My eyelashes are so light you can hardly see them.''

"That's what makes your face so interesting. You have red hair yet your lashes are blond.''

"Interesting?'' She looked at him as if he'd just told

her he liked her shoes because one was for the left foot and one was for the right.

The waiter came with their order, boxed and ready to go. Garret settled the bill, then ushered Krystal from the restaurant, grateful they didn't need to pass by Samantha and her companion.

For the first time since the night they'd spent together, he felt as if their relationship was back to where it had been before they'd made love. Instead of being uncomfortable around him, she seemed to enjoy his company. It was a good sign and gave him hope that by the time the baby arrived, they might actually be very good friends instead of acquaintances.

After they finished eating they took a walk down by the river, where they sat on a park bench and watched the barges slowly navigating the water. When a paddle wheeler went by with a load of passengers who waved at them, they waved back.

"That's the *Jonathan Padelford.* I haven't been on that since I was a kid and we went with our Cub Scout troop," he remarked.

"I've never been on it," she told him.

"You're kidding."

"No. You're forgetting I didn't grow up here. Where does it dock?"

He pointed to his left. "Over there at Harriet Island."

She shaded her eyes with her hand. "There's another paddleboat there now." She continued to gaze at the landing. "It looks like people are getting on. Do you need to buy tickets ahead of time?"

He shrugged. "I don't think so."

She jumped to her feet and stretched out her hands to him. "Then let's go take a ride."

"Now?"

"Sure, why not?" When he hesitated, she pleaded with him, "Come on. I've never been on a paddle wheeler. Please?"

The smile she gave him reminded him of the one she'd lured him to bed with. He knew he shouldn't respond to it, but he couldn't help himself. He had thought that because he'd slept with her, he'd destroyed the fantasy. Now he knew it wasn't true. She would always be a temptation for him.

"It's a bit of a hike," he warned. "And we might get there just as it's leaving."

"Then we'll have had a walk on a beautiful day." She tugged on his hands. "Please say yes."

He couldn't disappoint her. "Sure. Why not? There probably won't be many more September days like this."

They walked the short distance and discovered that the *Harriet Bishop* would be making one more trip on the Mississippi that afternoon and there were still tickets available. Garret thought Krystal was like a little kid, nearly jumping up and down with excitement at the thought of getting on the boat.

"Let's sit on the top," she said, then led him by the hand up the narrow staircase to the upper deck.

"It'll be sunny," he warned.

"I know but I don't want to be indoors." She found two chairs at the back of the boat where they could see the big wooden paddle wheel turn. "Isn't this great?" she said as the engine started and the wheel began to spin.

"Great," he agreed, and he didn't mean the boat ride.

It was the most pleasant hour and a half Garret had spent in a long time and he was sorry when the boat returned to the dock. He wanted to prolong their time together and suggested they get an ice-cream cone on the way back to his apartment. As they walked he told her he couldn't remember the last time he'd had such a relaxing afternoon.

"You work too much," she told him, licking chocolate from her fingers. "I know you're a dedicated doctor, but you need to make time for the fun things in life. You're far too serious."

"Doctors aren't supposed to be clowns, Krystal."

"Patch Adams was and his patients loved him."

He smiled. "That was a movie."

"Based on a real person."

"You love movies, don't you?"

"Mmm-hmm. Now that I'm pregnant my ideal job is being a taster for Ben & Jerry's ice cream. But when I was a kid I used to dream about directing movies. I wanted to travel all over the world and say, 'Lights! Camera! Action!'" There was a wistful gleam in her eyes.

"How come you never went to film school?"

"When you grow up in Fergus Falls, you don't think about going to film school."

"So you became a stylist instead of a cinematographer?"

"Mom said it was more practical than trying to make movies."

There was no regret in her voice and he knew it was because she liked styling hair. She'd told him that when she'd cut his hair for him that day of the hospital ball. No matter how hard he tried, he couldn't keep his thoughts from returning to that night. But then, why shouldn't they? With the wind blowing the fabric of her shirt against her body, he could see the gentle swell of her stomach where his baby was growing.

"Did I tell you I like that outfit on you?" he asked.

She looked down, as if she'd forgotten what she'd put on. "I guess the one nice thing about my pregnancy no longer being a secret is that I can now wear my maternity clothes and be comfortable." Her hand flew to her mouth. "I did it again, didn't I?"

"Considering we've been together all afternoon and there have only been a handful of references to—" he deliberately omitted the words "—I'd say you've done quite well."

She grinned. "I have, haven't I?"

"Want to talk about it now?"

She shook her head. "Why spoil a good day?"

He stopped and had her face him. "I don't want it to be a negative in my life, Krystal."

"I'm sorry. I shouldn't have said that. I don't want it to be a negative, either. It's just that lately I feel talked out on the subject."

He wanted to remind her that it was probably because she'd had over four months to talk about it. He'd only known about the baby for a few weeks.

He decided to let the subject rest. There would be plenty of time for them to discuss the issues that needed to be resolved. For now it was enough that the awkwardness between them was now gone. Because of the baby, their lives were forever going to be entwined. They needed to be friends. He wanted them to be friends. Not just for the baby, but for himself as well.

IT WAS MONDAY MORNING and Krystal's first appointment of the day was Ida Longley. Wash, blue rinse, set, dry and comb out. Krystal had the routine down. Ida had been one of her first clients when she'd started at the salon. Like her friend Gladys, she was more than a customer to Krystal. She was like the grandmother she no longer had, and Krystal took great care to make sure she was satisfied each time she came in for a wash and set.

"So tell me the news. Is it a boy or a girl?" Ida asked the minute she saw Krystal.

"I don't know. They couldn't tell."

"What?" she squawked. "I thought that's why they did an ultrasound."

"Actually, they do it to check to make sure the baby's developing as it should. Getting to know the sex is just a bonus. And in our case, we did get the good news that the baby is right on schedule, but no bonus information. The legs were crossed."

"Have you noticed anything unusual about your breasts?" Ida asked her.

From anybody else it might have been an embarrassing question, but Krystal had become accustomed to hearing off-the-wall remarks from her. "They're larger, which is to be expected."

"Yes, but is one bigger than the other?" Ida asked as she handed Krystal her walking stick.

Krystal frowned. She hadn't really noticed. "Is that normal during pregnancy?"

"Oh yes," she said with a wave of her fingers. "And if it's the right one that's larger, it means you're having a boy. If the left one is bigger, you're having a girl."

From the way Ida was staring at her, Krystal was relieved she had put an apron on over her regular clothes and her breasts were well hidden. "I'll have to remember that," she said, helping her into the styling chair.

"Personally, I think it's more fun when you don't know the sex of the baby. You get a big surprise."

"That's true, but it would have been nice to know.

Want me to take that for you?'' She reached for Ida's purse so she could set it on the counter.

"Yes, but before I forget, I have something for you.'' She reached into her bag and pulled out a small plastic bottle. "They're papaya tablets. I read they're good for indigestion and they're all natural.''

"Why thank you. That is so sweet of you,'' she said, examining the label on the jar. She opened her cupboard and set them inside.

Now that most of her regular clients knew about her pregnancy, she'd been getting advice on everything ranging from how to prevent stretch marks to what drugs to take during delivery.

"I don't know if they work or not, but I thought it was worth a try. I know how you like taking natural remedies,'' Ida told her.

"I'll give them a try,'' Krystal told her, draping the plastic cape over Ida's shoulders.

"Did you buy the support hose I told you about last week?''

Krystal lifted her long skirt to reveal a length of her leg. "Got them on today.''

"Good. You don't want to have trouble with varicose veins.''

"I try to sit with my legs up during my breaks,'' she said, snapping the cape in place.

"You must be taking good care of yourself. You look great. You've got that healthy pregnant glow.''

Krystal glanced in the mirror and knew what her client said was true. She did look good and, to her amazement, she felt even better. It was as if she'd crossed the midway point in her pregnancy and a switch had been flipped. She went from feeling terrible to feeling fantastic practically overnight.

"I'm doing all right.''

"What about that feller of yours?"

Although it was no secret that she was a pregnant single woman, only a handful of people knew Garret was the father. Ida was one of those people. That's because on Monday mornings there was seldom anyone else around and she was a good listener.

"You know I don't have a feller, Ida," she gently chastised her.

"When a man wants to marry you, he's your feller," Ida told her with a wag of a finger.

"Yes, but if he's in love with someone else, he's *her* feller," she argued.

"But he didn't ask *her* to marry him. He asked you."

"Only because of the baby. I don't want a man marrying me out of a sense of duty," she said as she backcombed Ida's curls.

"Why think of it as a duty? Why not think of it as a gesture of love—love for a baby? You said he's a good man."

"He is."

"And that you trust him."

"I do."

"And he's very concerned about the baby."

"He is."

"So what's the big obstacle?"

She sighed. "His mother for one."

She flapped her hand. "Don't pay any attention her. She'll get over it."

"You think I should accept his proposal, don't you?"

"Hell, yes. Good men are hard to find. At my age, they're practically extinct. I'd settle for one that was alive," she said with a chuckle.

Krystal smiled and handed Ida a mirror, then swiveled her around so she could see the back of her hair. "What do you think of that?"

"Perfect, as always." Ida handed the mirror back to her. "Now I feel as good as you look."

"You look good," Krystal told her, handing her the walking stick and the purse.

"Thank you, dear, and I'll see you next Monday," Ida said, pressing money into her hand. "Take good care of yourself until then and try not to worry. Things have a way of working out for the best."

Krystal hoped she was right.

ALTHOUGH KRYSTAL KNEW that one of the things she needed to work out before the baby was born was housing, she hadn't given it too much thought until she came home after work one night and found Carly's suitcases in her room.

"Are you leaving?" she asked her sister.

"We're going to Grandma's," Emily answered.

Krystal looked at Carly. "Are you?"

She nodded. "First thing in the morning. I think we've overstayed our welcome."

"Did Leonie say something to you?" She couldn't believe that her landlady would do such a thing, but she needed to ask.

"Well, she's not exactly kicking us out. Apparently she has a tenant for that room who'll be moving in the first of November. When she told me I took it as a hint that I should find another place to live, like ASAP, which is just as well. I really don't feel comfortable here anymore anyway."

Krystal heard the implication in her tone. "I suppose you think that's my fault."

"Well, she was a lot friendlier before she found out about you and Garret, but I'm not blaming you. It's time Emily and I found our own place anyway.'' She shoved a manila envelope toward her. ''This came to-day.''

Krystal opened it and found a petition for a divorce. ''Carly, I'm sorry.''

She shrugged. ''I knew it was coming. Now you see why I need to find a place of my own.''

''Have you looked through the classifieds?''

She nodded. ''I couldn't find anything in my price range, so I phoned a rental agent who's going to take me to look at some places this evening. I was hoping you'd come with me.''

Emily tugged on her hand. ''I'm going to have a lot of room to play.''

''That'll be fun, won't it?'' Krystal said with a smile.

''You can live there, too, if you want. Mommy said so.''

Again Krystal looked at her sister. ''I thought it might make more sense for us to share a house. I mean, you're not going to be able to stay here much longer, are you?''

It was something that had been on Krystal's mind, especially since Carly's arrival. She knew the three of them were an imposition on Leonie's generosity when she'd been on good terms with her landlady. Now that Leonie's attitude toward her had changed, there was an even greater incentive to move.

At one time she hadn't been able to imagine wanting to live anywhere but 14 Valentine Place. Now she knew she really had no choice. She was going to have a baby and even if Leonie wanted her to stay, it wouldn't be practical.

''No, I need to find another place, but...'' But she hadn't given any thought as to living with her sister.

Financially, it was a good idea, but would it be good for their relationship?

"I think it would work out really well for us, Krys." Carly did her best to persuade her. "Soon we're both going to be in the same situation—two single moms trying to raise kids. And it's not like we don't know how to get along. We shared a bedroom when we lived with Mom. We certainly could share a whole house, don't you think?"

Krystal had her doubts but didn't express them. "Are you sure there's no chance of you getting back together with Joe?"

"Believe me, Krys. It's over. Why don't you come with us to see the rental agent tonight? Emily would like that, wouldn't you, Emily?"

"Uh-huh." The four-year-old gave her a big grin.

Krystal knew it would be a solution to her housing problem, but then so would marriage to Garret. For weeks she'd been thinking about his proposal. At times she thought it was a realistic solution, and other times she thought she had to be crazy to even consider the idea.

"First I need to make a phone call," she told her sister.

"Are you worried about what Garret will say?"

"He is the baby's father."

Carly stared at her, hands on her hips. "Don't tell me you're actually thinking about marrying him? Krys, you're the one who told me that you would never settle for anything less than the right man. And believe me, marriage is tough enough the way it is without starting with one strike against you already."

"And what strike would that be?"

"Another woman in the picture? Everyone knows Garret's been seeing your neighbor upstairs."

"He told me he wasn't."

"And you believe him?"

"Yes, I did. Even if I don't marry him, I still need to tell Garret what I plan to do as far as housing goes."

She walked across the room to the small alcove where her dressing table was and dialed Garret's number. Getting his voice mail, she left him a message, then said to her sister, "I'll go with you to look at houses tonight, but I'm not going to make a decision just yet."

"But I need to find something soon, otherwise I'm going to end up staying here with you. Krys, you can't have the baby here."

Krystal knew she had a point. "How long are you planning to stay with Mom?"

"As short a time as possible. She said she'd go with me to get furniture from the house. Emily needs her own bed. I need the rest of my clothes among other things."

"Have you talked to Joe about taking stuff out of the house?"

"Yes, he said I could take what I need."

"And what about moving it all down here?"

"Mom knows a guy who has a pickup and a trailer."

And if he was like most of her mother's friends, he wasn't necessarily the most reliable person in Fergus Falls. Krystal sighed. "This has all happened pretty fast. Are you sure you're ready to make such a move?"

"Yes. I need a new start." She waved the divorce papers under her nose.

Krystal could see by the set of her sister's jaw that she wasn't going to be able to talk her into taking some time to think about it. "What about a job? Do you want me to ask at the salon and see if they need a receptionist?''

"You don't have to. I found one on my own," she boasted.

"Doing what?"

"Helping out in an office. It's a small company, on the bus line and the best part is, I'll have a great boss." She had a cagey grin on her face. "Want to know who it is?"

"Is it someone I know?"

Carly nodded. "It's Shane. He needs someone to help out…you know, answer phones, do some paperwork, that kind of stuff."

"I thought Jennifer did that for him."

"Apparently she doesn't have time for that anymore, now that she's gone back to school. Sounds as if she doesn't have time for much of anything when it comes to Shane and Mickey."

"Who told you that?"

She shrugged. "No one had to tell me. I have eyes and ears."

A hint of uneasiness narrowed Krystal's eyes. In the short time Carly had been staying at 14 Valentine Place she'd undergone quite a dramatic change. The first few days she hadn't bothered to even get dressed. She hadn't fussed with her hair or makeup, too caught up in her unhappiness to care about her personal appearance.

Today she wore an emerald sweater that highlighted the green in her eyes and a pair of slacks that showed that although she'd gained weight since she'd had Emily, she still had a nice figure. Her blond hair fell in gentle curls around her face, a face that was beautifully made up. Even her nails had been recently manicured. She looked good—almost too good for someone recovering from a broken marriage.

Suspicion had Krystal asking, "How did Shane know you were looking for a job?"

"I told him. Mickey's in Emily's Sunday school class."

Which could explain the reason her sister had decided the past few Sundays she needed to get her daughter to church. The uneasiness grew in Krystal's stomach.

She'd thought she'd noticed something different about her sister recently and now she knew what it was. There was a sparkle in her eye. When she'd first come to stay she'd been depressed, sleeping away most of her day, uninterested in life. Now she had color in her cheeks, enthusiasm in her voice. Krystal only hoped Shane Donovan wasn't the reason.

There was enough tension at 14 Valentine Place because of what had happened between her and Garret. Krystal could only imagine the fireworks that would fly if Shane were to show any interest in her sister.

The thought of moving was getting more attractive by the minute.

BEFORE THEY MET with the rental agent, Krystal warned her sister she was not going to make an immediate decision that evening. Although she knew Carly wanted to get on with her life, she also knew that her emotional state wasn't the most reliable at the moment. She told Carly it was always best to sleep on important decisions and to sit down and do the math to make sure the house was what they could afford.

After seeing the first two homes, Krystal didn't think she needed to worry about her sister rushing into any deal. It was a shock for her to see how expensive housing in St. Paul was compared to rental rates in Fergus Falls. After living in an upscale two-story with an interior designed by a professional decorator, Carly found it hard not to find fault with the rental properties the agent showed them. The rooms were too small, the carpets the wrong color, the appliances too old.

Krystal was tired and ready to call it quits for the evening, but the rental agent insisted they look at one more place that had a great location and was perfect for kids. The only problem was that it was out of the price range Carly and she could afford. However, once her sister saw it, she quickly forgot that money had anything at all to do with her decision.

Krystal could understand why her sister wanted the bungalow. It was perfect for a small family. The rooms were painted bright, cheery colors, the floors polished to a shine. The backyard was fenced with a swing hanging from a large oak tree. The kitchen had been recently remodeled with brand-new stainless-steel appliances and an eating counter as well as a breakfast nook.

"Look, Krys. There's a nursery!" Carly told her as the real estate agent flicked on a light in one of the bedrooms.

It was painted a soft yellow with nursery rhyme characters stenciled around the edges. Krystal could imagine a rocking chair in the corner, a crib along the inside wall.

"I think we should take this place," Carly urged her.

"It's nice, but…"

"Ooh, please don't say but. This house is perfect for us. You can have the room next to this one and I'll take the smaller bedroom next to Emily's."

It *was* nice. Krystal chewed on her lip, trying to

figure out how she and Carly would be able to afford it. She pulled her aside to talk finances.

"Are you going to be making enough to pay half of the rent on this place? Don't forget we have utilities, food, upkeep...." She rattled the items off on her fingers.

"I'm going to be getting child support for Emily," she told her.

"Do you know that for a fact? I thought you said Joe was broke."

"He is, but his folks will make him pay for Emily. They told me they will." She tugged on Krystal's arm. "Please say you'll go in on this with me."

"It's a lot of money."

"I know, but it'll be worth it."

Krystal was tempted to sign the rental agreement, but finally said, "I think we should sleep on it."

It wasn't what Carly wanted to hear. She moaned and groaned and pleaded with Krystal to have a heart and warned her that if they didn't act tonight, tomorrow it might be gone. She used every argument she could think of, including the fact that it would only get more uncomfortable at 14 Valentine Place the further along she was in her pregnancy.

It was that last argument that nearly had Krystal agreeing. Then her cell phone rang. It was Garret.

"Is everything okay?" There was concern in his voice and she realized that her message had alarmed him.

She stepped into one of the empty rooms to have privacy. "Everything's fine. I just wanted to tell you that I was going with Carly to try to find another place to live."

"Did Mom ask you to leave?" His voice resonated with disbelief.

"No," she quickly reassured him. "But I'm going to need a bigger place eventually and Carly's looking for something for her and Emily so we thought we might share a house. Actually, we're in one right now that looks as if it would work for us."

There was a silence, then he said, "I see."

"It's small, but there's a nursery. And it's in a good neighborhood."

"Is that what you want? To live with your sister?" Before she had a chance to answer, he said, "Excuse me a moment."

Krystal could hear muffled sounds in the background, mainly a woman's voice. It was a familiar one and she realized it belonged to Samantha. She felt a twinge—something like jealousy. She shook her head. Why would she care if Garret still saw Samantha?

"I'm sorry, Krystal. What were you saying?"

Apparently what Samantha had to say was of more interest. Again the tiny jab of jealousy surfaced, which she knew was ridiculous.

"I think this house might be a good solution for now," she told him.

"It sounds as if you've already made up your mind. I take it marriage is no longer an option."

It wasn't what she'd decided at all, but the woman's voice in the background reminded her of Carly's words earlier that evening. Did she really want to consider marriage to a man who was attracted to another woman?

"No, it isn't, and I need a place to live, Garret, and so does Carly. Before I make a decision I thought I should let you know."

"Thank you for that at least," he said a bit tersely. "I'd like to take a look at it. Give me the rental agent's name."

He wanted to make sure it was an appropriate place for his child to live. She knew it was what she'd want to do if she were in his shoes. If he were looking for housing for her baby she'd want to see where he planned to live.

Later that night she couldn't help but wonder if he hadn't been relieved when she'd told him she wanted to move in with Carly. It was a thought that kept her from falling asleep that night. And one that was on her mind the next morning when she awoke. In fact it bothered her all morning long. It wasn't until she glanced out the window and saw Samantha walking toward her car, smiling as she talked on her cell phone, that she realized why.

The reason she didn't want to see Garret with Samantha had nothing to do with the kind of stepmother she'd make. It was because she didn't want to see Garret with another woman.

She was jealous.

CHAPTER ELEVEN

THE FOLLOWING MORNING when Krystal left for work she ran into a rumpled Samantha coming home. Her clothes looked as if they'd been thrown on in a hurry, her hair, which was normally pulled back in a chignon, hung loose around her shoulders and she had a look about her Krystal recognized as one that said, *I'm sneaking in after spending the night somewhere I hadn't expected to be.*

"Hi. How are you?" Krystal greeted her with the standard neighborly greeting.

"I'm great, thanks," she said with a grin that could only be described as *If you only knew how great, you'd be so jealous.*

"Good," Krystal said pleasantly.

"And you?"

"Oh, I'm great, too," Krystal replied, which was hardly the truth. She hadn't slept much and her back was bothering her.

"I'm glad to hear that. Have a nice day," Samantha said, and continued up the stairs, humming to herself, definitely pleased about something.

Krystal could only imagine what…or whom. Memories of her phone call with Garret last night flashed in her mind. Samantha had been in the background. Laughing.

Throughout the morning at work, Krystal's mind drifted back to her conversation with Garret. She wished she knew what was going on in his head. Had he been disappointed that she wanted to move in with Carly or had he been relieved?

But that was the trouble with Garret. One never knew what he was thinking. When she first met him she thought he was simply shy. Now she knew it was more a case of him not talking about what was on his mind. It wasn't that he didn't want to share his thoughts with people. He simply wasn't in the habit of doing it.

Which was why Shannon suggested that Krystal ask him what he thought about her plan to live with her sister. It did no good to make assumptions about his feelings.

When he called her on her cell phone she was determined to do just that. She was in the middle of cutting a client's hair but excused herself, knowing that if she didn't talk to him she might not get another chance.

Before she could bring up the subject of marriage, however, he said, "I only have a minute, Krystal, so I need to talk fast. I saw the house. It's great. I don't see any reason you and Carly shouldn't rent it. In fact I ran into Carly there and I told her the same thing. She said the two of you had talked last night and that you had already decided to take the place if I approved, so it looks like you have a house. Carly can fill you in the details. She has the lease."

Krystal gulped. "The lease? You mean it's a done deal?"

"Yes, I thought I just said that." He sounded a bit impatient and once again she could tell he was preoccupied.

"What about the rental deposit?" she asked, knowing her sister didn't have the money to cover it.

"It's taken care of," he answered.

"What do you mean it's taken care of?"

"I paid it."

"You shouldn't have done that!" she protested.

"Krystal, I have an obligation to this baby. Part of that obligation is to provide housing. This is a nice house. I wanted you to be there."

So she hadn't been imagining things last night. He *was* relieved that she'd decided to share a house with her sister.

"But the money—" she began but he cut her short.

"We can figure out the financial details another time. I really can't talk right now. I'll call you later." And with a quick goodbye he hung up.

She slowly clicked her cell phone shut and put it back in her pocket. Hearing Samantha's voice in the background during their phone conversation last night, seeing her on the steps this morning, and now hearing Garret's eagerness to have her rent the house all fed her suspicion that despite what he said, he was still interested in Samantha.

"Is everything okay? You look a little troubled," her client said as Krystal went back to her workstation.

"No, I'm fine. I'm just a little surprised at how quickly things happen, that's all. It looks like I'm going to be moving out of 14 Valentine Place."

KRYSTAL TRIED CALLING Carly numerous times that afternoon, but she had her cell phone turned off. After leaving a message three times and not getting a return call, she decided her sister was ignoring her. And rightly so. Carly had led Garret to believe that all that was needed for them to rent the house was his approval. It still angered her to think about it.

When she got home that evening she went straight

up to her room to tell Carly exactly what she thought of her methods. Only her sister wasn't there. She'd left a note saying she'd gone back to Fergus Falls to get furniture for their new place.

Krystal crumpled the note and threw it in the trash, then dialed her mother's number. She should have known better than to make that mistake. First of all Carly was not there and, secondly, her mother wasted no time telling her what she thought of her new living arrangements.

"Are you crazy?" her mother screeched in her ear.

"No, but I have a feeling I will be by the end of this conversation," Krystal said dryly, in no mood to be criticized by her mother.

"I can understand Carly not thinking clearly. She's devastated by what Joe's done to her, but you...you should know better."

"Well, Mom, this might come as a news flash, but I am not responsible for that house getting rented," she retorted.

"I can't believe you let a terrific guy like Garret Donovan slip through your fingers."

Krystal sighed. So that's what her mother was upset about. Not the fact that she and Carly would be living together, but that she hadn't accepted Garret's marriage proposal.

"For your information, Mother, I never had him in my fingers."

"Carly told me he wanted to marry you," she said in an accusing tone.

"Well I didn't want to marry him," she snapped back, although that wasn't exactly true. She wasn't sure what she wanted. Lately she'd been having feelings toward Garret that confused the issue, especially now that marriage was no longer an option.

"What is wrong with you?" her mother continued. "He's a doctor. Do you realize the kind of lifestyle he could have provided for you?"

Krystal knew it was pointless to argue with her mother so she changed the subject. "It's spilled milk, Mom. Give it a rest, will you? I need to talk to Carly."

"I told you she's not here. She went over to the house."

"Would you have her call me when she gets back? And while you're at it, ask her where the rental agreement is. I want to see what she's gotten us into."

"Don't you know?" The question was loaded with criticism.

"No, she went ahead and signed it without my knowledge. See how your 'always right, always perfect' daughter behaved?" She knew it was childish to attack Carly, but she'd had a lifetime of "you should be more like your sister" comments and she didn't need her mother acting as if she were once again the big sister leading the younger one astray.

"I gotta go, Mom. There's someone at my door," she told her even though it wasn't true. All they were doing was upsetting each other. She needed to end the conversation before things were said that they both would regret.

CARLY DIDN'T CALL HER BACK that night. Or even the next day. Krystal got tired of waiting for her to phone and went to the rental agent to get a copy of the agreement herself. It was only after she read it that she realized Garret had not only paid the damage deposit, but her portion of the rent. The lease was for a one-year period.

Now she knew why Carly had left town so quickly and why she didn't return her phone calls. Her sister knew Krystal would be upset with the way she'd misled Garret into thinking that the only reason she hadn't signed the contract was because she'd wanted him to see the house.

Krystal doubted she could feel any worse about the situation. She had lived with Leonie long enough to know that although Garret had finished his residency and had a position at the clinic, he also had the burden of a huge student debt from medical school.

Shannon laughed when she expressed her concern about his financial status. She told her that no matter how much student debt he had, he was still a doctor with a good income.

That didn't matter to Krystal. She hated being indebted to Garret, which was exactly how she felt. Again Shannon told her that she shouldn't look at it as being in his debt. He did, after all, have a financial obligation to his baby. To Krystal, that obligation hadn't been defined clearly and until it was, she would not be comfortable accepting anything from him.

That's why she decided to call him and ask him to meet her. He told her he would be at 14 Valentine Place that evening. As she hung up the phone she wondered if he was coming to the house to see Samantha or his mother.

When she arrived home from work she saw his car parked out back. Samantha's Volvo was not next to it. Krystal used the private entrance. The fewer people she saw, the better, which was why she'd brought dinner home to eat in her room.

She hadn't finished when there was a knock on her door. She opened it to find Garret standing outside.

"Oh, you're home. I didn't see you come in," he said as he stepped inside.

"I came up the side entrance," she told him.

"Still avoiding Mom?"

She shrugged. "It just seems easier."

"I just spoke to her. I didn't realize you hadn't told her about the house and I mentioned it. I'm sorry."

"It's okay. I'm sure she's relieved to hear that I'm moving."

"I think you're wrong about that."

He hadn't heard the conversation she'd had with Leonie and Krystal didn't see any point in telling him about it. "Maybe it would be better if we didn't discuss your mother."

"Probably," he agreed. "But I think you should know that you and I aren't the only reason she's unhappy. Shane told her today that he and Jennifer are having problems."

Uneasiness spread through Krystal like water on a flat surface. "You don't mean marital problems?" She hated to even ask the question. Seeing his nod, the uneasiness got stronger.

"Apparently Jennifer's been unhappy for a while," he said quietly. "They're thinking about trying a trial separation."

"But when Dylan and Maddie were here they announced they were going to try to have another baby," she said in disbelief.

"It turns out that was Shane's idea not hers. He hasn't said very much except that she told him she feels trapped and that she needs some space. Shane's frustrated."

And probably feeling lonely and hanging around Carly, who's emotionally vulnerable. Krystal didn't want to even contemplate the volatility of such a situation. "You don't think there's a third person involved, do you?"

"Shane says there isn't."

Krystal hoped he was right. She hadn't forgotten how her sister's face had glowed when she'd talked about Garret's brother. This did, however, explain why Jennifer was no longer Shane's assistant in the accounting firm.

"I hope they can work out whatever problems they're having," Krystal said sincerely.

He nodded, then pulled a card from his pocket. "There's something else I wanted to talk about with you." He gave her the card. "This is my insurance information. As soon as the baby is born, she—or he," he quickly added before she could protest, "will be covered under my policy."

"But I have health insurance," she told him.

"Yes, I know you do, but I'd like you to use mine."

First it was the clothes, then the rent, and now the health insurance. He was taking care of things she should have been taking care of herself and it bothered her. She didn't want to feel indebted to him, even if he was the father of her child.

She folded her arms together saying, "I appreciate you letting me know about this, but I would rather use mine."

"It doesn't make any sense to pay for yours when you can use mine. Besides, I have better coverage."

"How do you know you do?"

"When I went with you to your appointment I asked the claims rep at the clinic to look into it for us."

He was making decisions and taking control of things that should have been her responsibility. Intellectually she understood why he felt the need to do it, but emotionally she had trouble accepting it.

"I think we need to come to some kind of agreement as to just how much responsibility for this baby is yours and how much is mine," she said in a tone she hadn't meant to sound antagonistic, but she could see by the way his eyes narrowed that that was exactly the way he'd heard it.

"Why do you have so much trouble accepting help from me?"

"I don't. It's just..." She paused, wondering how to explain feelings she herself didn't understand. "I'm used to taking care of myself."

"Don't think of it as me doing things for you. It's for the baby. You're not telling me you're uncomfortable with me wanting to provide for my child, are you?"

She wasn't, so why was it so difficult to accept his help? "No."

"Then what is it you want me to do?"

She wished she had an answer to that question herself. She wanted him to be a father to her baby, yet when he made any sort of gesture that indicated he was acting in that role, she became uncomfortable. "I'm not sure how people handle a situation like this."

"We don't need to do what other people do. We can handle it any way we choose."

"Maybe it would be better if we waited until after the baby is born to discuss this." She could see by the look he gave her that he didn't like that suggestion.

"I'm sorry if you feel I'm forcing myself into your life, but you might as well get used to it, because I'm going to be there for my child, Krystal." He looked at his watch. "Now I have to go. If you need anything, call me."

He started for the door and she called out to him, "Garret." He turned to look at her. "Thank you...for putting the deposit down on the house—" she waved the health card "—and for thinking of this."

"You're welcome," he said, and left.

AS SOON AS GARRET LEFT, Krystal went downstairs to find her landlady. She found her in the great room, where she sat in the flickering light from the fire crackling in the fireplace. The rest of the room was in darkness.

"Leonie, could I talk to you?" she asked, walking into the room.

Her landlady glanced up and for just a moment Krystal caught a glimpse of sadness, but it was quickly replaced by a smile. She motioned to her, saying, "Come sit down and enjoy the fire with me."

It was the overture Krystal needed and she didn't hesitate to accept her invitation. "Thanks, I'd like that," she said, taking a seat on one of the chairs close to the fireplace. "This feels good. It's awfully cold for October."

"Yes. I've been chilly all day, but finally I'm warming up. I love the smell of birch when it burns, don't you?"

"Yes, it's nice."

There was silence except for the crackling of the fire as the dry wood snapped and popped in the flames. Krystal wished they could turn back the clock to the last time they'd sat and talked in front of a fire. It had been spring and life had been so uncomplicated back then. Her biggest worry had been how she was going to juggle dating three different guys. Now she was trying to figure out how she was going to juggle a baby and a career.

Leonie must have been having similar nostalgic

thoughts for she said, "This has always been a popular spot in the house."

"Yes, it has. It's a good thing those bricks can't talk. We've had some pretty wild discussions in this room."

"It has seen its share of girl talk, hasn't it?" she said with a faint smile.

"Yes. I'm going to miss it," she said quietly. "I know Garret told you that Carly and I have found a house to rent."

"Yes, he did."

"I'm sorry you had to hear the news from him. I was going to tell you myself, but it all happened rather suddenly."

Leonie held up a hand. "You don't need to explain, Krystal."

"Yes, I do. And not just about the house. If I had explained things a long time ago, maybe these past few months wouldn't have been so miserable for me and maybe I wouldn't have hurt you."

"You didn't hurt me, Krystal."

"I disappointed you."

Leonie sighed. "Well, that's true. A mother doesn't want to hear that her grandchild is coming into the world without the benefit of having two parents who love each other. But I've talked with Garret and I realize that although it's not a perfect arrangement, it's the best possible one for right now."

They were words Krystal needed to hear. "Thank you for saying that."

"You don't need to thank me. This is the era of blended families. I advise my clients to be open to family situations and I guess I should apply that advice to my own situation."

"One thing you can count on, I'm going to do my

best to be a good mother,'' Krystal stated with conviction.

"I know you will and I know that Garret will make a good father.''

"I think so, too.''

"He's a fair man, Krystal. You know that no matter what the future holds for either of you, he'll never make unreasonable demands when it comes to custody arrangements.''

The word *custody* made her shiver. It reminded her that no matter how much she didn't want to think about the baby in such terms, it was inevitable. She and Garret wouldn't be living together and the possibility existed that both of them could marry other people.

"And as long as you're both willing to try hard to make this arrangement work, that's all anyone can ask,'' Leonie continued. "It'll help that you and Garret are friends.''

"We are and I want it to always be that way.''

"I'm sure he does, too. Now tell me about this house,'' Leonie said, switching topics. "Garret says it's nice.''

"Oh, it is. And it's not far from here. Maybe a fifteen-minute walk. So I'll be able to bring the baby over here or you could go there…if you want.''

"I'd like that. When do you plan to move?''

"The house is available the first of November, which is when Carly will move in, but I want to give you a sixty-day notice, so I probably won't move in until you find someone to take my room.''

"You don't need to worry about your lease with me,'' Leonie said.

"Yes, I do. It's not fair of me to leave you on short notice.''

"I don't think I'll have any trouble finding a replacement for you. Garret told me Samantha may know a couple of nursing students at the hospital who are looking for housing."

Garret and Samantha. Again Krystal wondered about their relationship. Were they seeing each other? She was tempted to ask Leonie, but she couldn't bring herself to do it.

"I should get to bed. I have to work in the morning," Krystal said, rising to her feet.

Leonie got up. "I'm glad we had this talk."

"Me, too."

"It's important to keep the lines of communication open."

"I agree. There's one other thing I wanted to tell you, and that's thank you for all the kindness and understanding you showed Carly while she was here," Krystal said with a heartfelt sincerity.

"I'm glad she's going to be all right. I was worried about her when she first arrived."

"I know. So was I, but she's slowly getting back on her feet." Krystal wondered if Leonie knew that Shane had offered Carly a job. Considering what Garret had told her earlier that evening, she decided it might be better not to mention it, as she was fairly certain it would be Jennifer's place Carly took at the accounting firm.

"Emily's a sweet child," Leonie remarked. "I hope she can get through this without any emotional trauma. Divorce can be devastating on children." Again the sadness came into her eyes. "I don't know whether Garret told you, but Shane and Jennifer are having problems."

The fact that she brought up the subject gave Krystal hope that in time they would be as close as they had been before her pregnancy had put a rift in their relationship. ''I'm so sorry, Leonie. That's not the kind of news anyone wants to hear. I hope they can find a way to resolve them.''

''I do, too,'' she said quietly.

Later, as Krystal lay in bed thinking about their conversation, she knew she needed to talk to her sister about Garret's brother. It would be very easy for Carly and Shane to be attracted to each other. They were both vulnerable. Each had a spouse that had rejected them. It was a prescription for trouble and Krystal only hoped that her sister would think before jumping from the frying pan into the fire.

In the following days, neither Garret nor Leonie mentioned anything about Shane offering Carly a job. Although Garret did tell Krystal that Shane had hired someone from a temp agency until he found a permanent replacement for Jennifer, he gave no indication that Carly was in line for that position.

The last thing Krystal wanted was for Carly to be Jennifer's replacement in Shane's personal or his professional life. The tension in her relationship with Leonie was slowly easing and she didn't need her sister to complicate everything by getting involved with Shane. Each time she tried to warn Carly to be careful when it came to Garret's brother, however, her sister told her to mind her own business. Krystal thought if it was a preview of how they would get along once they were sharing the same house, they were in trouble.

Because Krystal knew Carly would need help with the move, she rearranged her work schedule so that she could drive up to Fergus Falls a day early and help with the packing. She knew it would be a little cramped staying at her mother's with Carly and Emily there, but it would only be for one night.

When she arrived at the trailer park, her mother looked startled to see her. "You must not have gotten Carly's message."

"What message?" Krystal had a feeling she wasn't going to like the answer to her question.

"There's been a change in plans."

Krystal shrugged out of her coat and tossed it over the arm of the sofa. "Why? What's happened?"

"Carly went with Joe to the Cayman Islands."

Krystal shoved her hands to her hips. "Is that where they went to get a divorce?"

Linda grimaced. "She didn't tell you, did she?"

The niggling doubts of suspicion that had been with her ever since she'd arrived at her mother's became one big concern. "Tell me what, Mother?"

"They're trying to work things out. That's why they went to the Cayman Islands. They want to see if they can recapture some of the magic. It's where they spent their honeymoon," she reminded her.

Krystal's mouth dropped open. "Magic? The last I heard he was planning to marry another woman."

"Oh, that's over," her mother said with a flap of her hand.

"Really." Krystal had trouble believing that one. "And where did they get the money to go to the Cayman Islands? I thought he was filing for bankruptcy."

"Apparently his parents are going to help him and Carly get back on their feet."

"Are they going to put a choke collar on him so he can't go to the casino?" She shook her head in disgust. "How many times are they going to bail him out?"

"They're good people, Krys."

She didn't comment. "Where's Emily?"

"She's with her other grandparents."

"The good people," Krystal stated dryly.

"I know you wanted Carly to come back to the city so you'd have someone to live with you in that house you rented—" she began, and Krystal cut her short.

"*I* rented? No, Mom. *Carly* rented the house, not me. She wanted *me* to live with *her.* And now she's left me with a one-year lease on a place I can't afford."

That silenced her mother.

Krystal paced the small space in the trailer home, rubbing her brow. "I can't believe Carly did this."

"You don't want her to try to save her marriage?"

"Yes, but..." She also wanted her sister to be responsible for her obligations and one of those was a house in St. Paul that Krystal was now going to have to occupy by herself. "I can't believe she did this to me!" she repeated, although it really wasn't quite true. What she meant was she couldn't believe she'd been so foolish to even contemplate setting up house with her sister when her life was in emotional turmoil.

Krystal should never have taken her to look at rental houses until Carly had worked through her problems. She should have waited until the divorce was final, until Carly could at least make decisions without weeping.

"I'm screwed," she said in frustration.

"Watch your language in this house, young lady," Linda said in a stern voice.

"Well, what would you call it? Mom, I'm six months pregnant, I have no furniture other than the few things in my room at Leonie's, I have bills piling up, I don't know what I'm going to do for day care, and now my sister runs off with her ex-husband to some tropical island and leaves me footing the bill for her mistake!''

''I have some money saved. How much do you need?'' Linda offered.

Krystal knew her mother saved very little money and what she did have was for those rainy days when illness kept her from working. She couldn't take away the small bit of security her mother had.

''It's all right, Mom. I'll figure something out,'' she said. ''I'm going to go.''

''You're driving back to the city at this time of night?''

She nodded. ''I can't stay, Mom. Please don't ask me to.''

''Don't be angry at your sister, Krystal. She's got a child to think about.''

''You know what, Mom? So do I,'' she said, and walked out the door.

''WHAT ARE YOU DOING HERE?'' Shannon asked her the following day. ''I thought you were helping Carly move today.''

''I was supposed to be but she went to the Cayman Islands with Joe.''

Shannon was as shocked as Krystal had been. ''You're kidding, right?''

''No, I'm not.''

''They're getting back together?''

''It sounds as if they might be, but with my sister, who knows? All I know is I no longer have a roommate.''

''Oh, Krys, I'm so sorry. What are you going to do?''

Krystal shrugged. ''I don't know. Maybe get a part-time job and see if I can swing the rent on my own.''

"There has to be another solution than for you to work two jobs. I mean, you can do that for now, but what about when the baby comes? If I hadn't just renewed my lease, Josh and I would move in with you."

She waved her hand. "It's all right. I'll manage somehow. I'll have to."

"Maybe if you talk to your landlord and explain the situation he'll let you out of the lease."

"Maybe," she said thoughtfully. "I'm still going to have to find a place to live. I've given Leonie my notice and she already has another tenant who has signed a lease. Anyway you look at it, I have to move."

"Maybe Garret can help you. Have you discussed this with him?"

"I can't ask him for help. Everything is going good right now. Leonie and I are talking again and I don't want money getting in the way and messing things up. Besides, I don't want to look like a charity case."

"From what I know about the Donovan family, I don't think any of them would think of you in that way."

"Probably not, but I do have my pride."

"Are you sure that's all it is?" Shannon folded her arms across her chest.

"Why are you looking at me like that?"

"Krys, are you sure you haven't fallen for Garret?"

"No!" She was quick to deny the accusation. "He is so *not* what I'm looking for in a guy."

"Are you sure?"

She wasn't, but she didn't want to admit that to Shannon. "You can't honestly think that I'm falling in love with him? We're friends for Pete's sake."

"Friends who went to bed together," she reminded her.

"Yes and you know why."

"Oh Roy shmoy. You were never in love with him."

"Shannon! How can you of all people say that?"

"Because I don't think you were. Krys, haven't you ever wondered why you could go to bed with Garret so easily that night of the ball? I mean, Roy had cheated on you before, yet you never went to bed with another guy to get over the pain."

Shannon wasn't saying anything Krystal hadn't already said to herself, but she didn't want to be having this discussion. "There's no point in talking about this. Roy's gone and out of my life for good and Garret's attracted to another woman."

"Again I ask you, are you sure?"

She sighed. "Yes. You saw how fast Roy bolted when he discovered I was pregnant."

"I meant are you sure about Garret. Looks like he's your man, to me."

"Didn't you hear what I just said? He's attracted to another woman." She made a sound of exasperation. "Can we not talk about this?"

"I'm sorry, Krys. I didn't mean to upset you."

Krystal sighed. "It's all right. The trouble is, this isn't getting my housing problem solved."

"Maybe Carly will come back from the Cayman Islands and tell you she and Joe gave their marriage one last chance and it didn't work."

"Maybe." There was still that possibility, Krystal realized. But long after she and Shannon had gone back to their workstations, it wasn't the housing dilemma on Krystal's mind. It was Shannon's suggestion that she could be falling in love with Garret.

Yes, he was different from any man she'd ever known. And they were having a baby together. It was only natural that she'd have some feelings for him. But love? It just wasn't possible. Or was it?

CHAPTER TWELVE

THE FOLLOWING WEEK Krystal applied for several part-time positions at various department stores, but she knew that even if she worked the extra hours, it was going to be difficult to earn enough to afford the house. Every time she went over her budget figures she ended up drawing the same conclusion. Without Carly, she couldn't make the rent.

When her sister phoned her after her trip to the Cayman Islands, she tried to keep her emotions under control, but it wasn't easy, especially when Carly's voice held a hint of petulance. "Mom warned me you were going to be angry,''' she told Krystal.

"Can you honestly blame me, Carly? Why didn't you at least call me and tell me what was going on?"

"Because I knew you'd be upset! You know how awful my life has been these past couple of months. And I didn't know if you'd try to talk me out of going with Joe."

Krystal knew her sister had a point, but didn't comment.

"Would you have been able to be objective at that time?" Carly didn't expect an answer and continued on. "I went with Joe because I needed to make sure I was doing the right thing for me and for Emily. St. Paul is a long way from Fergus Falls."

"I know it is, Carly, which is why I suggested we not rush into getting the house in the first place," she reminded her. She sighed, knowing that it did no good to bring up the reason they were in this mess. It wouldn't change anything.

"I'm really sorry, Krys. Truly, I am."

"So are you and Joe getting back together?" Krystal had a feeling she already knew the answer, but she needed to ask the question anyway.

"Yes. I know you're upset about the house. Mom says you're worried about the legal ramifications, but you don't need to worry. I'll call the landlord and explain the situation. The worst thing that will happen is we'll lose our deposit."

"Carly, that money's not ours. It's Garret's. Do you realize what an uncomfortable position you put me in because of this?"

"I know and I'm sorry, Krys, but if you could have seen how Emily cried when she saw Joe. It just broke my heart. For her sake, Joe and I have got to try to make this work."

As frustrated as Krystal was by Carly's behavior, she knew that more was at stake than a rental deposit and a lease agreement. "I understand that and I'm not criticizing you for wanting to save your marriage. It's just that your actions have put us—and especially me—in a big financial mess."

"And I told you—I'm going to get the mess with the house straightened out," she insisted.

"How?"

"Don't worry about it. I've talked to Joe's dad and he says there's no lease that can't be broken. He's amazing when it comes to straightening out financial messes."

Krystal wanted to say he must be if a near-bankrupt Joe had been able to take Carly to the Cayman Islands. "Will you do it today?" she asked, needing the peace of mind of knowing that it was resolved without Garret's involvement.

"Yes. Trust me. It'll be fine."

Krystal had her doubts but decided there was no point in worrying until she heard from her sister that there was a problem. To her surprise, Carly called a short while later with the news that the original lease agreement had been voided. Since there was another party interested in renting the house immediately, the landlord agreed to only deduct a cancellation fee from the damage deposit.

"I hope you told him to take it out of your check?" Krystal told her sister.

"Of course I did," she replied. "It was my fault we didn't take the place. You can relax. No one lost any money and everything's fine."

"It's not quite fine, Carly. I still need to find a place to live."

"If you want me to come down and go looking with you, I will," she offered.

"No, it's all right," Krystal said in resignation.

"You were there for me when I needed you, Krys, and I really appreciate it. I only hope you can understand why I went back to Joe and try to be happy for me."

"I do want to be happy for you, Carly and I hope that this reconciliation with Joe works—for your sake and for Emily's," she said sincerely. She didn't add that she wasn't convinced it would work. She wanted to believe that her brother-in-law could make changes in his life and be the husband and father Carly and Emily needed, but she'd spent the past five years wanting to believe that Roy could change into something he wasn't.

"You should be happy I'm not going to be living

in St. Paul,'' Carly continued. ''At least now you won't have to worry about anything happening between me and Shane Donovan.''

''I wasn't worried about that,'' she lied. ''I knew you were just being friends during a time when you both were going through some problems.''

''Yes, we were. How are things between him and Jennifer?'' Carly asked.

''I'm not sure. I haven't seen Shane recently,'' Krystal answered, not wanting to discuss Garret's brother and his wife. She changed the subject, asking her sister about Emily. By the time they said goodbye, the tension that had been in their relationship at the start of the call was gone.

Carly's last words were, ''I'm glad everything's okay between us, Krys.''

Krystal expressed the same sentiment and hung up the phone, relieved that Carly had taken care of the problem involving the house. It was one less worry for her and meant she wouldn't have to feel indebted to Garret. She only wished that the rest of the issues she had with him could be resolved so easily.

GARRET WASN'T ONE to surprise people. He himself didn't appreciate getting caught unaware so he seldom sprang anything on anyone. Only sometimes the surprise was warranted, which was why he was on his way over to 14 Valentine Place with a trunk full of moving boxes to give to Krystal. It was not what she would be expecting to have dumped on her doorstep on a Monday morning.

Actually, she wouldn't be expecting to see him, either. It had been a while since he'd last seen her, and not because busy schedules had kept them from running into each other. He was fairly certain she had deliberately been avoiding him. Why else wouldn't she have told him about Carly wanting out of the house lease?

If it hadn't been for the fact that his name was on the rental agreement, he doubted that he'd even know there had been a problem. That made him all the more determined that today she would be the one getting the unexpected news.

When he pulled into the alley behind 14 Valentine Place, he parked next to her car, then opened his trunk and removed the cardboard boxes he'd stowed there last night. When he went inside he found Krystal and his mother in the kitchen eating breakfast.

"Well, good morning," his mother called out when she saw him. "This is a surprise."

"A good one, I hope," he answered.

"Of course," she said with a smile. Seeing the startled look on Krystal's face, he was fairly certain she didn't share his mother's opinion. "We're having muffins and coffee. Want to join us?"

"Sure, but first I need to get rid of these." He raised the boxes slightly. "They're for Krystal." Seeing the quizzical look on her face, he added, "My neighbor was going to toss them but I thought they'd make good moving boxes."

"They're the right size—not too big so that you won't be able to lift them once they're full," Leonie commented. She looked at Krystal and asked, "Do you want him to take them upstairs right away or should I put them in the storage room until you're ready to use them?"

"I should probably take them upstairs," Garret answered for her, then gave her a pointed look. "Now that Mom's found a tenant for your room, you're probably going to want to move before the weather turns nasty and cold.''

She looked reluctant to take him up on his offer, but she finally said, ''You can put them in my room.''

He followed her up the steps, admiring how slender she looked from the rear. Unless she turned to the side he couldn't even tell she was pregnant. She held her door open for him as he carried the stack of boxes into her room and set them on the floor.

''Looks like you could use some help. You haven't started packing,'' he said, glancing around.

She bit on her lower lip, then said, ''It's probably a good thing you came over this morning. I need to tell you something. Carly and I aren't moving into the house.''

He feigned innocence. ''Why not?''

''Joe convinced Carly they should give their marriage another chance. She decided to stay in Fergus Falls, so she won't be needing a place to live here.''

''Well, maybe she doesn't, but you still do,'' he pointed out.

''An apartment maybe. Not a whole house. But you don't have to worry about the money you put down. Carly called the landlord and explained the situation. He was very understanding and let us out of the lease agreement.''

''Is that right?''

She nodded eagerly. ''He said you'll get your damage deposit back within ten business days.''

He shook his head. ''I don't think so.''

Krystal looked puzzled. ''Sure you will. I told you, Carly was able to cancel the lease.''

''No, she was able to get her name off the lease because I was willing to keep my name on it,'' he told her.

He had definitely surprised her with that information.

"What are you talking about?" She eyed him suspiciously.

"When Carly called the landlord and asked to get out of the lease, he called me. I assured him that even though Carly didn't want to live at the house, I knew someone who did." He wiggled his brows. "You."

"But I can't afford that place!" she protested.

"Maybe not, but I can."

"Are you saying the reason Carly was able to get out of the deal was because you absorbed her responsibility?" He could see she was flustered. Her cheeks had more color than he'd seen in a long time.

"Yes. So you'll still be able to move in next week. The only thing that's changed is that you won't have Emily and Carly as housemates."

He expected her to smile and say thank you, that it was a very thoughtful thing for him to do, but she frowned and looked at him as if he'd done something to personally offend her.

"I wish you hadn't done that," she said stiffly.

"I thought you wanted to live there? Carly said you especially liked the place because it had the nursery for the baby."

"It's a great house for a baby, but I can't afford to pay that kind of rent."

"And I told you I would take care of the rent for you."

She was more than flustered. She was upset. She folded her arms across her chest in a defiant stance and shook her head. "No, I can't let you do that!"

"Why not?"

"Because it makes me feel indebted to you."

"Why should it? I'm the reason you need to move.

It's my child you're carrying which makes me responsible for both of you.''

"No, you're not responsible for me," she stated adamantly.

The outburst of emotion surprised him. "What's with your attitude anyway? Do you realize how many women in your situation would be grateful to have the fathers of their babies behave in a responsible way?"

"I am grateful," she insisted. "It's just that I'm used to taking care of myself and if I let you pay half of the rent even though we're not..." She paused, as if searching for the right words. "Involved in any type of relationship, it wouldn't be right."

"We have a child together. Isn't that a relationship?" he asked.

"Yes, but..."

"And aren't we equally responsible for that child?"

"Yes, but..."

"So you agree it's a fifty-fifty deal."

"Yes, but..."

"Then I'll pay half of the rent and you'll pay the other half." It was said with an authority that dared her to challenge it. He expected she would and he wasn't wrong.

"I can't let you do that. You'd be paying rent on two places," she protested with indignation on his behalf.

"Not if I sublet my apartment and move into the house I won't be." It was an argument he had been prepared to use should the need arise. He was fairly certain she didn't want him to pay double rent. "I know you don't want to be married for the baby's sake, but we could be roommates—for the baby's sake, of course." She didn't have a response to that suggestion and he wasn't sure if it was because she was shocked or if she was trying to think of a way to tell him what an awful idea she thought it was.

He decided to use the silence to argue the advantages of such an arrangement. "Carly backing out of the deal could be the solution we've been looking for when it comes to figuring out how we're going to share parenting duties. You know I hate the thought of being a part-time parent and, with the hours I work, it's going to be difficult to arrange a visiting schedule. If I were living in the same house as you and the baby, it would mean I'd get to see her every day instead of whenever our schedules would allow it."

She still didn't say anything, which was unusual for Krystal. She normally reacted immediately and emotionally to everything he said.

"Was Carly wrong? Didn't you like the house?" he prodded.

Finally she spoke. "Yeah. I liked it a lot. But are you sure this is what you want?"

"I wouldn't be suggesting it if it wasn't," he answered.

"You told me you didn't believe in couples living together outside of marriage," she reminded him. "That it wouldn't be a good example for a child to see."

"We wouldn't be a couple, Krystal. We'd be roommates."

That brought more color to her cheeks. "Oh."

She appeared to give his suggestion some consideration, chewing on her lower lip as she mulled it over. "We'd have to agree to some things."

"Like what?"

"How we handle our private lives. Whether guests can stay the night. That type of thing."

Was she referring to her having men friends over?

He didn't think she'd been dating. "We can say no overnight guests without consulting each other."

She nodded. "What about *special* friends?"

"Are you talking about me wanting to bring women home?"

"You don't think it'll happen?"

"No. I told you. I'm not seeing anyone. Are you seeing anyone?"

Her hand pointed to her tummy. "With this?"

"You're every bit as beautiful pregnant as you are when you're not." It was the truth. He'd hoped that his physical attraction to her would wane with time, but it only grew stronger. "Actually, I think you're more beautiful now than I've ever seen you."

That caused her to blush and she looked away from his gaze. "I wish you wouldn't say things like that."

"Why not?"

"Because it—" she glanced around the room as if looking for the words "—it's distracting us from the issue here. We're talking about rules for being roommates. Having guests can be a serious problem."

"Not for me it won't be. I'm not having any."

"Me neither," she said, then quickly added, "—unless my sister or my mom come for a visit."

"Relatives aren't a problem. In case you haven't noticed, I have a few myself." He grinned, trying to lighten the mood. It didn't work.

Her brows drew together and she asked, "What about your mom? Do you think she'll object to us living in the same house?"

"Does it matter if she does?"

She hesitated only a moment before shaking her head.

"We have to do what we think is best for the baby, Krystal." He paused a moment, then said, "I'm not suggesting a lifetime arrangement here. Just one year until we get the hang of this parenting stuff.''

She hesitated only a second longer, then said, ''Okay. We'll give it a shot and see what happens.''

He smiled and thought surprises weren't so bad after all.

''SO ARE YOU ALL SETTLED in your new place?'' Most of Krystal's regular clients knew she'd moved out of 14 Valentine Place so the question came as no surprise to her.

''I'm getting there.''

''And how do you like it?''

''It's great having so much room,'' she said as she applied color to the woman's hair.

''Then you don't miss the boardinghouse?''

''I miss having people around all the time. It's so quiet.''

''What about your guy? He must make some noise, doesn't he?''

Garret wasn't her guy, but she didn't correct her client's mistake. She knew it was impossible to hide the fact that she was pregnant and single, but she didn't need to divulge the details of her relationship with Garret.

''I hardly ever see him. I think he works even more than I do.'' She didn't realize how many hours he did put in until he'd moved in with her.

''Last time I was in you said you'd signed up for the prenatal classes. Is he going with you for that?''

''He said he would, but last night was our first one and he had an emergency so Shannon went with me. Not that it matters. Being a doctor, he probably knows all the information they give at those classes anyway.''

"It's still nice that he wants to go with you," she remarked.

It was nice and Krystal appreciated that he'd made the effort to enroll in the classes. She only wished he was doing it for a different reason. Last night there'd been several couples in the course who were obviously very much in love and happy to be having a baby. For Krystal it had almost been a relief not to have Garret there. She didn't want anyone to see that he wasn't in love with her.

"Have you picked out any names?" her customer wanted to know.

"We both like Emma."

"What if it's a boy?"

"We haven't been able to agree on a boy's name. He's convinced it's a girl."

"Show me your hands," the client demanded.

Krystal set down the color and brush on the counter, then shoved her hands out in front of her.

"He's right. It's a girl," she declared on a note of glee.

"What makes you say that?"

"You showed me your hands with your palms up. If you'd had palms down, it would have meant you're having a boy."

Krystal chuckled. "I have a client who's convinced it's a boy because when I drink my tea I lift my mug by the handle."

"I haven't heard that one before, but I know the palm test works. It's been right twenty-three times in a row so far. You'll see," she said with a knowing nod of her head.

"So you're saying I don't need to worry that I haven't a boy's name picked out?" Krystal asked with a dubious grin.

"Nope, you won't need it. You're lucky your guy wants a girl. Most men want a son the first time around," she remarked.

It was true that Garret often referred to the baby as she, but Krystal honestly didn't know if he was truly hoping it was a girl, because he hadn't told her his preference. Garret kept most of his thoughts about the baby to himself. Unless she asked him specific questions, he seemed content to go about daily life without much conversation at all.

Being a people person, she found it frustrating to live with someone who was perfectly content to keep to himself. She could have been living alone. When they were home together Garret closeted himself in his room with the door shut. Krystal wasn't sure what he did in there at night. Judging by the number of bookcases he owned, she figured he was probably reading.

That's why she was surprised when she arrived home from work one evening and found him in the kitchen cooking. She didn't think he did cook. He seldom left dirty dishes in the kitchen.

"Something smells good," she commented.

"It's chili."

Noticing the size of the pot, she asked, "Are you having guests?"

"As a matter of fact I am. I hope you don't mind?"

She shook her head. "No, go ahead," she told him, wondering whether they were male or female. "I'll make myself scarce."

"You don't have to do that. It's only Shane and Mickey."

"Not Jennifer?" she asked.

He shook his head. "No, they're still separated." He lifted the lid on the pot and stirred the contents.

"So you invited your brother and nephew over for supper. That was nice of you," she remarked.

"I have an ulterior motive," he admitted with a sheepish grin.

"And what would that be?" She rose to the bait.

"Look in the nursery."

She hung up her coat in the closet before walking down the hallway to the small bedroom connected to hers. It had been empty ever since she'd moved in, but now there was a bookcase filled with children's books along one of the walls. It was what was in the middle of the room, however, that had her mouth gaping. Scattered on the floor were various parts of what appeared to be a crib. She went back to the kitchen.

"Where did that come from?"

"I thought it was time we got that room ready. You never know when a baby's going to decide to arrive early." He clanked a lid onto a pan and faced her, a wooden spoon in his hand. "Bookcases I know how to put together. Cribs are another thing, which is why I called Shane. He knows his way around nuts and bolts much better than I do."

They hadn't talked about buying a crib yet. Although she and Shannon had looked at nursery furniture when they'd been at the mall, it was a purchase she thought she could delay until she was closer to her due date. It was also something *she* wanted to buy for her baby. Once more she had the feeling that he was making decisions and taking control of things that were her responsibility.

"I wish you had told me you were going to buy it," she stated as evenly as she could and trying not to sound unhappy.

"I thought I did tell you. It's been on my mind for quite some time."

"But that's just it. It was on your mind. You didn't tell me because you don't tell me anything!" To her dismay her voice rose, making it sound more like an accusation than a plea for understanding. It was exactly what she didn't want to have happen.

He put the spoon down and looked at her. "I'm sorry you feel that way," he stated calmly. He didn't speak immediately and she could see that he was carefully measuring his words before he did tell her what was on his mind. "We're in a situation that is new to both of us and, naturally, it'll take some time to adjust."

At that moment Mickey burst through the door like a whirlwind of energy. "We brought something for my cousin!" he boasted, his cheeks red from the brisk November wind.

Following behind him was Shane carrying a wooden cradle. "Since you're getting the baby's room ready I thought I might as well bring this over."

He set the cradle down in the middle of the kitchen floor and looked at Krystal. "This thing has been in the Donovan family for generations. Mickey here left his mark on it with a few crayons, but I sanded off his artwork and refinished it," he said, mussing his son's hair affectionately.

"Didn't Great-Grandpa Donovan carve this himself?" Garret asked, admiring the antique. "I thought Mom said you were going to ship it over to Dylan?"

He shook his head. "Maddie didn't want to risk anything happening to it in transit so Mom said I should give it to you and Krystal." He looked at her then and said, "I know Jennifer liked having it because she could keep it next to the bed at night."

When she didn't comment immediately, Garret said, "If you don't want it, I'll put it in my room."

It was an awkward moment and Krystal wished she had worked late instead of coming home. She wondered if she would ever stop feeling uncomfortable about her relationship with Garret.

"We probably don't need to decide what to do with it tonight, do we?" she said weakly, then added, "If you'll excuse me, I've got things to do."

"Aren't you going to have supper with us?" Shane wanted to know. "Garret makes a pretty mean chili…but you probably already know that. You live here."

She didn't know about the chili, but she was learning a lot about Garret that she hadn't known until she'd become his housemate. Like the fact that he worked the crossword puzzle every day in the paper while he ate his breakfast, which usually consisted of cold cereal and fruit. And he occasionally sang in the shower and he left his shoes in the same spot next to the door every night. And he did his own ironing and often forgot to take his clean clothes out of the dryer.

She'd always known he'd be a good doctor, but until she'd overheard him returning a phone call to one of his patients after hours she hadn't realized just how good he would be. He was dedicated to his work and passionate about helping people. It was why he was so solicitous of her health, so concerned for her well-being. He had a good heart, which was why she was living with him and not in a tiny apartment barely big enough for one person let alone a mother and child. It only made her feelings toward him grow stronger each day and wish that his actions weren't motivated out a sense of duty.

"You're welcome to join us," Garret seconded his brother's invitation.

Welcome to join us. Krystal noticed he didn't say,

Please stay. I want you, too. She tried not to let her emotions get the better of her, but she couldn't stop the self-pity. She felt like a big albatross around the Donovan family's neck. They tolerated her because they were good people and they wanted to do what they could to make everything go smoothly for the Donovan baby she carried.

But as she stood there in the kitchen looking at the Donovan heirloom cradle and thinking about the crib in the other room the two brothers were about to tackle, she didn't want him doing all those things for her because she was the mother of his child. She wanted him to do them because he loved her.

Mentally she shook herself. She stared at Garret and saw the same face, the same eyes, the same smile she'd seen every time she'd looked at him in the past three years. Only something was very different. Before, when she'd stared into those dark eyes, she'd seen a friend. Now she saw the man she loved.

It was an overwhelming realization, one that had her staring at him in bewilderment, wondering when it had happened. How could she have fallen in love with him and not been aware of it?

"Krystal, are you okay?" Garret asked.

She swallowed nervously. "Yeah, I'm fine," she mumbled, then excused herself and hurried to her room before either he or his brother saw on her face what was in her heart.

WHEN GARRET ARRIVED at the nursing home, he found Dolly Anderson in the solarium seated in a chair next to the window. She looked perfectly content as she gazed at the snow falling at a steady pace.

"So this is where you are," he said, walking into the glass-enclosed room.

"Isn't it lovely, Dr. G.?" she said, referring to the scene outdoors. "I know it's early to be getting this heavy a snowfall, but it's so beautiful." Her sigh was one of contentment. "They told me you might not be coming today. I should have known a little snow wouldn't stop you from doing your work."

"It's a little sloppy out there, but the road crews are doing their job and keeping the streets clear," he told her. "You ought to know by now, Dolly, that nothing can keep me away from you." He produced a box of gingersnaps from his bag.

Her eyes twinkled. "That is so sweet of you," she cooed. "I suppose now you want to take me back to my room so you can get me out of my clothes."

"The thought did cross my mind," he said with a flirtatious grin.

She giggled and struggled to her feet with his assistance. "A handsome doctor like you... I can't believe you're still single. Have I told you about my little gal who does my hair?"

"I believe you have," he said, helping her as she navigated toward the door using her cane.

"She's the sweetest thing," she said, her tone one of amazement. "And other people think so, too. I'm not the only one who thinks she's a gem."

"I'm sure she's very nice."

"Oh, she is. She listens to what you have to say. I mean really listens. I think you'd like her if you met her."

"I'm sure I would," he said with an indulgent grin.

"It's too bad you weren't here earlier this morning. She was here. You two could have met."

Sometimes being behind schedule wasn't such a bad thing, he thought as he helped her back to her room.

"You said she's pretty. She probably has a boy-friend."

"Uh-uh. She likes this one fella, but she said he's all wrong for her. Who knows? Maybe you'd be the right one, now that you're not going to the Doctors Without Borders program."

"I still don't have time for women, however," he told her.

"You need to make time," she advised him. "You should come to the party next week. She's going to be there. When she found out they needed someone to help with the entertainment, she volunteered." She sighed again. "Wasn't that sweet of her?"

"Very."

"What I like about her is she always has a smile on her face."

"Sounds like you, Dolly." They'd reached her room and he led her over to her favorite chair. "Now you sit right there. I'm going to close your curtains so no one sees what's going on between you and me," he told her with a wink.

"But the snow is so pretty,'" she protested.

"It'll just take us a minute."

"Boy, you are good, aren't you?" she quipped.

He grinned and wagged his finger at her. "Ah, Dolly, you are one sharp lady." As he reached for the cord on her drapes he automatically glanced outside to where his car sat in the parking lot. Although he'd arrived a short while ago, it was already covered with snow.

He had started to pull the drapes shut when he saw a familiar red head. It was bent over the windshield of a car, clearing away the snow. Its owner wore a dark green jacket, black slacks and a pair of chunky-heeled shoes that were totally inappropriate for the weather.

"Dolly, what did you say the woman's name is who does your hair for you?"

"You mean Kryssie?"

"Kryssie, huh?" he said, closing the curtain.

"It's really Krystal but she lets me call her Kryssie. Isn't she sweet?"

"You know what Dolly, I do believe she is." And with a smile on his face he got to work.

TUESDAYS WERE LONG DAYS for Krystal, because she spent her morning at the nursing home then went straight to the salon for a full day of work. Today she had brought her lunch, which she ate in the employee lounge while she balanced her checkbook and went over her monthly budget.

She and Garret had lived in the house well over a month, yet so far they'd had no utility bills arrive in the mail. Concerned, she made several phone calls during her lunch break and discovered the accounts were paid in full. When she asked to verify the billing addresses, she learned that although both of their names appeared on the accounts, the bills were mailed to Garret at his clinic address.

Without consulting her, he had assumed responsibility for the payment of the heat, electric and telephone bills. So much for his fifty-fifty division of expenses, she thought. As usual, when she tried to call him she reached his voice mail. She decided not to leave a message, but was determined she would talk to him about the matter that evening.

It continued to snow all afternoon and she was relieved when her final two appointments of the day canceled, meaning that as soon as she finished with her afternoon clients, she could go home. By the time she left the salon, many businesses had closed because of the winter storm. As she made her way through the parking lot to her car, she nearly fell, her feet sliding around on the ice and snow. After scraping her windshield and brushing off the car, her fingers were as cold as her toes.

Driving was difficult, but she managed to make it to within a couple of blocks of the house before she had any serious problems. Trying to avoid a collision, she ended up in a snowbank. The man driving the car behind her stopped to make sure she was all right and offered to call a tow truck, but she knew it was unlikely that on such a night anyone would respond to the call.

She decided to leave her car and walk the remaining distance since she was so close to home. As she climbed out she wished she had worn a different pair of shoes, but the severity of the storm had caught many people by surprise, including her.

She had trudged about half a block when she saw Garret's car at the corner. When he saw her, he got out. He didn't speak but came toward her with an intense look on his face.

Before she could say a word to him, he scooped her up into his arms and began to carry her toward the car.

"What are you doing?" she demanded.

"Rescuing you."

"You don't have to carry me. I can walk. I'm pregnant, not crippled," she told him.

He paid no attention. "Haven't you heard of boots?" he asked, looking at her platform shoes.

"It wasn't snowing when I left this morning." He stumbled and she thought they would both go tumbling to the ground, but he managed to stay on his feet. "Please put me down. I'm perfectly capable of walking."

He ignored her pleas and kept slogging through the snow until he got to his car, where he managed to open the passenger door and dump her inside. When he'd come around and sat in the driver's seat, he asked, "Where's your car?"

"Not far from here." She explained how she was forced off the road to avoid an accident. "How did you know where to find me?"

"I called the salon and they said you left for home an hour ago. I figured you'd be somewhere between here and there."

"Thank you for coming to find me," she said gratefully.

He didn't appreciate her thanks, however. "Why didn't you leave when they issued the winter storm warning?"

"Because I had clients with appointments."

"The salon didn't close?"

"Did the clinic?"

"Yes. Most businesses did."

"Well, mine didn't."

They had reached the house and the car skidded as he pulled into the snowy driveway. He turned off the engine and, without another word, he came around to her side to open the door. When she got out, he picked her up again and, despite her protests, carried her into the house, once more mumbling about the inappropriateness of her footwear.

It was warm inside and she kicked off her wet shoes and padded in her wet stocking feet across the kitchen floor. She was thirsty and hungry and went straight for the refrigerator.

When she opened it, he said, "You need to get out of those wet clothes."

Something in his tone set her off. "I don't need to be told what to do. I'm perfectly capable of taking care of myself."

"Oh really? Is that what you were doing when you ran your car off the road? Taking care of yourself?"

"That could have happened to anyone in this kind of weather."

"And how far do you think you would have made it in those shoes if I hadn't come along? For crying out loud, Krystal. It's a snowstorm out there. Don't you own a pair of snow boots?"

"And I told you, it wasn't snowing when I left this morning," she said, unwrapping her scarf from around her neck.

"It doesn't matter. Someone who's pregnant shouldn't be wearing shoes that look like they have Mickey's building blocks for soles," he shot back at her.

"The kind of shoes I wear is none of your business," she retaliated.

"Everything you do is my business. You're carrying my child."

She shoved her hands to her hips. So that's what this was really about. The baby. He wasn't worried about her health or her well-being. He was worried that she might do something that would harm his child.

When she'd first seen his car, she'd felt a rush of warmth at the thought he'd come looking for her. But now she realized the only reason he had was because of the baby.

Everything was for the baby. The house, the clothes, the food, the bills…at the thought of the utility bills, a fresh stream of anger rose in her. "And there's something I want to talk to you about. Since when did it become your responsibility to pay all of the utility bills for this house?''

"I do live here," he said calmly.

"So do I and we agreed everything would be fifty-fifty. Now I find you've paid the gas, the electric and the telephone bills without telling me!"

He stared at her in disbelief. "You're angry because I'm paying the utility bills?"

"I told you I didn't want to feel indebted to you." The quivering of her voice told her she was danger-ously close to losing control of her emotions, but she continued on anyway. "I know that doesn't matter to you. You don't care how I feel about anything! You just want to be in control." She shrugged out of her coat and threw it in the corner in frustration.

He stared at her, wide-eyed, then went over to pick it up. When he would have hung it up in the closet for her, she grabbed it from his hands.

"I don't want you hanging up my coat! I'll do it myself," she cried.

"You're obviously overwrought. Maybe you should go lie down," he suggested.

"I am not overwrought," she denied strongly. "What I am is tired of you treating me like a child. You keep doing all these things for me without even taking into consideration I might not want you to do them. How do you think that makes me feel?"

He didn't say anything for several seconds. He just stood staring at her. Finally he said in a quiet voice, "I do them because I care about you, Krystal, but I can see that's a misspent emotion. What does a man have to do? Walk out on you before you think he deserves your attention? Well, I can do that." And before she could utter a single word, he was gone.

Krystal found it difficult to swallow. Her body began to tremble, from emotion as well as from cold. She stumbled down the hallway to her bedroom, where she went inside and slammed the door. She peeled off the layers of clothes and hopped in the shower, needing the warmth of the water to chase away the chill in her bones. As she let the steam envelop her, there was only one thought running through her mind. How could she have been so stupid to fall in love with a man who saw her as nothing but an obligation?

CHAPTER THIRTEEN

IT HAD ONLY BEEN one week since the first snowfall of the season and already it had melted. Garret wished he could say the same thing about the tension in the house, but ever since that night when Krystal had made it perfectly clear what she thought about his efforts to make life easier for her, they had hardly said more than ten words to each other.

He'd tried to give her a peace offering—bringing home a book on breast-feeding. She'd interpreted it as a sign he was worried about her baby's IQ. He simply didn't know how to handle her mood swings and decided he might as well give up. It was easier not to have any contact with her than to get his head snapped off for trying to do something nice for her.

They were like two strangers living in the same house. Not a good environment for a child. And certainly not the way he wanted to live his own life. At least when he'd lived alone he was comfortable. Now he could hardly sleep nights and he knew that she felt the awkwardness, too. They were avoiding each other as much as possible and that was no way to live.

He'd been contemplating solutions to the problem and so far hadn't been able to come up with one. He'd sublet his apartment—not that he wanted to move back into it, because he didn't. He liked the house. And he liked living with Krystal in the house. The problem was she didn't like living in the house with him. Any way he looked at it, it was a mess.

He glanced at his watch. It was barely four. She wouldn't be home from work yet. He knew her schedule because she wrote her hours in red on the calendar in the kitchen. Today she worked until five. She also had karaoke tonight.

Karaoke. He didn't even want to think about her hanging out in some bar singing on a stage. But she had a different life than he did. She liked to have fun. How many times had he heard that from her? Too many, as an image of her in a smoky bar played in his head. She should have known better than to expose her unborn baby to all that secondhand smoke. She also should have known better than to go out in a snowstorm in platform shoes.

As he pulled up in front of the house he saw his mother's car out front. A glance in the driveway told him Krystal was home, too. Uneasiness filled him. Why would his mother be over unless something was wrong?

He quickly parked and went inside. Seated at the kitchen table were the two of them, laughing and having a jolly good time, as if the past couple of months had never happened.

"Garret! I didn't expect to see you so soon," his mother remarked when she saw him.

"It's my early afternoon," he told her, noticing how Krystal's laughter came to an abrupt halt. She averted her eyes, pretending to be fussing with the teapot sitting on the table.

"You look tired. You must be working too hard," his mother commented.

"I'm fine," he answered. He was about to excuse

himself and go into his room, but Krystal beat him to it.

"If you'll excuse me, Leonie, I'm going to change my clothes," she said, and made a hasty departure.

"Cavorting with the enemy, Mother?" he asked, shrugging out of his overcoat.

"Krystal's not my enemy, dear...or did you mean I was cavorting with *your* enemy?" she asked with a perceptive lift of one brow.

"What are you doing here?" he demanded.

"I was having tea with Krystal until you walked in and scared her away," she remarked.

He couldn't believe it. His own mother was looking at him as if the icy tension that existed in the house was his fault.

"Krystal doesn't frighten quite that easily," he retorted, then went to hang his coat in the entry closet. His mother let that comment slide.

"I thought you would be happy to see me here. You're the one who's been encouraging me to set aside my disappointment and try to look at the positive side of your situation. Now I have and you look annoyed."

He sighed. "I'm not annoyed. I'm glad...for your sake and for Krystal's. You are, after all, the baby's grandmother."

"And I'm Krystal's friend." She got up to clear away the cups and saucers from the table. "She needed both today."

He frowned. "Why was that?"

"Because she was upset."

"About the baby?"

"No, not about the baby," his mother said with a reassuring pat on his arm.

"Then what?"

"If you want to know what it is, why don't you go ask her and find out for yourself?"

He shrugged. "I will later. I thought she worked until five today."

"No, she had the afternoon off so we went shopping. You'll have to have her show you what I bought for the baby."

Leonie's cell phone rang and she excused herself to take the call. He could hear that it was a client by the tone of her voice, so he stepped into the living room to give her privacy. Spread out on the sofa were tiny little undershirts and nightgowns. Some were pink and some were blue.

He was standing over them when his mother walked in. "Aren't they tiny? I'd forgotten how small those things can be. It's been quite a while since Mickey was that size."

Just then Krystal reappeared. She'd changed out of a white T-shirt and jeans and into a black dress that sparkled when she walked. For a change her hair was worn in a rather simple style, brushed away from her face. She'd never looked sexier to him.

"Oh, you look lovely." His mother said what he wished he could have. "They make the cutest maternity clothes nowadays. Nothing at all like what I had in my day."

Garret hardly thought the dress should be described as cute. Elegant maybe, and much too nice for some bar. Again, the thought of her being with a bunch of people drinking beer and whiskey in order to get up the courage to sing into a microphone made him irritable.

"Garret, doesn't she look lovely?" his mother prodded.

He met Krystal's eyes then, and what he saw there

made him want to take her in his arms and hold her close to him. She quickly looked away as he said, "Yes, very nice."

"I'd better get going," she announced. "Dinner's early."

Leonie nodded in understanding. "I wish I could be there to see you perform."

"I'm sure it'll be fun," Krystal said as she pulled her coat from the closet.

There it was again. That word. *Fun.*

His mother gave him one of her looks which he knew meant he should do the gentlemanly thing and help Krystal with her coat. As he did he caught a whiff of the scent she wore and he had to fight the urge to wrap his arms around her and hold her close to him. Memories of the night they'd made love flashed in his mind. Before he knew it, she was out the door, eager to be away from him, as usual.

That's when his mother turned on him. She faced him with hands on her hips and said, "All right. What is going on with you two?"

"I'm sure Krystal's already answered that for you."

"If you mean did she tell me that you won't talk to her, yes, she did."

Leonie sounded angry with him. "Do you think maybe that *she's* the one who won't talk to *me?*" he asked.

That caused her to chuckle. "No, because I know better. Krystal cannot not talk to anyone. You, my son, can go for days without speaking and see nothing wrong with it."

"Well, thank you, Mom, for the compliment," he drawled sarcastically.

She slung an arm around his shoulder and gave it a squeeze. "That's not a criticism. It's just the way it is. She's a talker. You're a thinker. It's one of the reasons you're attracted to each other.''

"I'll let that slide.''

"What? The talker-thinker stuff or the part about you being attracted to her.''

"Well, it would be pointless to deny that I'm attracted to her, not with my sofa covered in baby things,'' he said dryly.

"You know I try not to interfere when it comes to your personal life.''

He held up his hands in supplication. "Then don't say anything, Mom. I thought renting a house together would be a good solution to our problem, but you know what? It's not working and I'm not sure I can do this…not even for the baby's sake.''

She grimaced. "That's what she said, too.''

A knifelike pain went through him. She didn't want to live with him. It shouldn't have come as a surprise. He'd only been fooling himself if he thought she was going to suddenly appreciate his interest in her. The phone rang and he went to answer it.

"I'm looking for Krystal,'' a man's voice said.

"She's gone.'' Garret was rather terse but he didn't care.

"Oh, shoot. I missed her. All right. I guess I'll just have to tell her when she gets here. Thanks.'' And the voice was gone.

"I take it that was for Krystal?'' his mother said.

"Just another guy. We both know there's been no shortage of men in her life,'' he said irritably.

His mother frowned. "I didn't think she'd been dating since she broke up with Roy. Not that it would matter to you,'' she added, scrutinizing his face closely.

"No, it doesn't matter,'' he lied.

"The same way it wouldn't matter to Krystal if I told her Samantha asked to be let out of her lease so she could move in with her latest boyfriend."

"Did you tell Krystal that?" he asked with interest.

"No, I thought I'd let you share that piece of information with her since she seems to think you're still interested in Samantha."

"That's ridiculous. I've told her half a dozen times that Samantha means nothing to me."

"Then if that's the case, just what is it that's keeping you and Krystal apart?"

"You make it sound as if we've had a lovers' quarrel and all we need to do is kiss and make up. We share a house, Mom. We're not lovers."

"Maybe that's the problem," his mother said, reaching for her coat, which had been slung over the kitchen chair. "Romance is my business, Garret. I know the look of love when I see it and it's in your eyes whether you want to see it or not."

"You think I'm in love with Krystal?"

"Yes. Now what do you plan to do about it?" She pulled on her coat and began buttoning it up.

"Nothing, because you're wrong. I'm not in love with her," he stated for his own benefit as much as hers.

"All right, so you're not." She gave him a kiss on the cheek and started toward the door. "I've got to get home. See you, dear."

"Mother, wait!"

She paused near the door. "What?" she asked impatiently.

"You don't think Krystal thinks I'm in love with her, do you?"

"Oh, good heavens, no. She thinks you're only living here because of the baby, that you treat her the way you do because of a sense of duty. She's given up hope that you'll ever fall in love with her.''

"You make it sound like she would want that to happen.''

"Why Garret, are you pumping your mother for information about a woman?'' she asked with a reproving look. "There's only one way for you to find out what Krystal wants. Go ask her. You saw how pretty she looked tonight. Why don't you do something impulsive—like get in your car and go after her.''

"Oh yeah,'' he drawled sarcastically. "Like I want to go to some smoky bar where she's singing karaoke to find out if we're a good match.''

His mother frowned. "Bar? What are you talking about? Krystal's not at a bar. She's at the nursing home.''

"Nursing home?'' He frowned, suddenly remembering Dolly Anderson telling him about Krystal volunteering to help at a party.

"It's their party night and she's hosting the karaoke for the seniors. Not that you'd want to go. I know how you hate parties.''

And with a wave and a bye-bye tossed over her shoulder, Leonie walked out, leaving Garret's mind racing with possibilities. Was Krystal hoping he'd fall in love with her? Or would he look like a fool if he showed up at the nursing home?

He paced for several minutes, unable to stop thinking about her. "You need to have more fun in your life.'' How many times had she told him that? Maybe it was time he showed her what a fun guy he could be. He grabbed his coat and keys and headed out the door. One of them was going to be in for a big surprise this evening. He could only hope it was Krystal.

"OH, MY! Don't you look beautiful," Dolly crooned when she saw Krystal. "All those spangles! It's too bad Dr. G. isn't going to be here tonight to see you."

Personally, Krystal was relieved he wasn't. For months Dolly had been mentioning her favorite doctor, who just happened to be single. Krystal was in no mood to have anybody matchmaking for her and she'd had enough of one particular doctor that she didn't care if she never met another one.

She couldn't think of Garret without her heart feeling as if it were being squeezed in a vise. When she'd first moved in with him she'd been determined to make their living arrangements work—for the sake of the baby. But ever since their huge fight last week, she'd been seriously thinking of looking for her own place.

She blamed herself. If she hadn't fallen in love with him, she wouldn't care that he ignored her. It wouldn't matter that he came home at night after she was in bed and was gone in the morning before she got up. But she did love him and she did care.

That's why today had been another painful reminder of why it would never work between them. When he'd come home and found her in the kitchen with his mother, she hadn't missed the surprise on his face. For one brief moment she had thought that maybe he was happy to see her, but then he'd looked away, as if he didn't need any reminders of his obligation.

"I made sure that you're seated at my table for dinner," Dolly told her, pulling her by the hand to where six other senior citizens already sat around the circular table. Introductions were made with Dolly bragging that Krystal would be in charge of entertainment after dinner.

The kitchen staff had just started to serve the food

when Dolly grabbed her by the arm and exclaimed, "Well, isn't that nice! He was able to come after all." She stared past Krystal in the direction of the exit.

Krystal assumed it was one of the older gentlemen residents until Dolly said, "It's Dr. G.—you know, the one I want you to meet, but he's sitting way across the room at a corner table. Maybe I can get him moved over here with us," she said, glancing around for a staff member.

"No, it's all right." Krystal pulled her hand down, in no hurry to be the recipient of Dolly's matchmaking attempts. "Let him eat. I'll meet him after dinner."

Dolly didn't protest, but Krystal noticed she glanced frequently in the doctor's direction throughout dinner. Krystal, however, kept her attention on the hot dish, green beans and gelatin salad on her plate, hoping that as soon as she was finished, her duties as a volunteer on the entertainment committee would keep her busy.

"Krystal, there's someone who wants to see you," Dolly said when they were on the final course—a scoop of ice cream.

Krystal knew the inevitable moment had come. She had to meet Dolly's doctor friend. She turned and was surprised to see Gladys Lingenfelser in a wheelchair.

"Oh, good! You're out of bed," Krystal said, giving the elderly woman a hug.

"I have something for you," Gladys said. She reached into her pocket and pulled out a beaded bracelet. "I made it for you."

"Why, thank you." Krystal's eyes misted with tears as she slipped the bracelet over her wrist. "That is one of the nicest gifts anyone has ever given me."

The elderly woman grinned and patted her hand. "You're such a sweet thing."

"Isn't she though?" Dolly seconded.

Then Krystal heard a male voice say, ''I think she just might be the sweetest thing I've ever met.''

Startled, she looked up to see Garret standing over her shoulder. Before she could utter a word, Dolly tugged on his sleeve. ''I'm so glad you came to the party. Now you can meet my friend Kryssie.''

Krystal looked from Dolly to Garret. ''This is Dr. G.?''

Dolly beamed. ''Yes, didn't I tell you he was good-looking?''

''You did.''

''And wasn't I right?''

Krystal looked at Garret when she answered. ''Yes, you were right.''

Dolly again pulled on Garret's coat sleeve. ''Say hello to Kryssie. Didn't I tell you she was pretty?''

''Yes, you did,'' he answered, amusement dancing in the eyes that gazed into Krystal's. ''Hello, Kryssie.''

''What are you doing here?'' she whispered to him.

''Looking to have some fun,'' he answered.

''Here?'' she squeaked.

He glanced around. ''There are a few more people than I like to see at a party, but I certainly can't complain about the guest list. And I hear the entertainment is worth the price of admission in itself.'' His eyes stared into hers as he finished his sentence.

''Kryssie, it's time to get started,'' Dolly interrupted them, pointing to the front of the room where the other volunteers now stood.

From the program that had been at her place at dinner, Krystal knew the entertainment consisted of three parts. A flutist, a magician and a karaoke specialist. She was the karaoke specialist, although she didn't want to admit to anyone that the only time she'd actually stood up in a bar and sung along with karaoke, she'd been a few sheets to the wind.

The flutist went first, followed by the magician. Both were received warmly by the elderly audience. When it was her turn, she took her place next to the karaoke machine, microphone in hand.

Dolly volunteered to sing "White Cliffs of Dover" because it reminded her of her husband. Music from the forties was very popular and Krystal was surprised at how many didn't need lyrics to sing along. When it appeared that everyone who wanted a turn had sung a favorite tune, Krystal was about to put the microphone away when Garret stood up.

"What about me. Don't I get to try?"

She stared at him in disbelief. He wanted to sing in front of an audience? She whispered close to his ear, "Are you sure? This isn't the shower."

He took the microphone from her and made his song selection. Before he started, he said, "Dolly, you know how you dedicated your song to your husband? Well, I'm dedicating this song to your Kryssie."

Krystal knew her eyes bulged. She couldn't imagine what it was he could possibly sing to her. Then he began and she nearly fell off her chair. The song was "Baby, I Need Your Lovin'."

Dolly nearly swooned over with joy. The rest of the audience grinned and applauded. Krystal couldn't do a single thing but cry.

She couldn't believe that quiet, unemotional Garret was belting out his love for her in a roomful of strangers. She knew how much he hated large groups of people. She knew how hard it was for him to shed his reserve and do something out of his comfort zone. Yet he was going on and on and on...

Suddenly she leaped to her feet and grabbed the

microphone from him and turned off the karaoke machine. She stared into eyes that were as dark and as rich as chocolate. "I need your lovin,' too."

Then she kissed him.

"So, Dr. G., what happens next?" she asked provocatively when they were the only two left in the cafeteria of the nursing home. "Do you have any other fun things you can show me?"

He pulled her into his arms and gave her a lingering kiss that would have continued a lot longer had they not been in a public place. "I've been wanting to do that for a long, long time."

"I wish you would have. It could have saved us a lot of misery," she said on a sigh.

He lifted her chin and stared into her eyes. "Have you been miserable?"

"Yes. Haven't you?"

"Yes." He brushed another kiss across her lips.

"I thought you wanted to be with Samantha and were only with me out of a sense of obligation to the baby."

"And I thought you wanted to be with Roy and were only with me because of the baby."

"He was never the right man for me and subconsciously I think I knew it all along. It's why one of the conditions I made when we got back together was that we'd have no sex until I knew it would last."

"But it didn't last."

She made a face. "Roy Stanton is such a loser compared to you...no, he's *nothing* compared to you." She smoothed her fingers across his brow. "You are good to the bone, Garret Donovan, and I can't think of anyone I'd rather have as a father to my baby."

That earned her another long kiss that ended with a

groan. "You don't know how many times I've fantasized about hearing you say that."

She stiffened and pushed away from him. "Then maybe I shouldn't have said it."

"Why not?" He gave her a puzzled look.

"Because that night we made love you said that's what I'd been to you—a fantasy. Then the next morning you told me it's all I'd been."

He pulled her back into his arms. "Because that's what it was for me. I've been a little in love with you since the day we met. For that one night you were the woman of my dreams. Then I awoke and found you crying and you told me it was all a mistake." He shook his head.

"I cried because I thought I'd disappointed you. That the reality of being with me hadn't lived up to the fantasy."

"It was so much better," he said, then kissed her in a way that convinced her she'd been wrong. A little breathless, he said, "I should have listened to Dolly sooner. She told me you would be perfect for me— only I didn't know you were the Kryssie she kept mentioning to me."

"I know. She kept calling you Dr. G.," Krystal said with a smile. "Is she the reason you came down here tonight?"

"Yes and no. She had told me about the party, but I also had a little help from a romance coach," he said with a grin.

"Your mother? But how did she know I was in love with you? I didn't say anything to her."

Garret grinned. "She knows her business. She also told me you were upset and that's why she'd come over."

"I was. I had some questions about becoming a

mother. And then she asked me how things were going between us and I said a few things I probably shouldn't have said.''

"So you did tell her you were in love with me?"

"Not in so many words, but…''

He kissed her again. "I told you she thinks of you as a daughter.''

"Yes, we're lucky she's going to be our baby's grandmother,'' she said, placing her fingertips on his lips so he could kiss them. "I never wanted you out of my life, but it was hard letting you in, especially when I knew that because of me you were going to have to sacrifice one of your dreams.''

"You're talking about going overseas.'' She nodded and he said, "That wasn't my only dream, Krystal. And there are other humanitarian projects I can become involved with right here in the States.''

"I admire you for wanting to help people.''

"Why? You're the same way. I've seen how you are with the residents here.''

In his arms she found a strength and a sense of rightness she'd never known before. "We're alike in some ways, but we're pretty different in a lot of ways, too.''

"Don't tell me you're trying to figure us out?''

She shook her head. "Uh-uh. I just want to hold fast to it and never let it slip away.''

He kissed her again. "That's exactly how I feel. It doesn't matter why you slept with me that night. What matters is that from our time together, something wonderful happened…and I don't just mean the baby.''

"Garret, I think we need to talk about that night.''

This time he put his fingertip to her lips, to quiet her. "It's not necessary.''

"For me it is. I know you think that night happened

because I was hurt. And when I went back to your apartment with you, I did want to be with a friend, but once I looked into your eyes, what I saw there made me want you in a way I'd never expected. Maybe it was because when I looked into your eyes I saw someone who really cared about me. Whatever the reason, it made loving you feel right.''

''Why didn't you tell me any of this before now?''

She shrugged. ''I can think of a few good reasons…like Samantha, for one.''

''I told you she was not my girlfriend,'' he said with a hint of impatience.

''Believe me, she wanted to be.''

He lifted her chin and planted another kiss on her lips. ''There's only one woman for me and now I'd like to take her home with me.''

''I think that's an excellent idea. Dolly says you could teach me a few things about love.''

''Dolly said that?''

''Mmm-hmm, but I have to warn you. It might take you a while.''

''And why is that?''

''I'm a slow learner.''

''Don't worry. We have a lifetime ahead of us.''

EPILOGUE

KRYSTAL AWOKE to find she was alone in bed. On the pillow where Garret's head should have been was a single red rose and a small book of poetry. She reached for the rose and inhaled its fragrance.

She'd been married exactly one week and she didn't think she could be any happier. Judging by the dedication Garret had written in the book of love poems, he shared her sentiment.

"I hope that smile means you like my valentine." The sound of his voice had her glancing toward the doorway.

"I do, but what are you doing out of bed so early on your day off?" she asked as he came toward her carrying a tray.

"Making breakfast for you." He sat down beside her, setting the tray in front of her. On a pink heart-shaped plate were two heart-shaped eggs, heart-shaped toast covered with raspberry jam, and a small red dish filled with freshly cut fruit.

She took his face in her hands and kissed him. "You are such a romantic and I love you, but I thought I was going to treat you to a Valentine's Day breakfast at that wonderful new French café."

"It's too cold this morning to be going out. Besides, I rather like the idea of spending the entire day inside with you," he said, stroking her hair.

"It works for me," she said with a grin.

Only it didn't work for either one of them. Before she'd taken a single bite of her breakfast, she felt a sudden warm sensation beneath her. "Ohmigosh!"

She didn't need to say another word. Garret could see what had happened.

"Is this…?" she asked.

He nodded. "You, my lovely wife, are going to have a baby."

"But…but I'm not ready!" she exclaimed as he calmly removed the tray and helped her out of bed.

With the onset of contractions, however, she changed her mind. She definitely was ready to give birth. She allowed her husband to drive her to the hospital, where she labored long and hard all afternoon to hear three little words.

"It's a girl."

As the doctor placed her baby on her bare abdomen, Krystal stared in disbelief at the tiny arms and legs flailing about. "I did that!" she said to Garret.

He kissed her. "Yes, you did. Thank you for giving me the perfect valentine."

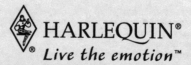

An offer you can't afford to refuse!

High-valued coupons for upcoming books

A sneak peek at Harlequin's newest line— Harlequin Flipside™

Send away for a hardcover by *New York Times* bestselling author Debbie Macomber

How can you get all this?

Buy four Harlequin or Silhouette books during October–December 2003, fill out the form below and send the form and four proofs of purchase (cash register receipts) to the address below.

I accept this amazing offer!
Send me a coupon booklet:

Name (PLEASE PRINT)

Address   Apt. #

City   State/Prov.   Zip/Postal Code

098 KIN DXHT

Please send this form, along with your cash register receipts
as proofs of purchase, to:

In the U.S.:
Harlequin Coupon Booklet Offer, P.O. Box 9071, Buffalo, NY 14269-9071

In Canada:
Harlequin Coupon Booklet Offer, P.O. Box 609, Fort Erie, Ontario L2A 5X3

Allow 4–6 weeks for delivery. Offer expires December 31, 2003.
Offer good only while quantities last.

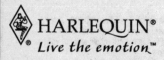

HARLEQUIN®
Live the emotion™

Silhouette®
Where love comes alive™

Visit us at www.eHarlequin.com

Q42003

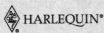

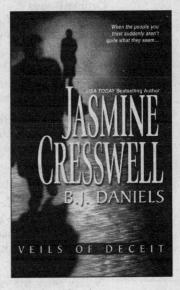

HARLEQUIN®
INTRIGUE®

Our unique brand of high-caliber romantic suspense just cannot be contained. And to meet our readers' demands, Harlequin Intrigue is expanding its publishing lineup to include **SIX** breathtaking titles every month!

Here's what we have in store for you:

❏ A trilogy of **Heartskeep** stories by Dani Sinclair

❏ More great **Bachelors at Large** books featuring sexy, single cops

❏ Plus outstanding contributions from your favorite Harlequin Intrigue authors, such as Amanda Stevens, B.J. Daniels and Gayle Wilson

MORE variety.
MORE pulse-pounding excitement.
MORE of your favorite authors and series.
Every month.

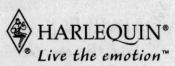

HARLEQUIN®
Live the emotion™

Visit us at www.tryIntrigue.com

HI4T06B

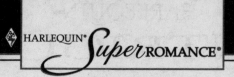

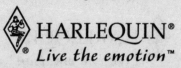